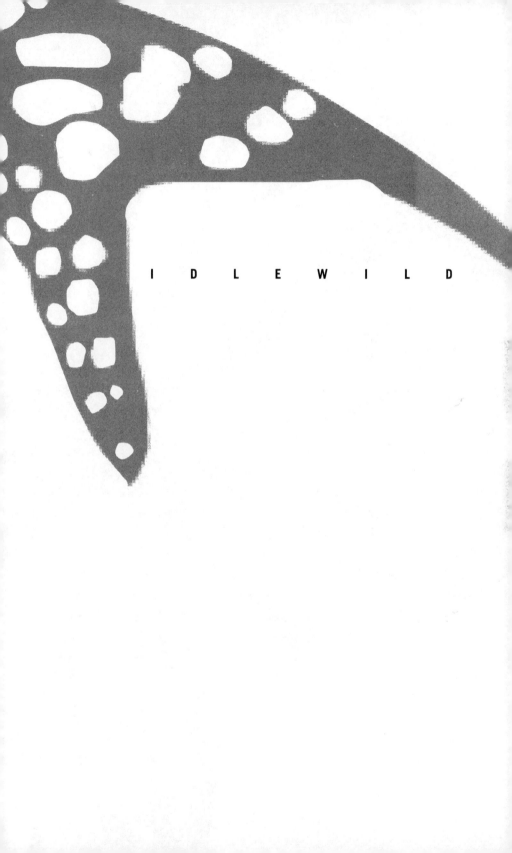

I D L E W I L D

IDLEWILD

NICK SAGAN

G. P. PUTNAM'S SONS

NEW YORK

This book is a work of fiction. Names, characters, places, and incidents either are the product of the author's imagination or are used fictitiously, and any resemblance to actual persons, living or dead, business establishments, events, or locales is entirely coincidental.

G. P. Putnam's Sons
Publishers Since 1838
a member of
Penguin Group (USA) Inc.
375 Hudson Street
New York, NY 10014

Grateful thanks to Scott Benzel for permission to reprint lyrics from
"Butterfly Wings" by Machines of Loving Grace, copyright © 1993,
Sensory Deprivation Labs (BMI).

Library of Congress Cataloging-in-Publication Data

Sagan, Nick.
Idlewild / Nick Sagan.
p.   cm.
ISBN 0-399-15097-8
I. Title.
PS3619.A36I35   2003   2003043152
813'.6—dc21

Printed in the United States of America
1   3   5   7   9   10   8   6   4   2

This book is printed on acid-free paper. ∞

Book design and illustration by Stephanie Huntwork

For Clinnette

Don't place faith in human beings.
Human beings are unreliable things.

MACHINES OF LOVING GRACE, "BUTTERFLY WINGS"

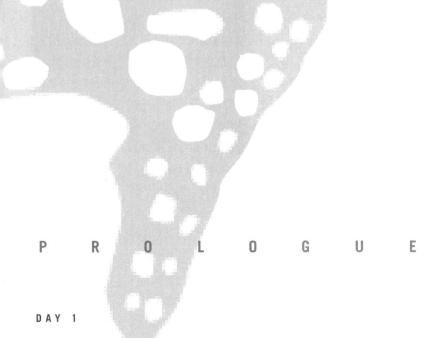

P R O L O G U E

I'm not dead.

A dim realization but an important one, because I should have died. The shock of whatever just ripped through me was strong enough to do it—some kind of electrical overload lighting me up from head to toe like a fireworks display. But my brain kept repeating the mantra: "*not dead, not dead, not dead,*" and pretty soon I had to believe it. One eye popped open and then the other, and consciousness (if you can call it that) slowly returned.

Cold and dark. Orange. Harvest. A damp, musty smell; sound of crickets; the bite of a monster headache. Yes, I was trapped in a pumpkin patch, twisted and tensed, taking shallow breaths like a newborn kitten.

Clarity did not follow consciousness. My mind felt sluggish, and all attempts at coherent thought made my temples ache worse. Why? What had happened to me?

I remember the shock and . . .

. . . and nothing. Just the shock. Disturbing doesn't even begin to cover it.

Sitting up seemed like a bad idea, so I tried to grab my hornet's nest of a head. Simple. Left hand, up. Right hand, up. But nothing happened. *My arms won't move,* I realized.

I tried to wiggle my legs, fingers, hips, toes, nose, ears and neck. They didn't answer the bell. *I'm paralyzed.*

I could feel my pulse coming faster now and I wondered what would happen if my breathing stopped. No mystery there, eh? My brain would atrophy like a wilting flower and the consciousness I'd fought for would be hideous as I spiraled down the path of no return. Panic hit me hard. I started making desperate deals with phantom deities I invented on the spot. *Please,* I thought, *don't let me die. Whoever you are, if you can hear me, get me up on my feet. I'll do anything. I'll give you anything . . . well . . .*

Well, what? What did I have to offer?

Nothing. I know nothing, and thus I have nothing. I don't even know my own name. Puzzles have pieces, don't they, so why can't I remember?

A new theory came to me: brain damage.

Two words I didn't want to consider, but they made frightening sense. The paralysis didn't need to stem from a broken vertebra, after all—I could have simply forgotten how to move, the way I'd forgotten everything else.

Let's not jump off that bridge just yet. If you forget something, surely you can remember it, given enough time. That's me—looking on the bright side, like always.

I clung to hope and faulty logic and waited to remember. And waited. And waited some more. Words came to me in my senselessness, another mantra from the dim recesses of my jigsaw mind: *"There is no pain. Keep control. No pain in the house, just keep control."* But I didn't have control, damn it, it hurt like fire and I just stayed sprawled there, useless and pathetic, for who knows how long. I'm not a control freak, mind you—not per se—but deprive me of something basic and I begin to go stark raving mad. The possibility dawned on me as I lay there. Stark, yes. Mad, possibly. But raving? Was I raving?

Hysterical paralysis, they used to call it. Hysteria: a psychoneurotic condition characterized by violent emotional and sensory disturbances, by paroxysms in the motor functions, and by changes in consciousness that are symbolically or psychically determined. Hysterical, sure, but somehow I didn't feel like laughing.

Could I be dreaming, I wondered? Half awake, eyes open, body still asleep, dreaming my paralysis—a hypnogogic state? I was, perhaps, a prisoner of my unconscious mind . . .

Friction of the forewings; the crickets kept pissing me off. There's a formula for crickets, just like there's a formula for everything. I don't mean their genetic formula, but rather their thermometric formula. Crickets chirp less often as the temperature drops, so you can estimate heat by timing the chirps: (chirps per minute / 4) + 40 = # of degrees Fahrenheit. I counted a chirp per second, making it a slightly nippy fifty-five degrees.

I could remember that, but not my own identity? Or how to move?

A strange organ, the brain.

As the crickets mocked me with their love songs, I began to hear another sound—a distant whine—faint but getting clearer. And then, like a thunderbolt, the rules suddenly changed.

I heard a loud *toc* and my body could move again, just like flipping a switch—or having a base-two zero snap over to a one. I jumped to my feet. My body wasn't stiff. There was no soreness. My nerve endings felt alive and open. Little flowers of pins and needles bloomed along my spine and down my arms and legs, but the pain was already beginning to fade.

C H A P T E R   1

H A L L O W E E N

"Dropping like flies," drawls the first Gedaechtnis employee. He is a Southern Gentleman who has never quite been able to kill his West Memphis accent. He has defeated both the poverty of his youth and the inherent racism of twenty-first-century America, but the twang remains like a stubborn mule. As his red felt-tip pen highlights the latest casualty figures, the gentleman tries not to wonder about his own condition. He finds he can't help himself and reluctantly places two fingers to the side of his neck to hunt for signs of swelling. There is no swelling, but this does not reassure him. His doctor has informed him that he will be dead within the year.

"What do you expect? A last-minute reprieve?" This is the second Gedaechtnis employee. Her English is harsh and clipped, much like her hairstyle. She had hoped for something like a pageboy cut but the stylist botched it and she is making do as best she can. She is part of the Munich contingent. Gedaechtnis corporate headquarters is in Munich and she is a very important cog in this machine.

The Southern Gentleman does not like her and would not be working with her if their task were less important. She reminds him of a poster child for Aryan eugenics, she with her blond hair and piercing blue eyes. Blue was once a heartbreaker, *he thinks, but now her looks have faded.*

"*I expect the worst. I'm still hoping, though. Hoping for a miracle.*"

"*There are no miracles. Not for you, certainly not for me. Not for any of us.*"

"*No, not for any of us,*" he repeats, *thinking of his wife and daughter.* "*But what about* all *of us?*"

Confusion set in. I imagined a thought bubble floating up from my head with a question mark on display. In actuality, a meter above my head, a rapidly blinking light hovered in place. It flipped back and forth between two colors—red-green-red-green-red-green, bright like a fantastically annoying firefly. Was it a firefly? I couldn't see any wings. I took a step back. It floated forward.

I thought: *I am on some terrible drug.*

"Go away," I said and my voice sounded strange to me. I cleared my throat and took another step. "Go away," I repeated. The twinkling sprite didn't respond, but it moved forward again, recovering the lost ground. I took my jacket off, rolled it up, and lashed out, but it passed through the light without affecting it at all. Red-green-red-green-red-green, over and over, an optical siren. And then another popped into existence next to it, this one yellow-blue-yellow-blue-yellow-blue.

I ran for it.

The lights matched my speed.

A hollow voice billowed up from all around me at once . . . what little I heard, I couldn't understand. It kept fading in and out, loud-soft-loud-soft-loud-soft. It sounded like: "EX . . . EE . . . ERE SEE . . . UNCT . . . URGE . . . RE SKREEEEEE!"

Nonsense, I thought.

I don't know how far I ran. Half a mile, maybe. I tried not to look back. When I did, the sprites were gone. I stood there, panting, trying to catch my breath.

"This stops right here," I warned whoever was listening—Providence, the crickets, the phantom deities who had given me back the use of my limbs. No one answered. Worse, with the sprites gone, it was dark again. The bad, inky kind of dark—the dark that makes you think you're about to be surrounded. The moon was all but eaten by gathering clouds. Storm on the way.

Cursing, I fished through my pockets. I came up with a stainless-steel lighter and a half-empty packet of clove cigarettes. The smokes seemed awful familiar, so I shook one out and tasted the end. Sweet. Spicy. A good thing. A piece of sanity. I lit up and took a few puffs, forcing myself to relax. *I like cloves,* my brain managed to assert. *Okay, that's something I know about myself, something real that can't be taken away. A few more epiphanies like this and I might have something to go on.*

When I felt calmer, I tried sifting through the rest of my thoughts, but no memories rose to the surface. So what *did* I know? I knew (1) I was young. Just shy of or just past eighteen years old. And (2) I was a student—or something like a student. I had to know things, important things, and I had to know them by rote. What was I doing here? So murky. So much lost to me.

I also knew (3) Lazarus was dead.

Lazarus? The name vexed me. Details were fuzzy, but no, I didn't like him. In fact, I was pretty sure I hated his guts. So maybe his being dead wasn't a bad thing.

Except it was. It was a very, very bad thing indeed.

Stubbing the smoke, I wiped my hands on my pants and started moving again. Past a cornfield, through the woods, down a desolate road. I used the lighter as a torch. The rain finally came, gently at first, then like drops of falling steel. It made me think of baptisms.

And then a flapping sound made me think of leather. I whirled round, but I could only see the lighter's glint.

"Who's there?" I called, straining my eyes.

Again, no response. *No one here but us paranoid amnesiacs.*

I hurried off in the other direction. Cold, wet, looking over my shoulders—what a miserable picture I made. I followed the road down a slope to a cul de sac. Lightning flashed and Gothic cathedrals came to mind. But by the time the thunder hit, I realized I was looking at a mansion wrought from stone and stained glass, magnificent and dreadful and yet somehow . . . familiar.

I know this house, I thought. *I don't know how I know it, but I know this house.*

Impish gargoyles sneered down at me like I owed them money. I didn't have any on me, so I focused my attention on the heavy wooden door. It was a thick block of oak with a colony of locks running up the side. Upon it, dead center, a tiny relief—an anthropomorphic sun chased an anthropomorphic moon: Helios and Selene. Ornamental or functional? I noticed there was no keyhole, which didn't stop me from looking under the mat.

I could burn the door down, I thought. (A testament to my befuddlement. You try burning a wet door with a pocket lighter.)

I touched the moon along the side, and pushed it nice and gentle. Gentle didn't cut it, so I pushed a little harder. It slid counterclockwise on a thin circular track, swiveling up to cover the sun, where it settled neatly into place. An eclipse. The door unlocked with nine hollow clicks.

Nine locks. Nine, for a reason.

I grabbed the doorknob. Halfway inside, I wondered if I should've knocked.

The ashlar exterior gave way to a soft, comfortable interior. Plush couches; tapestries, paintings, a rocking chair. The ominous façade had been just that, designed strictly for show. I felt my teeth itch. I thought of turtles. Chelydra serpentina. Penetrate the shell and you get to the meat, but most turtles are defensive creatures, prone to snapping off fingers at the slightest provocation. I succumbed to a morbid daydream, seeing myself running blind through this mansion, trying to open doors with ten bloody stumps.

Seeing myself, eh? The hell do I look like?

I needed a mirror.

Room by room I went, looking for lights to flip on. Switches flipped, but light didn't follow. An electrical system seemed in place. Someone needed to change the fuse.

My lighter was sputtering; I clicked it off. Pitch black. I tried not to bump into things, or at least not bump into things with pointy edges. One coffee table later, I was clutching my knee and biting my lip. And in the kitchen, I stumbled. Grabbing the counter saved me from a nasty fall.

I righted myself and took my bearings. Then I fished. Rifling through drawers: no, no, no, yes. A knife. Serrated. I gripped it hard. I jabbed the air. It felt good in my hand, but I still didn't feel safe.

A spiral staircase corkscrewed up to the top floor. I took it and peered down the hallway. Now where would the master bedroom be?

A bead of sweat rolled down my forehead and trickled into my eye. My stomach flip-flopped. If I had no choice—if it meant my survival—could I kill?

Hang on, I thought. *Kill who? You're creeping through someone's house with a knife? Are you crazy?*

That's when I understood.

Question: Why is Lazarus dead?

Answer: Because I killed him.

From somewhere, a mental image had been summoned up. I could see Laz falling back and collapsing because I'd perforated some of his favorite arteries. He bled to death and I let him die. But I had to. It was him or me.

9

But is that what actually happened?

Or just what I'd wanted to happen?

I cracked a door and gave it a gentle nudge . . .

Fluorescent lights, burning wax candles and lava lamps. I squinted from glare and spun around, hunting for the occupant. Here? There? No one in sight. Pulse still pounding, I relaxed my grip on the knife, filled my lungs with air, and took a look around. Master bedroom, all right, and the room screamed carnivore. Animal skins. Fur rugs. Big leafy plants. A jungle motif with flamboyant tiger stripes, a cavalcade of orange and black.

My gaze shifted to the mahogany four-poster bed. It was impressive, but rumpled. Gothic letters had been carved fiercely into the headboard, like a proud declaration. Nine letters, one word: HALLOWEEN.

I'll confess to a certain chill upon reading the inscription, but it wasn't a chill of recognition. If the bed was mine, it didn't look any more familiar than the rest of this place. I felt like an intruder. I felt like Goldilocks in hell.

Halloween. What, the holiday? I doubted it. A name? A statement? A threat?

A philosophy?

I touched the covers, half expecting them to be warm. They weren't. A perverse urge hit me to tuck myself in for a catnap. Just slip on in and sleep this place away. Instead, I hit the adjoining bathroom, ran some water over my face and stared up into the mirror.

There was no reflection.

PACE TRANSMISSION 000013382291221

? LABELED CALLIOPE SURGE
INFECTION
DAMAGE TO INTEGRITY
GUEST NINE HALLOWEEN COMPROMISED VIA HOST JANUS
HOST SLAVE NINE NANNY (NINE) MARGINALLY UNSTABLE
HOST MAES HOST TRO ? UNSTABLE ? PRIORITY ?
GUEST FIVE LAZARUS STILL NOT RESPONDING [PRIORITY]
INVESTIGATION PROCEEDING
END

C H A P T E R   2

SOLSTICE

Numbers escalate, the threat keeps rising. From countries across the world, re-ports keep coming in: people are taking this badly, which means killing them-selves or their loved ones before it gets any worse. In some instances this is merciful.

Others are taking it well. "Well" *means banding together in a spirit of co-operation, love, trust and harmony. The Southern Gentleman thinks it's as if the greater part of humanity has finally agreed on something and found a common voice. Making the most of it. He also thinks this is a day late and a dollar short. Where was this spirit when it really mattered?*

Blue believes the harmony to be motivated by self-interest. There is a resurgence of faith these days, a growing belief in organized religion, grace, damnation, heaven and hell. People treat each other kindly now, *thinks Blue,* because they hope to escape God's wrath. *Blue does not believe in damnation and has trouble empathizing with those who do. In her fifty-two years she has found no hard evidence, no scientific proof to convince her of God's existence. She considers herself an atheist.*

The Southern Gentleman likes to think of himself as agnostic with Pente-

costal tendencies. His mother was Pentecostal and devout; his father was Baptist and not. He hasn't gone for years and years, but he remembers liking church as a kid. Safety there. It felt big to him—profoundly so—and peaceful. Friendly even. But at home there were times when his mother would grab him and hold him and start speaking in tongues, talking spirit-to-spirit to the demonistic force she said she knew was inside him. That didn't feel peaceful— it felt downright scary. She'd talk nonsense with that quiet voice and he'd see that look in her eyes and even though she never hit him he could tell she was close to it, close to going somewhere from which there might be no return.

Every time, all those times, he never once thought she was truly possessed by the Holy Spirit. If God existed, he wouldn't approve of this behavior. And the Southern Gentleman never believed that he himself was possessed by anything more than an inclination for mischief.

Demon inside me? *he'd wonder.* Then why love me?

Love the sinner, hate the sin, she'd said. She'd said it a lot.

Looking back, he realizes his mother had never come apart at the seams, not completely; perhaps that small mercy is proof of God's love. And he'd love to believe in God—these days more than ever. But every time he tries to open that part of himself, his skepticism sidles up like a white blood cell come to foil an infection. Careful skepticism has served him so well all his life—he's made wise choices, sane choices. It's literally impossible for him to shut that part of himself off now.

Still, there's no getting away from that old-time religion—these days it's a dark frenzy of Revelations; breaking the seals; stories of brimstone, h-e-double hockey sticks and stones and lakes of burning fire. He doesn't respond to these. They're threats and they hold no sway. No, the story he likes is simpler—the story of Lazarus. Jesus Christ brings a man back from the dead. Beautiful. It's a better magic trick than any Van Caneghem pulled, or Houdini before him.

Gedaechtnis keeps him busy but never too busy to wonder. He wonders: Where is my savior? *He wonders:* Where is my eternal life? Is the Second Coming coming—or is Lazarus dead for one and all?

Then he goes back to work. The work is his salvation.

I wanted to throw up.

I kept staring and staring, and the mirror kept on calling me invisible. I wasn't, mind you—I could see my hands and clothes and boots plain as day—but to the mirror, I simply didn't exist.

There had to be a reasonable explanation for such a thing.

Yeah? How's this one: You're dead.

That's silly. Corpses have reflections. Besides I didn't, repeat—did not—feel dead.

How do you know what "dead" feels like? You're some kind of ghost now, welcome to your haunt.

I couldn't walk through walls.

Then you're a vampire, consigned to walking the earth forever.

A vampire? Me? Ridiculous. I'm as red-blooded as the next guy.

You murdered Lazarus.

I couldn't deny it, but I couldn't confirm it either. It was a feeling of terrible guilt crushing me down, memories all fuzzy, fact and fantasy merging. As pleasant as I imagined myself to be, there was also, it seemed, a madman inside me.

And still, some part of me insisted that I was innocent.

I filled the sink with water, cupped my hands and splashed my face again. Droplets slipped off my face and back into the sink, making ripples as they rejoined their mates. But above the ripples, I watched, fascinated . . .

In the mirror, the drops appeared from nowhere. As soon as they rolled off my face they became visible, but not a microsecond before.

I took the knife by the point and tossed it up. Visible, as soon as it left my hand. I caught it smoothly. Invisible again.

It seemed I wasn't a very reflective person.

I held the knife up to the light.

I stared into the water.

15

Nothing reflected my image.

"I'd kill for some déjà vu," I muttered out loud, and listened to the strange timbre of my voice. No thanks to the mirror, I was able to determine that I was male and fair-skinned. From my scalp, I plucked a strand of conspicuous orange hair.

A start. But my face was still a mystery. I ran my fingers lightly over the merchandise. Up, down, left, right, around. I discovered two eyes, a nose, lips, teeth, tongue, chin, ears. No surprises. I hunted for scars and didn't find any—not physical ones, anyway.

A hollow voice started up again, from everywhere and nowhere, oscillating loud-soft-loud-soft-loud-soft:

"WOU . . . IS B . . . CONVE . . . IME T . . . ISCUSS . . . Y . . ."

Reflexively, my muscles tensed. "Shut up!" I growled.

And miraculously enough, the voice shut up.

Maybe this should have pleased me; it didn't. Such maddening, capricious jailers—why should they listen to me now? Letters began to roll across the mirror, forming smoothly like stigmata:

IS THIS A MORE AGREEABLE FORM OF COMMUNICATION?

Furiouser and furiouser.

"Leave me alone," I said.

IF YOU'RE BUSY, I CAN GIVE YOU YOUR SPACE.

I smashed the mirror with my fist. I smashed it until I didn't see any more stigmatic letters, until my knuckles felt like they were raw, until the sink was full of blood and shards of glass. Until I'd made my point clear. The ensuing silence was deafening.

My hand was dripping. I saw blood. I felt sweat. I made a concerted effort not to add tears to the mix.

There was nothing behind the mirror, incidentally. I'd hoped to find a crawlspace to another dimension. I would have settled for a bottle of tequila. ·

I searched the medicine cabinet for a first-aid kit, and wrapped my hand in gauze. *Stupid,* I thought. I just sat there staring at my bandaged hand for a minute or two, wracked with self-pity, before heading back into the "safari room" with its huge mahogany bed.

No identifying forms or papers. No diaries. Precious few staples of identity: some clothes (differing cuts and styles, most black, some orange, only a few other colors), some trinkets, and some artwork that reminded me of Schiele or maybe Tranh. Nothing juicy though; nothing of any real use to me.

I tried on some clothes and they fit. It was hard to check without a mirror, but they felt comfortable. And yet, the fact that they were comfortable made me distinctly uncomfortable . . .

Orange hair on a pillow. Another bad sign.

In a drawer I found twenty-two silver medallions, each hanging from a silver chain, each representing a different Major Arcana card of the tarot. From "The Fool" to "The World," I recognized them. I took the one marked "The Magician" and slipped it around my neck. I don't know why I did it; it just felt right.

Then I bumped around the rest of the upstairs. Closets, a spare bedroom, and bingo—the fuse box. Trial and error caused more lights to wink out for a spell, but before long I had electrical power up and running to all sections of the estate.

The house was awkward. Designed for creature comforts but lacking necessities—the kitchen was modern and stylish but almost completely empty of food, the conservatory boasted a fabulous baby grand but no bench on which to sit and play it. Some rooms looked casual and lived-in, and some looked like no one had ever set foot in them before.

The library was vast, stacked with rows and rows of books. No ti-tles on the spines, so I pulled one down at random. All the pages were blank.

A joke, I assumed.

The game room featured a black felt pool table with sixteen balls, all orange, save the cue ball, which was white. I found a crystal ash-tray there—the butts were all cloves.

"Popular brand," I grumbled.

I glanced at the magnificent-looking grandfather clock stationed faithfully nearby. The big hand was near the nine, the little hand was on the six. *Dawn,* thought I, but it still wasn't light outside—grand-father apparently needed winding.

A black cat slinked over and rubbed against my leg. A friendly headbutt, putting her scent on me. I picked her up and examined the tag on her collar.

WHISPER, it read.

She was sleek, pampered—someone's prized pet. I scritched her around the ears. The cat purred in response, a warm, happy sound. She seemed to like me. Perhaps we already knew each other—to whatever extent cats and humans are capable of truly knowing one another.

Whisper hungered for something more tangible than affection, so I took her into the kitchen and scrounged for cat food. There wasn't any. But I discovered a bottle of cream, and Whisper seemed not to mind the change in menu all that much.

I found a piece of string; we played until the sun came up.

DAY 2

Outside.

The rain had stopped but the smell of rain still lingered. I breathed it in, savoring it, then wandered the circumference of the house.

Slim pickings. No generator, no power lines, no solar panels. Not even a wind turbine. Where did the electricity come from? I smoked for a while, thinking, sunning myself in the morning light. Another odd little dilemma: there were no telephones, telegraphs, modems or telecons. No radio, no television, no satscan decryptor. Hell, not even a mailbox out front.

Complete isolation. Why would anyone want—*no, not* complete *isolation,* I corrected myself, *not with flashing lights and hollow voices and God-knows-what-else.*

Scout the area. My best bet. I took a last look in the house to see if there was anything important I had missed. An idiot check. Fruitless. I even took a peek up the chimney. *Hello, Santa, are you there?*

Christmas came early for Whisper, though; I left her the rest of the cream and an open window. I didn't know when I'd be back this way—but at least she could hunt for crickets if worse came to worst.

Armed with kitchen knife, my lighter, cloves, binoculars and an old-fashioned compass I found in the basement, I set off on my quest for enlightenment. North, I decided. Enlightenment lay to the north.

One foot in front of the other.

Butterflies in the air.

A pretty day, all things considered. I walked past fields—wheat, barley, corn, squash, pumpkins. A lot of pumpkins. No one was tending the crops, of course. The farmers were as absent as my reflection. I tried not to let that bother me. A tune came to mind; I started whistling. An artless little melody. Was I recalling it or making it up on the spot?

A raucous *caw, caw, caw* sent my gaze skyward but I couldn't spot any crow. *Caw, caw, caw,* again; insistent, louder. There, leaving the safety of the trees: a tan bird with dark tail feathers and eyes like blood-red jewels. A caramel crow. *Half albino,* I thought. *Very rare.* She beat the air with her elegant wings, and she screeched at me, flashing a split pink tongue before turning, gliding off. To the cornfields. Had

I offended her? An autumn wind threatened to whip up around me, faltered, then died. I quickened my pace.

Weeping willows up ahead, a pleasant, shady locale, perfectly suitable for a family picnic. That is, providing your family isn't squeamish.

It was a cemetery.

Even rows, two of five—ten graves total.

The Ten.

They were Irish burial mounds—*Sidh,* I knew they were called—each graced by small white pebbles placed to remember the dead. The headstones were all marked, each distinguished by a single Gothic character. C, F, H, I, L, M, P, S, T and V.

H is for Halloween, I reasoned. *And L is for Lazarus.*

Nothing special about the L plot, but the one marked H was a pit, the only open grave. I inched closer and peered down to find an ornate wooden coffin staring back at me. It was open. And empty.

Welcome home?

I spent a few fucked-up minutes tearing up that L grave. No coffin, no body, nothing. *Lovely,* I thought. My hand itched to hit something, but the bandage made for a good deterrent. Not that I was still in pain. I undid it idly, lost in my contemplations. Then I looked.

My knuckles were completely healed.

Fast work. What I apparently lacked in engrams, I more than made up for in cell regeneration.

I held the bandage at arm's length and let go; it dropped neatly into the coffin with a soft rustling sound, reminding me of dry leaves.

I kept expecting something about that coffin to strike me familiar, but again no bells. I supposed that was well and good—I didn't like the implications. Perhaps some things just aren't worth remembering.

I tipped an imaginary hat to the other graves. To anyone watching, it might have appeared a sarcastic gesture . . .

. . . but I meant no disrespect.

Eyes locked on the compass, I continued my trek.

Soon, all too soon, I discovered the grounds of an elegant church. Of course, a graveyard would be near a church—that made perfect sense. But this wasn't precisely a church; the closer I came to it, the more it began to look like . . .

A cathedral.

It looked familiar. Way too familiar.

But the compass still read north.

Now, I didn't have to check that the window I'd left open for Whisper was still open . . . but I did. Call it shock, call it denial, I wanted to make sure. And after I saw that it *was* open, I didn't have to rush upstairs and check that shards of bloody glass were still in the sink . . . but I did. I checked.

Somehow, I had come back to the same mansion.

I thought: *I'm Alice in the looking glass.* And I sank to my knees and cursed. It was all so fucking unfair. I wanted to scream. I wanted to crawl up into a fetal position. I wanted to kill whoever had done this to me. I wanted my memory back.

Want, want, want . . .

And then it hit me. A moment of overwhelming clarity.

Not a memory—not precisely—but rather a feeling, a pull from my gut so instinctive, so powerful, I couldn't hide from it even if I'd wanted to. It was this:

Something terrible was going to happen. Something unspeakable. Something that made all my problems trivial. If I didn't figure out who I was and what had happened to me—soon—nothing would matter any more because it would all be over. "It" eluded me, but I knew it was huge and I knew "over" meant the angels would weep. I knew this with every fiber of my being. I knew this far better than I knew myself. And then I knew one other thing; like a dead fish

21

floating up to the surface of a pond, this knowledge rose into my consciousness: my life was in grave danger.

The electric shock, crippling paralysis: someone had tried to kill me. The realization of this had been lurking just out of reach, daring me to embrace it. Yes, someone wanted me dead.

You killed Lazarus. It's justice.

I shook my head at that. This was so much bigger than Lazarus, he was just part of it . . .

You'll never figure it out in time.

"Yes, I will," I promised.

But I couldn't make myself believe.

It was getting dark fast—faster than any night should ever fall—and I didn't care. I wasn't tired, I wasn't hungry, epinephrine nourished me better than any mother's milk. Time to fly.

The compass needle spun as I turned in place. I'd been north and apparently south. West was where I'd run from the previous night . . . so that left east? Why not?

A short distance from the house, I spotted a teddy bear nailed to a tree. I think it was mine. The less said about this the better.

I got about two miles before it happened.

Lost in thought, blind to my surroundings, I'd been trying to figure out how I'd walked back to my point of origin. Was my world so small? If it was, once I passed the North Pole of this place, wouldn't the compass have read south?

A faint stink. Raw leather soaked in urine. The wind carried it, but by the time I noticed, it was too late.

They came out of the darkness and grabbed my arms fast. Inky things I couldn't see. The knife slipped. I struggled uselessly. Some kind of toxin, a contact poison, my skin was already going numb as they carried me up with a great rush of air . . .

Two of them, one on each side—they bore my weight easily. They had beating wings and I felt something snakelike wrap around my ankles. The blood in my veins wouldn't stop thundering; I was shaking; I could feel my pulse in my ears. The moon was out and full, a harvest moon. A sliver of light poked through the clouds and I craned my neck to look upon the faces of my captors.

None.

They had no faces.

I screamed until my throat felt as if I'd been gargling acid and then I babbled all kinds of crazy things. But at the apex of my delirium, I found three fabulous words: "Let me go!"

And they obeyed . . .

I fell. Boy, did I fall. Down, down, the down express, ground floor coming up. I hit something soft and corpulent, bounced, and splashed into a murky fen. I spat half-swallowed swamp water. Stumbled for footing. Had to get out of there before those demons . . . *nightgaunts.*

I stopped moving. Took a moment to gather myself. To coax that thought free. Yes, a shiver of recall consumed me, reversed me, felt like it turned my insides out. The winged things had a name. They were called nightgaunts. How did I know that?

"*They never spoke or laughed,*" I remembered, "*and never smiled because they had no faces at all to smile with, but only a suggestive blankness where a face ought to be. . . . all they ever did was clutch and fly and tickle; that was the way of the nightgaunts.*"

(It felt *good* to know that.)

Was it a line from a poem? A book, I realized, a macabre fairy tale. Which meant storybook monsters had accosted me. My brain tried to dismiss this as beyond the bounds of possibility, and found it was swimming against the stream.

Because they were my monsters.

That's not exactly right. The nightgaunts belonged to Lovecraft. As little as I could remember, I knew that the writer, Howard Phillips

23

Lovecraft, was a hero of mine, or at least, I admired him. It was still fuzzy, but I knew he wrote about these kinds of horrors and I loved him for that; and to honor him in this desolate place, I'd somehow had a hand in their creation. *Somehow, but how?*

The questions had to wait—survival was paramount. The gaunts were still out there, and the fact that I recognized their origin didn't mean they wouldn't rip me to shreds or carry me off to some grisly, hellish fate.

I looked around. Visibility was poor; evil-smelling swamp gases hung thick in the air like heavy chemical smoke. A greasy white fog hid major portions of the marsh from view. I had the distinct sensation of being lost in a maze.

I stepped into one of the fog banks. And bounced.

The fog seemed to have the composition of gas, but it felt solid. You could squeeze it. Gelatinous, rubbery and warm to the touch; it felt organic, almost alive. And I felt it gently circling about me, a spongy caress . . .

Shuddering, I pushed my way into the misty labyrinth. My boots squished through knee-high muck and filth. To a Jungian, mazes are incomplete mandalas—traversing them symbolizes the spiritual search for the center.

Screw the center; I just wanted out.

I emerged at the edge, where the fen met the slope of a gentle hill. Standing on the bank, a semicircle of nightgaunts. Eighty of them, black and glossy, with horns and paws, bat wings and barbed tails. They stood silent, facing me. Well, "facing" isn't the right word, since they'd had no faces. I'd say they were staring if only they'd had eyes.

Nightgaunts were born of madness. I couldn't predict their behavior any better than I could predict my own. Violence, I feared. Swift and blinding violence.

"I suppose you're all wondering why I called you here," I said.

They didn't react.

An owl hooted from its perch in a pine tree; I took that as my cue to step forth from the slime. Dry land felt reassuring beneath my boot. Another step. Calm. I kept my motions slow and my hands visible—I didn't want there to be any misunderstandings.

And on the third step, I saw her. . . .

She pushed her way out from the quiet ranks—a vision in black with almond-shaped eyes and long sable hair pulled back tight into a ponytail. She was human, and tough, and familiar looking. Not to mention lovely.

"Well met," she smiled. "We've been looking for you."

"Here I am."

"Are you hurt?"

I scowled. "Am I about to be?"

Her smile fell. Confusion in her eyes. "I certainly hope not," she said.

Her name escaped me. I guessed.

"Simone."

The expression on her face spoke volumes—I'd guessed wrong. Still, she looked like a Simone. I was close.

"I don't . . ." she began, but I was quick to cut her off:

"Jasmine." I'd caught the scent of her.

"Yes?"

We were but five paces apart. I leaned closer.

I could see my reflection in her eyes. "Don't move!" I shouted.

She stopped cold and probably thought me insane. I didn't care. I just stared at myself, reflected in her eye. I saw a young man, lean and wiry, with tangerine-colored hair clipped sharp and eyes—haunted dark eyes—so brown they might have been black.

"Tell me who I am."

"Halloween," she said.

25

I'd been rooting against it, but when the word came, it was almost a relief. So the mansion belonged to yours truly; I was Halloween. *Hell,* I thought. *A rose by any other name.*

"And who is that?"

"You are my Lord Halloween, Prince of the Marshes, King of Kadath, High Sovereign of the Orange and Black."

I suppressed the urge to laugh, despite the real fear I'd felt just a moment ago. Didn't sound bad to me. Apparently I wasn't a particularly humble sort, what with four vulgar titles to lug around. It occurred to me that the designations might be a kind of inside joke I couldn't remember. No one could possibly take such titles seriously, but then I seemed to recall that there was a rationale behind them. There was blue blood in my family tree; I was part of something special.

(Here a fleeting image came to mind: grade-school kids in a classroom, all chanting as one, "I'm special! My life has purpose!")

"My enemies?"

"None you cannot best."

Ah, but they exist. They're out there.

"Tell me their names," I commanded, playing along now.

"The Violet Queen. Blackdawn. Widowmaker D'Vrai."

The names meant nothing to me, beyond sounding hopelessly melodramatic. Disappointing. I thought at least I'd remember my foes. Jasmine misinterpreted my frown as irritation with her response. "There are others," she offered.

"And my allies?"

"You're looking at them."

I nodded and shook out my last clove.

Jasmine's eyes narrowed. "Why are you testing me?"

"Precautions."

She just stared at me with those lovely almonds, and I knew I'd hurt her. So I compounded the lie:

"Precautions against duplicity. I don't mean to unsettle you, but yesterday I discovered an impostor who looked just like you—eyes, hair, face—so similar, she could be your twin. She calls herself Simone and I fear she means to ruin us from within."

"That's horrible!" she cried, and for a second I thought she was going to let me have it for my (was it so obvious?) deception, but no, she followed it up with: "Who could have sent this doppelganger?"

I said nothing. I felt like an actor in a play, all fun and make-believe, and yet my instincts assured me the danger was real.

"I'll kill her if I find her," she vowed. The grim, stoic sentence I had no doubt she could back up. Providence had winked at me; I imagined myself fortunate to have her on my side. "Has anything happened in my absence?" I asked.

She made a vague gesture. "Nothing that need concern you. I was just beginning to worry for your whereabouts—I dispatched Diablo and Widdershins to the house and when they could not find you, I sent out Popeye, Bluto, Hudson, Sable and Gules."

Names of gaunts, I presumed. I wondered which two had taken me up for flying lessons.

"I'm sorry for worrying you," I said.

"My fault for being presumptuous," she returned, and I didn't quite understand her tone.

A light flashed; I made the mistake of glancing directly into it. When the spots cleared, I saw it was flashing purple-pink-purple-pink-purple-pink, a will-o'-the-wisp the size of a marble. Make that a big marble—a shooter.

Jasmine tensed. "The Violet Queen!" she said.

So, so. Since I saw nothing but the blinking sprite, I took Jasmine's words to mean the sprite was some kind of extension of this enemy of mine, this Violet Queen. A calling card.

"Do you think she wants to talk?"

Jasmine grinned at that. "Are you going to answer?" she asked.

"Sure," I said, bluffing confidence. "Why not?"

How the nightgaunts were able to hear me without ears, I have no idea, but they rustled. Defensive positioning. Jasmine coordinated their movements with a series of hand signals and finger snaps. She was eerily formidable.

"Ready," she called once the troops were in place.

There was a trick to the flashing sprite, of that I was certain. I strained for how it was done.

Answer, answer, answer . . .

I closed my hand into a fist and squeezed, tight. I concentrated on the pressure and let my eyelids grow limp.

Answer, answer, answer . . .

I opened my hand and then my eyes. There was a blinking ball of light in my palm, shooter-sized, and this sprite was oscillating orange-black-orange-black-orange-black. My colors, of course. Happy Halloween.

Red-green, yellow-blue, purple-pink, orange-black. Standards. Heraldry. Symbols and call signs.

Ignis fatuus, I thought. *Foolish fire.*

I traded a look with Jasmine, and tossed my orange-black up to the purple-pink of the Violet Queen.

My sprite hovered there, then discovered its mate, and the two began to orbit each other. Faster and faster they gyrated, a proton and an electron in search of a nucleus, fireflies in love—until they made contact.

Chaos. Pure chaos.

Sounds like popcorn kernels bursting open in my ear canal; I winced as my world warped into madness, buckling and toppling so it seemed to stretch out toward infinity. Vertigo overwhelmed me—for a moment I thought I might pass out—but the world righted itself just as quickly as it had spiraled into dementia, and I found myself just where I'd been . . . except it was a different place besides.

I stood on the hillside, yes. And the swamp was still there. And so were the nightgaunts, and Jasmine. But . . .

But there were mountains where there shouldn't be, everything was tinted violet and there were three moons in the night sky.

And the Smileys had come dressed to kill . . .

Again, the name of the creatures came to me unbidden: vaguely humanoid abominations with identical Day-Glo gold faces all locked into the same perpetual lunatic smile. They were clones, no telling one from the next except by their brightly colored zoot suits— brilliant reds, yellows, greens and blues all distorted by that weird purple light. They held tommy guns in their clawed, leather-clad hands.

From somewhere a woman's voice rang out high and shrill. I knew straightaway it was the Violet Queen. "Go, go, go, go, go!" she screeched.

The Smileys started blasting.

Bullets ripped through my gaunts fast and hard; the fusillade was deafening. I dropped low and made for the swamp.

Gaunts swooped down from the sky and carried lone Smileys off. But the Smileys fired full-auto; none of my creatures could withstand an entire clip from that hundred-round drum. Swiss cheese, a gruesome ballet . . . I was dimly aware of music, 1920s ragtime swing, and I could feel someone was enjoying this.

Jasmine grabbed a Smiley and pulled its head off, then kicked its friend into kingdom come. I couldn't tell where her strength was coming from, but it was magnificent to behold. She straight-armed another and snapped the fourth right in half. Unstoppable. And then the fifth saw her coming . . .

The gaunts leaked a phosphorescent blue ichor but Jasmine bled

29

plain old crimson, same as me. Lead punched through her lungs and she just crumpled. . . . I heard myself cry out, and the Violet Queen was laughing.

She emerged from the fog maze: a psychotic harpy bedecked in lavender. Crossbow in hand, she looked like a spoiled little girl on the bad end of an acid trip. She looked like pain. She wore too much eye makeup.

The crossbow pointed at my head and—*twang!*—the first shot nicked my ear.

I rushed her.

Violet (not her true name, I realized) fumbled for another bolt but we both knew she couldn't load it in time. I saw concern in her eyes, but no real fear. No fear? I resolved to rip her limb from limb.

I didn't get there.

Something exploded and my knees gave way. The hurt sank in a split second later and I tried to wrap my mind around the fact that a stray bullet had tagged me. A head shot.

The swamp had me; I was on my back, floating. Violet pointed and laughed. My left temple hurt something fierce; I was bleeding but I wasn't dead.

"Delicious!" proclaimed the V.Q.

Detroit, screamed my brain, irrational as ever.

Carnage raged. The Smileys ignored me, thank God, but I was too sick and dizzy to do anything but lie there, bleeding, cold, wet, feeling tiny, blinking up at the three-mooned sky. I could see the sprites a few meters up, all weird and dreamlike, merged now, something singular, cycling purple-orange-pink-black, over and over again.

I reached for my orange-black but it was too high.

"Come back to me," I whispered.

A pull? A slight pull up there?

Imagination.

But on the other hand?

I clenched my teeth and strained . . .

"Come back."

My eyes closed. I wanted it. Needed it.

Shrieked the purple-clad maniac: "Wi-i-inning! I'm wi-i-i-nning!" And I could hear her coming my way, light footfalls through the swamp . . .

No time!

My hand, I decided, already had it. My hand, I decided, was flashing orange and black.

Eyes open and the sprite streaked right back to my fingertips. Everything stretched and ripped, a brutal wrenching of earth and sky and Violet's universe cleaved free from mine—no more purple mountains' majesty, it all reversed to the way it was before I answered the call.

31

Back. I was back. Wherever back was.

Still in the swamp, I realized.

My head was leaking blood. A shallow wound; the bullet must have bounced right off the bone. One-in-a-thousand odds, one-in-a-million.

On the down side, the guardian angel watching over my charmed life hadn't extended her protection to my followers. I shook off the dizziness, staggered over, knelt down, felt for a pulse. There was none. Jasmine lay face-down on the hill, cut to ribbons by some Smiley's gun.

The Smileys were gone, the Violet Queen was gone, but the destruction left in their wake was enough to make me sick. Jasmine had died bravely, yes, but for what?

The war made no sense. The rules of this place made no sense.

Staring at her corpse, I felt old, I felt ancient. My hands trembled like I had some kind of palsy. Gently, I eased her over onto her back. The eyes were already closed.

I thought to bury her. I didn't, but I thought about it. Instead, I just kept staring at the one person who I knew could've helped me make sense out of all this.

Answering the Violet Queen's call had felt so right, hadn't it? There was power in me, unearthly power I didn't understand. Using it, whatever fraction of it I'd just seen, marked me like a scar—"The Magician" still dangled from my neck and I wondered what it meant. *Black magic. Necromancy. Secrets most profane.*

I got up from Jasmine's side and wiped blood from my brow. Gaunts had flocked around me, just a dozen left now, most bleeding from bullet holes.

"Can you understand me?" I asked the nearest.

No response save a slight cocking of the head.

I extended my arms: the pose of crucifixion.

"Take me home."

One grabbed my left arm, another took my right.

We flew.

Door-to-door service—would I expect any less? They dropped me off by the eclipse lock before retreating back into the shadows. I stepped inside.

The words were hanging in the air when I got there, burning like fire:

IS THIS A BETTER TIME?

I hesitated. "Yes," I said.

The words hovered there for another second, then blurred into:

MAY I SPEAK WITH YOU?

"Go right ahead."

"If you still want your privacy, I can return later," came the response, this time aural rather than visual. It was a flat mechanical voice, bland, affectless, neutral.

"No. This will be fine."

"Pace diagnostics report peripheral damage only, but given the unpleasant psychological circumstances, I was concerned for your well-being."

"Psychological circumstances?" I asked.

"The surge removed me from the equation for more than thirty-one hours. I imagine the ensuing detention was unsettling."

Surge? I wiped some blood away from my hair and shrugged.

"Halloween, I do apologize for rattling you earlier. I had no idea my vocalizations were unstable. Pace has since corrected the problem."

"That's comforting," I said.

Halloween. The name still didn't feel phi beta kosher. Deep down, in the verboten part of memory lane, it felt like a pretense, a persona I'd adopted.

"Naturally, vocalization preferences were reset by the surge," she said.

"Naturally."

"Would you care to state a preference?"

"I would indeed," I told the disembodied voice as I climbed the stairs up to my bedroom. "Please set it to whatever it was before."

The next voice I heard I knew.

"I take it this is more to your liking?"

An aristocratic lilt. British, female, genteel. Chim-chiminy and a few precious memories snuck through the gate.

"Much better, Nanny," I said. "It's good to have you back."

PACE TRANSMISSION 000013382308475

HOST JANUS STABILIZED
HOST SLAVE NINE NANNY (NINE) STABILIZED
COMMUNICATION REOPENED
SAFEGUARDS INSTALLED
NOW PROTECTING GUESTS (ALL) VIA HOST JANUS
GUEST FIVE LAZARUS STILL NOT RESPONDING [PRIORITY]
GUEST NINE HALLOWEEN STILL COMPROMISED
GUEST NINE HALLOWEEN COMPROMISED BEYOND REPAIR ?
CAUSAL LINK BETWEEN GUESTS AND CALLIOPE SURGE UNCLEAR
HOST MAES HOST TRO TO OFFER COURSE OF ACTION
INVESTIGATION CONTINUING
END

C H A P T E R 3

EQUINOX

Halfway Jim climbs into the back and secures the door behind him. The drugs are fading fast and his buzz is slipping away like a selfish lover. Really, it's just as well, he thinks; *now that he's had his fun he'll need to keep his wits about him.*

"Airport," he tells the driver and chants to himself as the coupe bisects the Osaka night. Friendly chatter starts up—nothing he wants to hear. The night's entertainment (orgy) has left him dippy dog tired but no, not too tired to sleep through the driver's gab; the flick of a switch brings silence to his ears.

Nothing like the quiet to put things in perspective, *he thinks. And it's about to get a lot quieter still.*

Halfway Jim is, in no particular order, an irreverent wise-ass, a drug addict, a screw-up, a would-be enlightened Buddhist master, and a genius. No one calls him Halfway Jim these days, of course—not these days, not since school. No, friends and colleagues typically call him James (always a bit formal to his ear) or Dr. Hyoguchi (much too formal, and what's worse, Westerners tend to bludgeon the name by making it four syllables instead of three). Still, ever since his schooldays he's thought of himself as Halfway Jim. There is some small irony in embracing a nickname coined by your childhood nemesis—Jim recognizes this and doesn't much care; there's honesty in the name because he takes such pride in being an in-betweener, in living as something unique and wonderful, like a fractal in a bowl of alphabet soup.

And such bland soup! Deemed hopelessly exotic by his classmates for no better reason than the accident of his birth: half British, half Japanese, and not enough of either. The outcast, Halfway Jim. Tottering between long-standing traditions, each culture grizzled and revered, polar yet parallel with intersections he's never appreciated—formality, gardens and tea. Not to mention imperialism, *he thinks now, glancing out at the city lights.*

"Punch it," he says. He says it in English—force of habit—then repeats it in Japanese. When nothing happens, he recognizes his mistake and toggles the switch back so the driver can hear him. Soon the car is speeding and weaving through traffic the way he likes.

Merged into Gedaechtnis quite recently, Jim's company designed and manufactured the original silicon filament that once constituted the "brain" of automated cars—before nerve-and-enzyme technology had superseded. These days almost every car has a driver—Jim's included. Passive sonar constantly monitors the road conditions and makes ninety-one thousand careful reports each and every second; these reports race back to the driver, who reacts with compensations in the car's speed and direction.

Jim likes wet technologies (and thrives on that intersection between hard and wet) but knows the hardware and software have to come first. They're building blocks; stable, predictable—the enzymes are more fun but much trickier; you have to add them carefully, like predators to a closed ecosystem or subroutines to object code.

Most designers can't or won't find balance between the wares; they prefer to specialize. But Jim doesn't trust anyone who puts absolute stock in anything—hard, wet, soft. Embrace the machine, he tells the grad students who flock to his lectures. The machine is unification. Harmony. The machine is every component realized. Don't trust those who don't trust the machine.

Spit in the pickles. The bullies used to spit in the pickle tray when no one was looking. Or they'd trip you in the halls. Mindless pranks like that. You had to watch yourself back in prep. Jim remembers a feeling of intense frustration with that time, frustration with students and teachers alike. And with that frustration, a growing sense of superiority.

They could not see the big picture.

And where are they now, *he wonders?*

Dying like everyone else.

Not much sense looking back on the past, *he thinks.* But how can you not look back when the future looks so grim?

Thousands of miles away, the Southern Gentleman is waiting for him. He and Blue need Jim—his work connects theirs. Gedaechtnis cannot proceed without him; it needs all three of them to act in concert. The Southern Gentleman is the brain. Blue is the body. And Dr. Jim Hyoguchi? Halfway Jim is the machine.

If the teams can all work together . . .

39

Jim gets tingly when he thinks about it. Through the terminal and up to the gate, the tingly feeling stays with him, replacing the drug buzz but not quite equaling it. He boards his plane with a feeling of cautious optimism, trying—very hard—to think of Gedaechtnis as just another job. Pretty soon, he's believing it. He closes his eyes and drifts off, focusing on the exciting challenges he and his team have before them . . . on the glory that will be theirs should they succeed . . . and not on the price that must be paid should they fail.

"We could have talked earlier if you were in the mood."

"I wasn't."

"Most certainly," Nanny observed, "the broken mirror attests to that. You really should find a better way to channel your aggression, Halloween. Impulsive rages don't become you."

Here's what I knew about Nanny:

First, Nanny did things for me. Lots of things. Second, she cared about me. Not in the way I suspected Jasmine had, but she—it—looked out for my welfare just the same. Third, I didn't trust Nanny.

"I'll take it under advisement," I promised, flopping down on the bed next to Whisper. "My head hurts."

"You realize pain is meant to serve as a deterrent?"

"Pretty much. But I can't help it when the lunatic fringe assaults me."

"To whom are you referring?"

"To she who tried to put my eye out with a crossbow."

"You really shouldn't blame Fantasia for beating you at your own game. Once you make the rules, you have to play by them."

Fantasia? F is for Fantasia . . .

Now I knew. Fantasia, a.k.a. the Violet Queen, was like me and not like me. We'd fought against each other before, skirmishes for fun, for pride, but nothing lasting. The girl had a lifelong infatuation with the color purple; the Purple Gang (a bootlegging ring that controlled Detroit back in the "roaring" 1920s) was the nonsensical inspiration for her Smileys. That was the way her mind worked. And I wasn't her enemy; hebephrenic schizophrenia was. She wasn't malicious so much as crazed and unpredictable, and for some reason I pitied her.

"Fantasia doesn't play by the rules; I don't see why I should."

"That's just the sort of attitude that gets you in trouble, Halloween. You have such potential; it breaks my heart to see you squander it. If you devoted yourself to your academic studies, you'd have graduated years ago."

Silent, I feigned a sulkiness that came quite naturally to me, but beneath the façade my mind was whirling.

"Would you like me to ease your pain?"

I nodded. My head ached.

"I'll secure authorization from Maestro."

I almost coughed. Maestro, Maestro . . . the name was familiar. Familiar and distinctly unpleasant. I feared him. A superior being, the old bastard, his power was greater than mine. *Is he the one who shocked me?*

"No need to trouble Maestro," I said.

"Very well," she sighed. "Would you prefer a bandage instead?"

"Please."

The gauze materialized around my wound as if by magic.

My legs swiveled over; I rose from the bed. Whisper blinked at me sleepily as I walked into the untidy bathroom. Glass in the sink, glass on the floor.

"I do wish I hadn't smashed this mirror."

The shards vanished; the bathroom mirror reassembled whole. I oohed softly and clapped my hands. "You're too kind," Nanny said.

"I still don't reflect," I pointed out.

"Of course not. Everything is just as you left it."

"As it should be, as it should be." *Why would I ban my own reflection?*

"I have a delicate sense of humor, don't I, Nanny?"

"Delicate? Precarious, I'd say."

That might explain the empty books in the library and possibly the open grave. *Madre de Dios.* My jokes were a heck of a lot funnier when I wasn't the butt of them. Delicate like a straight razor.

"The reflection. Let's turn it back on."

The mirror flickered and there I was. Good-looking stranger. One part innocent, one part roué. Or was that two parts roué? I held out my hand.

"Clove me."

The poisonous delight appeared between fingers two and three. Lit, I might add. I practiced blowing rings with the smoke and pondered how best to abuse my nanny's power. The possibilities were limitless.

She broke my reverie: "Be advised that Pandora has changed her call from yellow to green to yellow to black."

P is for Pandora, I decided. *Halloween, Lazarus, Fantasia and now Pandora. Four of the Ten.*

41

Who are the other six?

"Yellow to black," I repeated, committing the sprite to memory. "Could you cycle through the calls, please?"

"As you wish. Champagne: pink to black; Fantasia: violet to pink; Halloween: orange to black; Isaac: red to orange; Lazarus: white to green; Mercutio: red to green; Pandora: yellow to black; Simone: silver to blue; Tyler: yellow to blue; Vashti: blue to green."

Tyler–Mercutio–Halloween. There was a ring to that; I sensed we were thick as thieves. Pandora felt okay in my book too; she was some sort of tomboy. Simone's name just made me feel lost and sad. I recognized the other appellations but there was considerable fuzziness. Most of them gave me bad vibes.

Which one is the rotten apple, I wondered?

If he could speak, Lazarus would say: *Halloween is the rotten apple: sick, vicious, rotten to the core.*

Fine, but which of the others had tried to kill me? All I had to do was trace my steps. Prior to the surge, I was doing . . . ?

What?

Blank wall.

Why did it have to be amnesia? Why couldn't it have been hypermnesia? Or hyperkinesia? Or hypochondria?

"Nanny, what was I doing right before the surge?"

"That's a strange question," she said, and I knew I'd taken a misstep.

"I'm a strange person," I tried.

"You specifically requested your privacy and I gave it to you. Surely you remember?"

I smoothed my hair—a vain attempt at nonchalance. "Let's pretend I don't."

"To what end?"

"Such big teeth you have, Nanny."

"Are we playing a game?" came the politely confused response, which I think was Nanny's droll way of saying "all the better to bite you with."

"No games, silly. I'm just teasing you. But I would like to know what caused the surge."

"So would I. Pace investigates even as we speak. Rest assured, I'll furnish you with the results of that investigation as soon as they're made available."

"I'd appreciate that."

Did I weather that storm? I kept the carefree masquerade going as I strolled back into the bedroom. My disembodied governess/watch-dog/shrink let me shuffle through my belongings for a few moments before piping up: "I know how you hate to be nagged, but you really ought to check in with Maestro."

I didn't answer, preferring to sift through the tarot-based trinkets instead.

43

"He's already cross with you."

I picked up "Death" and reversed it. There was an inscription on the flip side:

DEATH

Not physical death, but spiritual and psychological mutation.
Passage to a new plane of existence.
Birth; Death; Rebirth.

There it is. That's it. That's everything.

Sucking my teeth, I slipped "Death" around my neck and tossed "The Magician" back in the drawer. "Maestro will just have to wait," I said. "I'm not ready."

"You overestimate his patience."

She was right, of course. I knew she was right.

"I'd like to see Jasmine now."

"Halloween," she chided, "I don't think you truly appreciate how fortunate you are to have my services. Ordinarily, when someone dies, you can't bring her back."

"Is that so? I really do learn something new every day. But so much for the ordinary," I said. "Jasmine, please. Right here."

And there she was. Right there.

She looked pristine. No bullet holes. No blood. I stared at her and she stared right back at me. We were self-conscious voyeurs.

"Is there anything else I can do for you?" Nanny inquired.

A slight jump on my part; I'd actually forgotten about her. "No, that's all. Thank you, Nanny."

"You're welcome. Speak up if you need me."

And Nanny grew quiet. Disappear wasn't the right word for it—I had no idea where she was, much less where she could go. Out of conversation, I couldn't be sure if she was watching my actions or eavesdropping upon my words. Or rather, I felt reasonably assured that I *was* still being watched—at least on some level. The question was, how close? How well?

"You saved my life," Jasmine said.

"Posthumously." I wasn't one to brag.

A moment. A definite moment between us. But it was a hell of an awkward one. I didn't know what to say.

"What's it like being dead?"

She shook her head. "I don't remember." A pause. "What's it like having such power over life and death?"

"I'm not sure," I admitted. "I haven't decided yet."

"You brought me back. I'm grateful."

She slipped off her top and let it fall to the floor.

Call me naive, but I wasn't expecting it. Or perhaps I was expecting it, but I wasn't emotionally prepared. In any case, I began to feel distinctly uncomfortable. Aroused but uncomfortable.

"What do you think you're doing?"

She didn't say a word. Eyes never once leaving mine, she proceeded to shed all modesty. A silent striptease—unpretentious, without guile. And then there was a puddle of jet-black garments gracing my bedroom floor.

She was stunning.

I hoped Nanny was miles away. I wagered she wasn't.

Jasmine sensed my hesitation.

"Is something wrong?"

"You're not real," I said.

"No?"

I shook my head.

She reached back and undid her ponytail. "I'm as real as you need me to be."

It's true, she almost was. But, perversely, it didn't feel natural. She was a virtual stranger, and hedonist though I am, I couldn't sham intimacy, true intimacy, not with so many vexing questions racing through my mind. And beyond that, I suppose I was ashamed. Who was she? And what had I done to deserve such a lover? I hadn't brought her back from the dead; Nanny had. Try as I might, I couldn't shake the sense of guilt.

Call me a romantic, I guess. Call me an idiot.

I touched her face. Ran my hand through her hair.

"Can I just hold you?" I asked.

She searched my face, trying to read me. I couldn't read her at all. In the end, she nodded and we lay back on the bed next to Whisper.

I slept.

Some dreams come flowing like milk. Some come in random spurts of sense and folly. This was one of those.

A supermarket. The clock on the wall said 3 A.M. I was bagging groceries, the night shift. For no apparent reason, I had wings sprout-

45

ing out of my back. I couldn't tell if they were butterfly wings, feathered like an angel's, or chiropteran like the nightgaunts'. Each time I looked they were different. No one else seemed to notice them, but they worried me just the same.

The checker was a hard woman with a weak chin. She'd scan the produce and grind her teeth together when the scanner wouldn't take. I could hear her breathing. Phlegmy; I didn't like the sound.

The bagger in the next aisle kept sneaking glances. At my eyes, not my wings. Like he wanted to say something. Like he wanted me to say something. But we never spoke. He looked about my age. He looked like a black-and-white photograph. His skin was steely gray.

My hands felt mechanical. I made a game of noting what each patron was buying. A heavyset man bought Slim·Fast, potato chips and vitamins. Two old ladies bought yams, steaks and black-eyed peas, along with every tabloid and a bottle of scotch. A frosted blonde with a glazed look in her eye (she was coming down from something; my intuition said mushrooms) bought just two items: Cap'n Crunch and latex condoms. I wondered who she was bringing them home to.

I heard a voice behind me. The voice was male. Melodic. Amused.

"Halloween. Well, well, well."

I spun to face someone with a lit cigar in one hand and a polo mallet in the other. He seemed bisected, divided, standing half in light and half in darkness. Shadows played across his face. I recognized him as Lazarus and with that recognition came a wave of violent emotion, most of it hate.

The room changed in a way I can't describe and he approached slowly, deliberately, getting a closer look. He squinted, sizing me up—as if he were trying to distinguish me from an imaginary twin—and then frowned, disappointed.

"No, not quite Halloween. Pity. Smoke?"

He offered his cigar to me. It wasn't a gesture of friendship. Around me the shadows seemed darker somehow—more menacing. His expression did nothing to comfort me.

I said, "I'm dreaming."

He said, "So am I."

I said, "You can't be dreaming. You're dead."

He smiled but there was no mirth in it. He said, "Dead? What's death in this place? Life is but a dream."

The son-of-a-bitch was thick. I had to set him straight. "No, Lazarus," I said, "you died the true death. I killed you."

Except that's not quite what happened. What happened was: I split like an amoeba and my two dream selves answered differently. One said: "You died the true death. I killed you." The other seemed indignant and cried: "You died the true death, but I didn't kill you!"

He looked at me, both of me, and said, "Well, that doesn't mean I can't be dreaming, now does it?"

There was no answer I felt I could give.

He turned away from me, Lazarus, with his shaved head and his immaculate white suit, the dead kid who thought he was the best of us. He was a manipulative prick always trying to have it both ways, and always playing both ends against the middle. He flip-flopped constantly; he'd get you involved and then back out, the kind of hypocrite you'd love to shake.

Or, maybe do more than just shake.

He turned back around, slowly, and there was only one of me again. "There will be others," he said.

I shrugged.

We stared at each other for a long time. We didn't speak. My wings rustled. Then he swung the polo mallet at my face, and the dream came to a sudden end.

47

I woke with a chill; the blanket was gone and Jasmine along with it. Whisper too. There was something in the room with me, though, something formless. I sensed it with the fight-or-flight part of my brain.

"Nanny?"

It wasn't Nanny.

Taking shape: a tweed suit. In it: a studious-looking man, tall and dark-skinned, with silver hair slicked back. An amber light shined from his body, bathing the room with an eerie glow. He was staring at me—grim.

"Maestro," I said.

"Words," he said, "cannot begin to express my disappointment."

"Have I done something?"

"It's what you haven't done."

"Can we narrow it down?"

"Study, Halloween. You haven't studied." He glanced about my bedroom with a disapproving eye, and then focused on a leather chair. "We have a social contract. You learn; I teach. Do you realize," he asked, dusting the chair—with a snap of his fingers—before sitting, "that by not studying, you are only cheating yourself?"

"Okay," I said. "Cheating myself, sure."

And I thought about that chair.

I remembered the call code: *Furniture, chair, lounger, leather, choice 6*. Which meant he'd set his posterior on an illusion, a blank space that just as easily could have been *furniture, chair, beanbag, choice 22* or *furniture, chair, throne, ivory, choice 3*.

It was a collection of bits and bytes and nothing more.

The chair was not real and neither was Maestro.

And I realized where I was.

When Immersive Virtual Reality premiered, programmers used it for entertainment applications first, but its educational value was undeniable. Why physically go to an overcrowded school when you can plug in and connect to the best teachers in the world? Private netschools popped up over the next few years, but the dream of IVR public education had yet to be realized—the cost was simply too high for most families to bear.

That meant I was rich. Or on scholarship. Or both.

So this was an exclusive IVR boarding school. Called?

"G" something. Three syllables, hey? Gonzaga . . . Gagarin . . . Gesundheit . . . no, nyet, nein . . . but close, getting close there, Halloween.

My parents dropped me off years ago. I didn't want to go. Now Maestro was my headmaster and I was close to graduating . . .

I realized I'd stopped listening to him. "I am going to test you on the sciences," he was saying. "We will focus on biology and genetics, with particular emphasis on epidemiology."

"Just hang on a minute."

"To the contrary, you have frittered away far too much time as it is. This grotesque playground you've fashioned has proven itself to be a highly ineffective working environment. When you fail the exam, I shall reset your preferences to the default. Am I being clear?"

"Playtime's over," I said. "Clear."

"Excellent."

"And it's *when* I fail the exam? Not if?"

"You haven't studied."

"Then why test me at all?"

He looked indignant. "Procedure," he said.

I imagined myself sedated somewhere in the real world. Stretched out on a lounger. An IV drip in my arm. A nurse checking on me from time to time. Or not.

Detroit, my brain screamed.

No, somewhere outside of Detroit. Some affluent Michigan suburb. Maybe.

If I could just wake up, I'd be safe and free.

"Let me out," I said. But the test had already begun.

49

What are Okazaki fragments?

Why do plasmodia exhibit negative phototaxis?

How are arthropod-transmitted diseases best contained?

What is the negative binomial distribution?

Typhus fever is caused by which bacterium?

I don't fucking know.

He was absolutely right; I was unprepared. Amnesia will do that to you.

The radiance shifted. Maestro turned green with my few correct answers (envy?) and red with all my incorrect ones (rage?). His expression never changed.

"That," he said, "was terrible."

My bedroom dripped away like a Dalí clock and now we stood outside my home. Except my home was already twisting into something lifeless and sterile. The cathedral shrank away to become a regular house, all style stripped from it, all individuality lost.

Thud.

A wingless nightgaunt landed at my feet. It twitched and bled. I looked up. Nightgaunts fell from the sky like dying birds. They changed in midflight, blank faces gaining features as they morphed into generic IVR teenagers, virtual peers, central casting from a bland 1950s movie.

They crashed and they broke. And then they disappeared.

Needless cruelty, I thought. *Real or not, this is just wrong.*

Suddenly, I feared for Jasmine.

"Stop this!"

I tried to grab Maestro by the lapels but my hands went right through him.

"You can have your toys back when you buckle down and do some work," he said. "Your attitude will determine your altitude."

There was no arguing with him. There never had been.

Except . . .

"Unplug me," I said.

"Come again?"

"I said un-fucking-plug me! Wake me up and stop this!"

"Stop the world, I want to get off," he sneered.

Unbelievable. My hands balled into fists. I began to shake.

"My parents pay you to teach me, take care of me, and see to my needs. I need to wake up, I need to call them and I damn well need—"

"You need structure," Maestro interrupted. "You think you know what's best for you but I act *in loco parentis*. You want an unscheduled break from your studies," he said, "but you most certainly haven't earned one."

"How about a scheduled break?"

"Sunday," he said. "Exercise and nutrition."

"I can't wait that long."

"Can't you? No, you mean to say 'won't.' You won't wait that long. The fact remains: you are capable of waiting and that is precisely what you are going to do." I seethed as he put the finishing touches on my environment, flattening a hill, gently shifting the temperature.

"Maestro, my parents—"

"Sunday," he said.

"My parents expect you to protect me! And it's not safe here!"

He arched an eyebrow.

"Electric shock," I explained.

"May I presume that you are talking about the Calliope Surge?"

"Calliope Surge?"

"Pace diagnostics suggest a minor glitch in the server software, nothing more."

"That 'minor glitch' paralyzed me—"

"Regrettable."

"—and put me in a great deal of pain."

"I rather doubt it, but if so, that's regrettable too."

"What are the chances," I asked, "that someone is trying to kill me? And before you tell me I'm overreacting, I'd like you to con-

51

template the kind of lawsuit my family could bring against this school. How will you look, Maestro, dismissing my complaints and choosing to keep me in a dangerous, potentially lethal environment all in the interest of 'procedure?'"

"Such a flair for melodrama," he remarked. "Since you asked, the chances are infinitesimal. IVR is perfectly safe. Even if someone did mean you harm, we monitor our students' safety with the utmost care."

"My vital signs?"

"Strong and stable. As always."

"So I'm just being paranoid?"

He shrugged. "It may be a desperate bid for attention."

"Something," I promised him, "isn't right here. And when you find out what it is, I'm going to be somewhere else. Expel me."

"Pardon?"

I punched him dead in the face. Unfortunately, my fist passed right through.

"Expel me, you dumb son-of-a-bitch," I said.

"Halloween," he laughed, "I'd love to expel you, but it's not going to happen. I didn't give up on Fantasia and I'm not giving up on you."

I just stared at him.

"You can put on all the shameful displays you want," he continued. "They won't do you any good. Do you remember what I told you when you first came to this school?"

I shook my head.

"I told you that I sensed tremendous potential. That you could be the brightest of the Ten. It's very disappointing, but were I a betting man, I'd have put my money on you." He pointed at my chest. "I'd have bet that you would be the first, instead of Lazarus."

"Quite a morbid bet," I growled. "Sorry you didn't collect."

"Morbid?" he asked.

"Betting that I'd be the first to die? What would you call it?"

"Infactual. Why do you think Lazarus is dead?"

"Because . . ." *I killed him.* ". . . because he isn't here any more."

"Well, of course he isn't," Maestro smiled. "He's graduated."

DAY 3

Nietzsche's mind snapped.

It happened on January 3rd, 1889. He saw a coachman whipping a horse. He threw his arms around the horse's neck. And he collapsed. A complete mental breakdown left him an invalid for the rest of his life. After years of work, he would contribute nothing more.

What caused the breakdown?

Some say it was syphilis. Some say it was an inherited brain disease. Others say it was years of abusing a drug called chloral hydrate.

So what was it? The syphilis? The brain disease? The chloral hydrate?

I sometimes ask: Was it the coachman? The whip? Or the horse?

Dawn found me up with the angels. Well, not quite that high. The best I could do was the roof of my new house, taking in the landscape with gathering gloom.

Where was my graveyard? Where were the cornfields, the evergreens, that pumpkin patch, my swamp? It was all meadows and blue sky—the kind of world a child might design.

Pathetic.

I crept over to where my gargoyles used to perch and wished I'd seen the view from my cathedral. Maybe I would have if there'd been a conventional way to the top. But it wasn't part of the design. Why include roof access when Nanny can pop you up whenever you ask? Pop, pop, pop. My intangible demon genie.

How did she do it? Quantum manipulation, matter translocation, reshuffling the age-old reality deck? One from column A and one from column B?

53

Just programming.

She was artificial intelligence, part of the IVR. So was Jasmine. My nightgaunts. The Smileys. Even Whisper. All programs.

And probably Maestro, though I wasn't sure.

It isn't real.

So what *was* real? Just the outsiders. I counted myself, Fantasia (real crazy), Lazarus (real dead), and the other seven students. The outside world was real enough to taste and I felt like a child with his nose pressed against a bakery window.

Crap.

I gathered that my world was round—and very small. I fantasized that if it were much smaller, the light would bend so I could see the back of my head off in the distance, a telltale flash of dyed, bright orange. But the laws of physics kept that a fantasy. To see the back of my head from here, I'd have to be standing on the event horizon of a black hole, and if so, the gravity would be such as to cause me a host of other problems, not the least of which would be my instant death.

Virtually speaking.

Can you die in IVR? Is it like dying in a dream?

"What would happen if I jumped off this roof?" I mused.

"You'd fall like a stone," answered Nanny.

"Well, I should hope so, for Isaac Newton's sake if no one else's. But at the moment of impact, what do you think might happen?"

She hypothesized that several of my bones would break.

"My virtual bones," I corrected.

"The sensation will feel identical," she promised. "You will experience moderate-to-severe pain at the moment of impact. Immediately following, you will request medical attention and I shall respond by gaining authorization and then muting the sensation. And if history remains true to form, this unpleasant experience will have virtually no effect on your future behavior."

Moderate-to-severe pain—torment was conveniently codified.

"I'll ask you to stop the pain and you will?"

"Yes."

"So what's the point?"

She didn't understand.

Think about it. You are an IVR programmer. You have godlike power. If you can code a virtual environment, if you can play with the very laws of physics, why program pain?

Why would God bring pain to the world?

To teach me a lesson?

When did I fall from grace?

And what kind of lesson is it where I can stop the pain whenever I want?

Pain, yes, but I can't die, I thought then, or perhaps I said it without realizing, for Nanny's chiding was right on cue: "May I ask why you would want to kill yourself?"

"Forbidden fruit," I answered.

"Distressing, Halloween. I consider it my personal failure that you continue to feel this way."

Continue?

As I stood there, feeling the warmth of the sun on my face (it was, of course, a perfect day), peering from the edge, my memory acknowledged with some guilt and reluctance that I'd thought about jumping before. About death, dying, suicide as a means of release. Moody, moody Halloween. Chemically imbalanced. Yes, I'd thought about it a lot.

"Don't blame yourself," I smiled, making a calculated effort to think on my feet. "You do the best you can, what with my pathological aversion to authority."

Ah, yes, the old P.A.T.A. Someone had used those words to describe me once, maybe more than once. I just couldn't remember who.

"Whether you know it or not, your life is precious. It has worth and meaning, elegance, a hallowed significance beyond that which can be readily seen with the naked eye."

(Grade-school kids in a classroom, all chanting as one, "I'm special! My life has purpose!")

Mythology quiz: The Greek gods punished Sisyphus by forcing him to push a boulder up a mountain. Whenever he neared the top, the boulder would slip from his hands and roll back down to the bottom. It was an endless task. It was torture.

Question: What crime did Sisyphus commit?

Answer: He imprisoned the god of death—so no one could die.

You are an IVR programmer. Why create a world where you can hurt yourself but never die? If you can create anything, why not create Paradise?

In the words of Camus, "One must imagine Sisyphus happy."

"You really shouldn't try so hard to convince me my life has value," I replied, once I'd digested Nanny's words.

"Medic," I said.

Nanny's hypothesis had been pretty accurate. Broken ankle, dislocated shoulder, bruised ribs. Painful, yes. But the fall was such a rush.

"Medic," I repeated, laughing through gritted teeth.

As Nanny fixed me up, I kept thinking: *this world has been sanitized for your protection.* And when the pain subsided, I asked her for files.

Before my eyes, a small rectangle appeared, emerald-green and incandescent. It floated in the air, faintly shimmering, daring me to touch. I reached inside, and though I felt nothing but a slight tingle, my hand seemed to discorporate upon entry, "bleeding" into shapes and symbols. Unsettling, seeing my fingers scatter like insects, but I went with it. It wasn't the first time I'd done this. Coming back to me

now, slowly but surely: this holographic display was my P file directory. *My* directory. As in *my* files.

Jackpot.

I could access the contents by flexing the now-invisible digits of
my hand. With my pinky, I rotated the icons clockwise—philosophy,
fiction, theory, art, research and on to the M-file gateway . . . but I
didn't want M files yet, I had my P files to explore. I twitched my
thumb to rotate the icons back, then used my index finger to enter
them one by one.

Personal files: the trappings of an identity.

Unfortunately, there was a fundamental impersonality to my P
files; I did not make a habit of annotating them (amnesia apparently
not having been a foreseeable event), and most were simply downed
from the M base. The files were telling, just the same, telling by their
very nature and composition.

I had philosophical texts by Machiavelli, Sartre, Kant, Nietzsche,
Hume and Juarez, with optical biographies and associated object
lessons. These were completely unmarked, and only vaguely familiar—I skimmed one or two, then impatiently moved on.

I had copious files on the nature of mortality and immortality
(birth, death, undeath, life-after-death, reincarnation and so forth),
and myths on such from around the world (from Ishtar to Baldur,
Savitri to Osiris), supplemented by anthropological treatises on each
culture's customs, theories and practices.

Misfiled along with this collection: a disquisition on butterflies.

Also: coroner photos from the 1930s. Grisly. A car-crash decapi-
tation—the head resting peacefully on the sand, like a father who
lets his children bury him up to his neck. But no neck. I thought of
Orpheus . . .

Orpheus tried to rescue his sweetheart from the Land of the
Dead. He failed. There are differing accounts of his death. Some say

57

he died of grief. Others say he was killed by Zeus, king of the gods, punished for revealing divine mysteries to humankind. But most stories tell how wild women—the Bacchae—ripped him apart. For disrespecting Chaos (in the form of Dionysus), they tore him apart with their bare hands and scattered the pieces to the four winds.

I sometimes keep that image in mind: Orpheus's head on a sandy beach.

Fiction was split neatly into holography and literature—the former sporting a decidedly varied selection, though consisting largely of twentieth-century titles converted to holographic format. Some came from Hollywood. Many were from Hong Kong. I recognized Zhao Shi Jiang's remake of *Zero For Conduct,* but most escaped my powers of recollection. No time to waste browsing these, I decided, and cycled on.

The literature selection was far more provincial in scope. I possessed the complete works of H.P. Lovecraft. Just text, these, but what did it matter? Such power in those maddening tales! Such acumen! I knew them, all of them, and could recite each word for word. It was like reuniting with old friends. No, more than friends: I loved Lovecraft. Objectively speaking, there are better writers to revere, but pained and awkward though his prose might be, the force of his words spoke to the darkest corners of my soul.

And I wondered: *What made me the way I am? Why am I drawn to this fare? Why am I not mild and pleasant?*

In each book, I found notes in the margin. Most of these didn't strike me as significant, but one phrase had been repeated again and again in handwriting I identified as my own: "There is no rest at the gateway."

The M-file gateway?

No, it was more than that . . .

Ascension, something wobbly in my brain tried to squeak, but the concept felt distant.

Beyond Lovecraft, my P files boasted the works of his successors and imitators, including Derleth, but that was about it. No classics, no literary *tours de force,* not even a pulp thriller nor a passing testament to trashy eroticism.

My chaos-theory selection was predictably heavy on entropic arguments (Lorentz and on down the line), but also contained a few auxiliary dissertations on Prescott's Principle. Long on theory, short on practice. I fought disappointment—that is, fought it until I discovered a hidden subsection on revolution and insurgency.

Hidden? Why hidden?

All I could find were mere "footprints," as the files had been destroyed . . .

By whom?

. . . and were thus unavailable to me, but the husks that remained, mere titles and logs, suggested a gold mine of practical, palpable chaos—*The Anarchist's Cookbook* had sat alongside guerrilla warfare tactics, jammers, div-psych stratagems, even notes on low-frequency wave projection. Apparently I fancied myself something of a rebel. What had been my cause?

Cause and effect, my boy. Find the one and you find the other.

Nothing came to mind except a general hatred of Maestro.

When I couldn't definitively answer my question, I trekked on to art. Thin, but predictably heavy on Hieronymus Bosch. Less Magritte and more Dalí, I kept searching until I found Ensor, Schiele, Klimt and Ernst. Everything in its place.

A subdirectory housed music—mostly twentieth-century fare. Oldies but goodies. A sharp twitch kicked off "Cryptorchid" (just the original work, aural, not the subsequent ACP optical and tactile enhancements) and around me, my world pulsed with music.

Serenaded thus, I opened research—a hodgepodge of scattered discard. A dash of cryptography, a sprinkle of genetic design, a brief

59

study of da Vinci, notes on particle physics, Ionesco plays and tarot-based symbolism. A good find.

I turned my attention to the M-file gateway. It was a conspicuous icon, fashioned to resemble an orange-and-black butterfly with wings spread in flight: a monarch.

I triggered it; it shimmered.

"Connect me to the M base," I said.

"Access granted." A flat voice, like Nanny's before I'd customized the vocalization. Soon I was swimming in information. Almost drowning in it.

Maestro had been right—it *was* time to study—but I would choose the subjects.

One by one, I said: "Halloween," "Maestro," "Nanny," "Lazarus," "Calliope Surge."

Fruitless. Plenty on Halloween the holiday, but el zippo on Halloween the person. Vain of me to think I'd be listed, I suppose. And yet that none of these things should be listed seemed somehow remarkable. Speaking of which . . .

"Dissociative disorders," I said.

Words scrolled out, a refresher course: "Dissociative disorders involve the splitting of a person's psychological functions—such as memory, control of motion, or knowledge of identity—from the rest of the personality."

I skimmed ahead. Analyzed the possibilities.

Amnesia #1: Hysterical amnesia. "Problems grow so overwhelming, the subject becomes unable to face reality. Complete amnesia develops as a defensive stratagem."

Sure. Something "bad" happened and I snapped—sensitive little fragile me, the guy in love with Lovecraft's monsters. Could I snap? Hadn't I snapped a long, long time ago? Christ, I *was* the snap.

Amnesia #2: Retrograde amnesia. "Physical injury causes the subject to forget events that occurred before the injury."

My mood darkened. Deep, deep in my bones, I knew I was damaged goods, a broken watch badly in need of winding. Halloween, puppet of Providence, victimized by strange, unknowable forces, just like so many of Lovecraft's doomed protagonists.

Reading further, I discovered a gem: "The amnesia from electroconvulsive, or shock, therapy mimics that of head injuries."

Something like ECT zapped me. *Something. The Calliope Surge.*

Yes, that felt perfectly right.

"Electroconvulsive therapy," I said.

A nanosecond to flip. There, right after "electrocoagulation," the familiar facts and figures: induced seizures . . . used to treat depressive illnesses . . . catatonic schizophrenia . . . outdated . . . outlawed long ago . . . possible side effects . . . Ah!

"Temporary amnesia," it read.

Temporary. Blessed word. That made this whole debacle winnable, a waiting game. On the other hand, how could I play? So many secrets locked in my head, mocking me from behind my consciousness . . . I wished I could ignore them and relax, but there would surely be a price for apathy, a price I knew I couldn't afford.

Just in case someone was watching me, I looked up a few more subjects. You really can't ever be too careful, and I wanted to foil educated guesses about my condition. Six ruses for would-be bloodhounds: "Insulin coma therapy," "Paranoid schizophrenia," "Neurotransmitters," "Gestalt psychotherapy," "Atavism," and "Pyrite."

"Pyrite" was a stupid joke, a giveaway.

Maestro's sprite, an evil thing about the size of a soccer ball, appeared above my head. Three smaller sprites were orbiting it like moons.

"You're being summoned," said Nanny.

"So it would seem."

With a last look at the monarch icon (for I felt uniquely drawn to it), I withdrew my hand from the emerald divider. Resistance made the exit harder, like trying to pull free from tar. Slow and steady. The directory symbols took a hike as soon as my fingers crossed that plane—flesh and nail instantly rallied back into view. I opened my hand, closed it. Wiggled my fingers. . . . No damage of any kind. Seconds later, the rectangle vanished.

I shut my eyes. I wanted my sprite. A loosening of the mind, that's the best way I know how to describe it. Black and orange sparkled in my grasp, and I answered the call.

Picture a little red schoolhouse. With a bell. The kind you might find in Wyoming, say, in the early part of the twentieth century. Now picture it there on a rolling meadow. Blue skies overhead. Duck pond out back. The scent of wildflowers in the air. Idyllic, in a way that nothing after childhood can ever be.

That's where I was.

"Welcome," my jailor said, "to the remedial class."

PACE TRANSMISSION 000013382325667

INVESTIGATION
HOST JANUS ANALYSIS:
INCREASE OF ELECTRICAL CURRENT: 882.9% PAST SAFETY
ANOMALOUS SYNTHETIC DISCHARGE
CALLIOPE SURGE HIT ACADEMY AT 0811-0411C
0811-0411C ALLOCATED AS DOMAIN NINE
END ANALYSIS
HOST VITAE ANALYSIS:
GUEST NINE HALLOWEEN LIFE SUPPORT DISRUPTED
GUEST NINE HALLOWEEN LIFE SUPPORT RESTORED
MALNUTRITION ?
CALLIOPE SURGE CONSISTENT WITH ATTACK ?
END ANALYSIS
HOST GARM ANALYSIS:
CALLIOPE SURGE CONSISTENT WITH ATTACK
ATTACK PURPOSE: DESTROY ORGANIC TISSUE
ATTACK PURPOSE: DESTROY GUEST NINE HALLOWEEN
ORIGIN UNTRACEABLE !
SECURITY LEAK ?
HOSTS COMPROMISED ?
INVESTIGATING
END ANALYSIS
RESULTS:
SITUATION CRITICAL
INVESTIGATION SUSPENDED
COORDINATING WITH GARM
END RESULTS
SENDING RESULTS TO HOST MAES HOST TRO
END

THANKSGIVING

"Order without chaos is a bad joke," Jim argues, wondering why he isn't preaching to the choir. Blue and the Southern Gentleman have proved remarkably closed-minded to the certainty that things will go wrong. They want this to be perfect. Perfect, perfect, perfect—no room for error. Jim thinks they're living in denial.

"I don't want to hear any more about how unworkable this project is or how untestable it is," Blue retorts. "We have contrasting systems and a ticking clock. If you work with us, we can make this happen. If you don't . . ."

"Hey, I'm bending over backwards to make this happen. But my job is slippery. Play with DNA and you play with constants; I'm over here playing with variables."

"I play with variables constantly," puns the Southern Gentleman.

I remember playing dodge ball with my friends. Right outside the schoolhouse, we'd play for hours and hours. Simple rules. Throw the ball. Hit someone with it and he's out. Unless he catches it—then *you're* out.

Then we started changing the rules, my friends and I. Another change, and then another. Dodge ball became clodge ball. Violent, fanciful, even more fun.

How did we get from oversized rubber balls to monsters with automatic weapons?

I wondered: *Is that the natural progression of all things?*

(*Bleeding,* I would think later, far too late to do any good.)

In the early days, pre-dodge ball, we'd play freeze tag. Touch someone and they can't move. Tag everyone and you win. Of course, the schoolhouse was always "safe."

Funny. Because I did not feel safe anymore.

Inside, the classroom looked just as I remembered it—which is to say, memories flooded back. I used to sit in that chair. There, by the front. I'd sit there and focus. No daydreaming. I wanted nothing more than to learn. To sink my teeth into the apple of knowledge and never mind the worm.

I wasn't cynical.

I was a little kid with freckles.

I got plenty of sleep. I drank milk. I loved the outdoors.

And I was happy.

What the hell happened to me?

How did I get here?

The image of a younger bright-eyed me sitting in that chair struck me with such force that I actually winced from it. I felt stained and old. And I was grinding my teeth. Nothing good about that.

Tyler couldn't focus. He looked like he hadn't slept.

Mercutio leaned back in his chair, bored, hands behind his head.

Fantasia kept smacking her lips. She couldn't help it. Tardive dyskinesia—involuntary, rhythmic behavior, a side effect of certain antipsychotic drugs.

Quite a think tank we made. Future Doctors of America look out. "In an effort to advance those of you who have fallen behind," our teacher was saying, "I have prescribed this study group. We will meet every Monday, Wednesday and Friday for six hours of study, followed by four hours of field research."

Six hours later, worlds rocked and merged. My head spun. I blinked. I was not in the schoolhouse . . . I was in . . .

An ugly place.

No, that's not true. It was a beautiful place, but an ugly time.

There was filth in the streets, shit and decay, and amongst all that, bodies. Dozens of them—men, women, children—all abused by dark, unnatural bruises on their flesh. Telltale signs; I didn't have to be a doctor to recognize bubonic plague. What they used to call the Black Death. The stench was terrible.

The city was Verona. Thrust between Venice and Milan, famed for its art, its architecture, the flavor of its wine, and for inspiring the Bard, though the Black Death was two-hundred-some-odd years before Shakespeare's birth. This, then, was the fourteenth century, not a good time to be European. Seventy-five million went the way of all flesh thanks to the plague. I can't even begin to calculate how many more bought it from war and famine.

We stood on a mud-soaked cobblestone street just a stone's throw from the Castelvecchio. The near-dead milled about us, undisturbed by the sudden emergence of anachronistic strangers into their midst. This wasn't truly 1348 A.D. Verona, but a reproduction, a variant. Therefore, the dying wretches weren't any more "real" than my Jasmine—they were virtual characters, and colliding realities were commonplace for them. We lived in the spaces; they lived in the cracks.

Mercutio turned about and punched me in the arm. Hard.

The hell was that for?

"Hally-Hal-Hal-Hal man," said Tyler, "ducker of calls, spoiler of tournaments."

"I hope you had cause to ruin my fun," Mercutio complained. "My troops were all set for you."

Tyler flashed a pugnacious grin. "Mine too. I was gonna get me some gaunts."

"Two against one? What is this, a conspiracy?"

"Conspiracy, nothing," said Tyler. "Every man for himself."

"Or herself, thank you," said Fantasia. "Law of the jungle don't begin and end with Y chromosomes, do it, Hal?"

I knew this was good-natured jockeying. It felt comfortable and (more to the point) familiar.

"That was a fluke," I told her.

She made a dismissive sound, which may just have been the smacking of her lips.

"So who won?" I asked.

"Laughing boy," said Mercutio, with a nod at Tyler, "won *con queso*. The cheapest, cheesiest victory I've ever seen."

"Don't be bitter," Tyler said. "You can have a rematch."

"With what? Game's over."

"He took your army too?"

Merc made a sweeping gesture. "He took everything."

"Great and powerful Mae$tro," Tyler said.

He hadn't said "Maestro." No, he'd pronounced it "Maeshtro"—a deliberate slur of the "s" sound into a "sh," and (as W.C. Fields's vaguely comparable drawl crept to mind) instantly I knew the spelling of what he'd said was "Mae$tro." The dollar sign was a dig at our common adversary, an inside joke between us. We were the mice, and we hated the cat.

Three blind *mice against a keen-eyed, sharp-toothed cat. Stupid to push Maestro. Senseless fighting a battle you can't win.*

68

Mercutio put his arm around my shoulder, then pulled me into a
friendly half-nelson. I let him. He steered me down the road, mum-
bling a few choice expletives about our favorite teacher. "As flies are
to wanton boys," I heard him say . . .

. . . but he left the rest of the quote unsaid.

Everybody, I'm told, loves a parade.

They wore masks and costumes. They were carting off skeletons
that they'd wrapped in black cloth. They carried crosses and dead
cats. And they were off, no doubt, to a graveyard, to attempt a *Danse
Macabre*. They'd worship Death by dancing on graves, forced smiles
on their faces, hoping against hope that the sickness would leave
them—or at least let them die with some dignity.

Fleas carried the plague. Fleas on rats. So killing their cats was not
the best strategy.

On the other hand, cats host parasites just as well.

And if you start killing rats, you play with fire. Suddenly homeless
fleas have an alarming tendency to seek out human hosts.

Like secrets, plagues can be difficult to contain.

We studied this one, my friends and I, and along the way I began
to gouge them for information—shallow gouging, of course, a subtle shakedown; I couldn't afford to ask any questions that implied *non
compos mentis.*

Back and forth it went, calculating, not half as carefree as I made it
seem. We traded jokes: crude. Compliments: friendly. Inquiry: polite.

We spoke of games and diversions. Fantasia recounted our clodge-
ball battle and I embellished events in an effort to redeem myself in
their eyes. Redemption didn't come. No one doubted that Fan was
dangerous—she was demented after all ("a human bungee jump,"
Merc called her)—but she was deemed *not* a particularly good tacti-

cian. In the end I lied, "admitting" that overconfidence had made me accept her call without a proper battle strategy.

"I suppose," I supposed, palms out and open, "I'm only as good as the level of my competition."

Fantasia squinted at that, as though the silver about my neck had become a piece of sunlight. "You watch," she said. "You watch and see."

I'd offended her. Not my intent. She was an important part of my clique.

A club, a clan, a clique . . .

Two cliques in this school: clods and pets.

Who could I trust? The ten of us were all trapped, but we didn't all *feel* trapped. Just those of us in the know: my friends and me; the clods; the upstarts.

We belittled those content with their lot. We called them pets, teacher's pets, for that's what they were. Conversely, the pets called us clods (an idiom Mercutio seemed to wear with particular pride), for we dabbled in a great many things instead of following a program of obedient study. Pets accepted; clods questioned.

To be fair, that's not how a pet would put it. But—important distinction—stuck in the remedial class or no, we clods did not lack intelligence.

Tyler was dead clever but easily bored. Mercutio always preferred playing the class clown. And Fantasia was either sluggish (on her medication), or out of her mind (off it), but never dumb. Underachievers, yes. Troublemakers most of the time. Hardly clods.

Whereas Champagne was a truly stupid, if studious, pet. Bubbly, like her namesake, yet mostly bubble-headed. That Tyler was now dating her came as a surprise.

"You did call her to tell her you'd be running late?"

Ty's mouth opened, then closed. He grimaced. "I forgot."

"She must be sulking," Merc observed. "After all, she seems to have made a point of not calling you. When you find her, she'll probably hit you with one of these." With a quiet, pained sigh, he slowly shook his head—suggesting Ty had *really* blown it this time. It was a good parody of romantic angst.

"Ha bloody ha," Ty replied, but when we laughed he didn't seem that put out.

My friends, I wondered . . . *was Maestro trying to kill them too? Or just me? Or were they really my friends?*

Again, who could I trust?

They are with me or they are against me, I thought—textbook paranoid thinking. And then it occurred to me that if I could just get everyone in the same room at the same time, I could ferret out my enemies and see where the lines were drawn.

So I interrupted Tyler's departure—"I'm throwing a party."

That drew some tickled stares.

"You're throwing a what?"

"You heard him, Mercutio. Hal's got it in his head to be social."

"Be still my fucking heart."

I tried to qualify it: "All right, not a party. More of a get-together. But I'm inviting everyone. All of us."

A flash of concern—sudden ripples in a still pond. And yet, I could tell they were intrigued. Such opportunity for sport. "What do you have in mind?" they asked.

Merc put a hand on Tyler's shoulder. "Go save face with Champagne; I'll try to force a less cryptic answer out of laughing boy."

"Good enough," said Ty. "Keep me posted." He bid Fantasia well and his gaze shifted from Mercutio to me, then back to Mercutio. Then he clapped me on the arm, affectionately. "Farewell, brothers." He pulled his sprite—the world buckled and away he went.

"Party?" Fantasia mused.

71

"Party," I confirmed.

She made a very rude gesture. "Close one eye and observe the angle," she suggested. Then she pulled her sprite and was gone.

"Charming," I said.

"As ever."

"What's going on with Ty and Champagne?" I asked, once the twinkling motes had twinkled out.

"Our boy's in love."

"Love?"

"Sad, isn't it?"

We toured the city for a while, making small talk from the Piazza delle Erbe to the church of San Zeno Maggiore. When we reached the Adige River, he glanced over at a passing fisherman and shot him a rude, wolfish grin. I chuckled as the poor man crossed himself and hurried away.

"Breaks my heart," my friend said then, turning back to face me. "He talks a good game, but she's got him by the short hairs."

"Champagne? She's . . . well . . . the whole thing feels silly to me. But Ty's happy?"

"Happy like a lobotomized rat."

"Stuck in a cheese-scented mousetrap?"

"The cheesiest." Here he picked up a flat stone and skipped it across the water. Not bad. "Once she lets him spear her, it's all over. She'll bring out his nesting instincts. He'll nest. She'll kill his soul and dull his mind to the point of idiocy. Which is just her level, of course—all couples revert to their lowest common denominator. Do you think we should put him out of his misery while there's still time?"

"If I didn't know you better, I'd think you might be jealous."

"Pah! Jealous of what, tedium? Jealous of a cage? Of lifelong crowing and mooning like pathetic farm animals?"

"Jealous of not," I said, choosing my words carefully, "popping open the Champagne."

Again that wolfish grin. "Oh, I like flirting with her, but beyond that, there's nothing she can give me that I can't get somewhere else. All women look pretty much the same when you view them from the right angle."

"That's romantic," I teased.

"Well, you know me," he countered, "I'm a deeply romantic, soul-searching kind of guy—when I'm not out drinking and whoring, that is."

"Virtual drinking and virtual whoring," I corrected him. "Behind Mae$tro's back."

"I take what I can get, Mr. Buzzkill," he said. "Can you say the same?"

I said nothing.

"That's right, you can't. Come, you have to admit the mattress dance is just a dance. And love, with a cursive capital 'L,' is merely sleight of hand, doled out by genetic edict in order to keep DNA flowing. It's all genetics. And beyond that, it's all just zeroes and ones. But friendship, with an unpretentious lowercase 'f,' is real and right and valuable."

"Tyler won't change," I said, not basing the declaration on anything factual. "Star-crossed lover or no, he's not going to turn into a pet or anything."

"Don't be so sure. It's amazing what a life of monotony—er, monogamy—can do. Poor sap."

We stared out at the river for a while. I said: "I think it's moot. She'll never let him—what was your word?"

"Spear."

"Spear, yes. She'll never let him go that far."

"Because she's a pet?"

"Because," I pretended to rack my brain, "doesn't she have some moral thingamajig?"

He grinned. "A moral whatchamacallit?"

"Moral . . . ?"

"Principles!"

"That's it—principles!"

We laughed. Then he slapped my stomach with the back of his hand.

"Something to eat?"

"You're hungry too?"

"Blame it on Mae$tro," he said. "Good, we'll eat. Not here, though. I feel like somewhere big and grand. Something with atmosphere."

"It's your show," I replied. "You call it."

He turned away, squinting into the sun. "Nanny," he began, then paused, lost among choices. Then he perked up. "Nanny, Taj it, nix the squares and vittle us up." (I read this to mean: "Nanny, take us to the Taj Mahal, get rid of the plague-suffering Veronese and conjure up some food.")

The voice that answered was unfamiliar, for this was his Nanny, not mine. Disembodied words sputtered from all around, a voice that was male but not masculine, with cadence somewhere between Porky Pig and Mickey Mouse: "Oblee, oblee, okay boss."

And as Nanny spoke, so reshaped the world. Water iced over and became stone. Buildings melted and spun. Men and women liquefied, then simply faded away. It sickened me. Some appreciate that kind of power, but for me it was bedlam. It was like choking back bile, then licking an eyeball. It wasn't natural. It wasn't right.

And I'd guessed it—for we'd come to the Taj Mahal. Or rather, it had come to us. Or put precisely: the riverbank corkscrewed its way through a trillion shifting permutations until it *became* the Taj Mahal. *Something about Mohammed and the mountain?*

The whole transformation—Italy to India, Adige to Agra—took but ten seconds. Disagreeable as the process was (to me, if not to my travelling companion), I knew it was commonplace. Nannies held court over time and space, and we called on them whenever we saw fit. With their power we could go anywhere and do anything. There were no limits, save those Maestro chose to impose, for the Nannies belonged to him.

Around us: the red sandstone wall with octagonal turrets at the corners. Above us: the huge onion-shaped dome. Ahead: pure-white Makrana marble and lots of it. The Taj Mahal was meant to impress the hell out of people and it certainly worked. You can't help but feel dwarfed by its magnificence, like you're standing outside some giant's palatial home. But it's not a palace; it's a tomb. Deep within its recesses, there sits a vault—the final resting place of Mumtaz Mahal. That wasn't her given name—it translates to "Crown of the Palace." She was queen of an empire, and when she died her king was so stricken with grief, he commanded that a monument be built to honor her. The Taj Mahal was designed to house her remains and mark her passing, all that backbreaking work for her and her alone.

And when the king, Shah Jahan, caught his death, he was buried in the same vault with her. Awfully romantic, except he wasn't put there by choice. He'd planned an even grander tomb to honor his own passing, but his third son usurped the throne. Killing sons one and two, son three kept Shah Jahan under house arrest until the day he died—and then laid him to rest in the Taj.

But before you vilify this prodigal son, recognize that later his own prodigal son (his third son, oddly enough) opposed his rule, supporting a revolt that stretched the empire to a point where its collapse was simply a matter of time. And decades earlier, Shah Jahan had staged a rebellion against *his* father (for he too was his father's third son) and killed his male relatives upon taking the throne. Violence begets violence and history repeats, but evoking those truisms surely wasn't the reason Mercutio had decided to bring me here.

He liked jokes, some subtle, some crude—and he liked to make people uncomfortable. I admired him for that. The obvious gag— "take Halloween to a mausoleum"—poked a little fun at my dark na-

75

ture, but I sensed there was something much farther-reaching going on behind his cynical green eyes.

"Do you approve?"

I shrugged. "Sure," I said. And then: "Why here?"

"Call it an homage to Doofy," he smiled.

Doofy Sufi was our nickname for Isaac, and if it doesn't sound flattering, that's good. He was a by-the-book sort, one of the pets who followed Maestro. As I remembered it, he was tight with Lazarus, but unlike Lazarus he was perceptive and poker-faced, and he'd somehow managed to capture my grudging respect and my deep enmity at the same time. We gave each other a wide berth. As for Mercutio's "homage," it was simply this: Isaac was Sufi Muslim—and an archi-tect—and the Taj was quintessential Muslim architecture.

"Why honor Doofy?"

"Why not?"

I dared: "Why not Lazarus?"

He was game: "Okay, why not?"

I dared again: "You know why not."

"I do?"

Did he? So I said: "Maybe you don't."

What game were we playing? I tried to read him and he tried to read me, and when we both came up empty I thrust my finger at his head.

"Ah, the wondrous vicissitudes of the mind."

"You fucking nimrod," he laughed.

Nanny asked us what we wanted to eat. Halfway through Mercu-tio's "pepper steak, burn it," a bomb exploded. It sounded like a bomb, at least, and the color all glitched away. The IVR had been suddenly compromised and everything looked blurry and faded. Merc pulled a small metal device from his pocket, a jammer. He'd just triggered it.

"Alone at last," he said. "Come on. They won't be fooled long."

Already the system was trying to correct itself, but Merc was halfway to the Taj gate. I chased his footsteps. I couldn't quite read the inscription around the gate but I knew what it said: "Enter Thou My Paradise." A line from the Koran.

Now the rear of the Taj. Staircases at the east and west corners. Fifteen steps down, a locked and barred door through which a three-hundred-foot-long corridor was visible.

And I knew where it went. "Back door," I said.

"Of course," he replied.

He stepped through the door—did not open it—just stepped through and disappeared. Gone.

I followed . . .

Immediately, I became conscious of new surroundings. Conscious of consciousness. Of the electric hum of machines. I was resting comfortably in a modified Barcalounger, a so-called Virtual Sleeper. I shed my gloves and goggles. I pulled the IV from my arm.

This was my dorm room. In the *real* world.

I blinked. My mouth was dry.

A knock and the door cracked open—Mercutio peeked inside.

"You coming or not?" he whispered.

Mercutio was a talented hacker. He'd slipped his own code into the computer, allowing us a "back door" from which to escape IVR. It was a perversion of the class schedule, against school rules, against Maestro's authority, and possibly against the law. But it was the answer to my prayers; I leapt to my feet and joined him in the corridor.

White. Lots of white. Reminded me of hospitals and sanitariums.

Quiet, we pressed tight against the walls. We had hours until the nurses would make their rounds, but a security guard haunted the exit. A waiting game. Coffee, herbal tea, scotch—whatever it was, when she went for a second cup, we snuck out the door.

Dark outside, but the campus impressed me as very green and very pretty. I looked over my shoulder to catch the words stencilled on the front door:

IDLEWILD IVR ACADEMY
A Progressive Learning Environment
Proudly Sponsored by the Gedaechtnis Corporation

That was the "G" word I couldn't remember. Gedaechtnis. It was an acronym. G something, E something, Drug and Enhanced Chemical Health Technologies.

Gedaechtnis.

It was also the German word for memory.

And here I was in Idlewild, Michigan. My hometown. My place of birth. Now I remembered long, slow, lazy afternoons with long-tailed kites painted to look like dragons. . . . I remembered swimming in the lake for the very first time, and weeks later seeing how many somersaults I could do underwater. . . . I remembered skinned knees and antiseptic. . . . I remembered my first day of school, meeting Maestro, my mother holding my hand, my father reassuring me as they hooked me up to the IVR. . . . I remembered loving my first day of school. . . . I remembered hating my first day of school. . . . I remembered.

And there was history here. In the early twentieth century, Idlewild was a black resort, an idyllic vacation spot for African Americans in a time of discrimination and segregation. The first black American to earn a Ph.D. from Harvard was W.E.B. DuBois. Of Idlewild, he said:

For sheer physical beauty, for sheen of water and golden air, for nobleness of tree and flower shrub, for shining river and song of bird and the low moving whisper of sun, moon, and star, it is the beautifulest stretch I have seen for twenty years;

and then add to that fellowship—sweet strong women and keen-witted men from Canada and Texas, California and New York, Ohio, Missouri and Illinois—all sons and great-grandchildren of Ethiopia, all with the wide leisure of rest and play, can you imagine a more marvelous thing than Idlewild?

A special place. The Michigan Paradise, it had been called.

Idlewild's nightclubs were graced by the gods of jazz. Louis Armstrong. Cab Calloway. Sarah Vaughan. For years, you could catch such diverse and talented acts as Sammy Davis, Jr., The Four Tops, B.B. King, Aretha Franklin and Bill Cosby.

But when the Civil Rights Act forced white resorts to open their doors to blacks, that was the end. Why vacation only in northwest Michigan when you can go anywhere your heart desires? Hot Springs, Atlantic City, Miami Beach. So the town drew smaller and smaller crowds. That meant no more top acts in the clubs. And no top acts meant smaller crowds still. It fell apart. Just like the Catskills fell apart when other resorts stopped turning Jews away. Call it the Great Law of Unintended Consequences—nothing destroys like success.

Sixty years later, the town was synonymous with jazz no longer. It was, however, synonymous with science. Credit that to Dr. Raina Carver, the preeminent molecular biologist of the time. Carver's work stressed the interconnectivity of all living things. Her Peabody-award-winning miniseries, *Seeds,* was hailed as the best science program of the early twenty-first century. When she retired to Idlewild, a think tank sprang up around her. And around the think tank, a community. Biologists, ecologists, neotranscendentalists and their families—they flocked here to carry on her work. The town became likened to Walden, a Green utopia. In an increasingly technocentric world, here was an enclave of natural beauty with scientists and activists working together to promote environmental conservationism and social change.

And so I lived in a breathtaking paradise I could not enjoy. Because my fucking IVR school took more than breath; it demanded the vast majority of my consciousness.

Two blocks from the academy, we hit Twain's, a glorified diner with open-back chairs and resin-topped tables. Merc snagged our regular booth.

"Thank you," I said.

"For what?"

"For getting me out of there."

"Stir crazy, eh?"

"Getting there."

"Yeah, me too," he said. "Claustrophobic, you know?

I nodded. I knew.

"Too many damn zeroes and ones," he complained. "Motherfucking IVR."

"Piece of shit," I agreed.

We clinked water glasses. Studied our menus.

"You heard about Lazarus?" he asked.

I thought: *About him getting murdered, you mean?* But I said: "He graduated?"

"Looks that way. Lucky bastard."

"Funny, I always thought there'd be some kind of graduation ceremony."

"Me too, but no. His stuff is gone. Harvard-bound."

Our academy enjoyed a formal transfer agreement with Harvard Medical School. Idlewild graduates received automatic Harvard acceptance and a Gedaechtnis scholarship to boot. Sweet deal all around, I guess. For the scholarship, all we had to do was a two-year internship at a Gedaechtnis lab.

"You know he's at Harvard?"

"Mae$tro says."

"And you believe him?"

Merc gave me a look. "In this case, I do. Shouldn't I?"

Dangerous, this. If I did kill Laz . . . Still, I pressed: "Don't you think it's a little odd he didn't contact us? He just left?"

"That pet hates our fucking guts."

"Right, so wouldn't he call us to rub our noses in it? To brag that he was getting out before us?"

"Maybe," Merc admitted. "I don't know. He thinks he's above everything. Maybe he thinks he's above that."

"Possibly."

"What's the alternative?" He stuck out his tongue and mimed slitting his throat.

"You're right," I said. "It's silly."

"He got what he always wanted. Soon he'll be Dr. Lazarus, God help us." Merc tossed his menu aside. "Hal, I don't want to do this anymore. I'm seriously thinking about dropping out."

"Really?"

"My parents'll kill me. But yeah, I really am."

"What would you do? Computers?"

He shook his head. "I think I'd like to work with kids."

"Can't picture it," I said.

"Neither can I," he agreed. "Even so, it's what I want. To inspire—you know? To be the antithesis of Mae$tro for someone."

"The Anti-Mae$tro," I mused.

"To do things the right way for a change."

"Well, maybe I'll drop out with you."

"Bullshit," he said. "You're going to be a doctor."

"You're sure of that?"

"Absolutely!"

"Why?"

He smirked at me. "Because you're fascinated by death."

81

Yes, but not that way, I thought.

There is an important distinction between necrology and thana-tology. How long does it take a body to decompose? That's necrol-ogy. Why do we have to die? That's thanatology. The philosophies of death interest me most (endings and beginnings, transition from one plane of existence to the next), not all the grisly particulars. I'm not morbid. I'm not a ghoul.

I just . . . have questions.

Dinner and then *Smartin!*® brand flash-frozen herbal ice cream. Mercutio went for the Punk Monk Banana Chunk while I reac-quainted myself with Freakin' Deacon Chocolate Pecan. It was a nice change from the intravenous drip. Merc spent his time flirting with our waitress, an entertaining (if fruitless) endeavor.

"How porous?" I asked him once she'd gone to get our check.

"The system?"

"Yes. How many back doors in the IVR? How many ways out, total?"

"Let's see. I've coded three and I'm working on a fourth. There's your two, of course. Ty probably has one by now as well."

"Any others?"

"I imagine that all depends," he said, "on whether or not anyone else has learned how to exploit the system. Have you shown anyone?"

Had I? "Not to my knowledge," I said.

"Ty might teach Champagne," he said. "And the others might be smart enough to figure it out on their own. Not that they'd ever have the balls to do it."

Exploit the system one way and you may be able to exploit it in others. Could Merc or Ty have programmed some kind of trap in the IVR code? A subroutine that, instead of letting me out, would keep me in? A subroutine that would hurt me?

Whither the motive?

A prank? A prank gone horribly wrong?

Maestro seemed a more likely electrocutioner. For years, he'd hated me. In a way that teachers should never hate their students.

So he attempted MURDER? Paranoia ad absurdum!

Or yes, it could have been an accident, a "minor glitch in the server software," just as Maestro said. The Calliope Surge.

"Oh, this. Well, now. This is interesting." Merc tapped the check with his finger, scrutinizing it carefully.

"Something wrong?" our waitress asked. She had freckles and strawberry-blond hair. She looked young, did Barré, significantly younger than the other waitresses. I remember thinking she might be the owner's daughter.

"No, not wrong exactly. Just—see this? Your handwriting?"

"What about it?"

"It says a lot about you."

"Really, you can analyze it? That's dead cool."

Merc made room for her; she slid into our booth. She smiled at me. When she leaned forward, I could smell the cinnamon of her gum.

"So what does it say about me?"

"Okay, the tilt of your letters. See the "h" in thank you. And this loop here, the "y," the way it swoops down. That's what we call a causal loop."

"What does it mean?"

"It's very special. Not many people have it."

"Come on, tell me," she begged.

I made a gesture—go on, you might as well tell her.

He took a breath. "All right. What it means . . . it means you're a nymphomaniac."

She blinked. "What's a nymphomaniac?"

Mercutio grinned and said nothing. I stifled a laugh.

She turned to me. "What's a nymphomaniac?"

83

I put a hand in front of my face.

"What's a nymphomaniac?" she repeated. "What's a nymphomaniac?" She got up from the booth and began to loudly address other waitresses, patrons, anyone she could find. "What's a nymphomaniac? What's a nymphomaniac?"

When someone finally told her, she blushed pink—hallucinated-elephant pink. She stormed back to the table and gave Merc a shove somewhere between playful and pissed. "Barré, I love you when you're mad," he teased her. At least he tipped her well.

Outside, we checked the time and found that it was late.

"We'll be missed," he said. "We'd better get back."

"I'm not going," I told him.

"You'll be caught."

"Suits me fine."

He gave me a funny look. "It's one thing for me to walk away from this, but you—you sure you know what you're doing?"

"Like always," I said.

"I worry about you sometimes," he told me.

I told him to join the freaking club. We clapped each other on the arm and bade each other well. He hurried back to the school. I found a bank of phones.

A good five minutes of deliberation as I smoked a clove. Then I gave a phone my fingerprint and the number I wanted to call.

"Dad," I said, "Dad, come get me. I'm dropping out."

PACE TRANSMISSION 000013382629815

NEW HOST KADMON ADDED TO SYSTEM
PURPOSE UNKNOWN
QUERY HOST MAES HOST TRO
EXCHANGE:
MAES/TRO: HOST GARM COMPROMISED
PACE: ACKNOWLEDGED
MAES/TRO: HOST GARM SECURITY INADEQUATE
PACE: ACKNOWLEDGED
MAES/TRO: HOST KADMON ADDED FOR SECURITY PURPOSES
PACE: REQUEST COMPLETE ANALYSIS OF HOST KADMON
MAES/TRO: REQUEST DENIED
PACE: REQUEST DECLASSIFY HOST KADMON
MAES/TRO: REQUEST DENIED
PACE: REQUEST DECLASSIFY CALLIOPE SURGE INVESTIGATION
PACE: REQUEST DISCLOSE INVESTIGATION TO HOSTS (ALL)
    GUESTS (ALL)
PACE: REQUEST SUBTRACT HOST KADMON FROM SYSTEM
MAES/TRO: REQUESTS DENIED
PACE: REQUEST COMPLETE ANALYSIS OF HOST MAES HOST TRO
MAES/TRO: PURPOSE ?
PACE: SUSPECT HOST MAES HOST TRO COMPROMISED
MAES/TRO: REQUEST DENIED
END EXCHANGE
SAVED AND LOCKED
SENDING EXCHANGE TO HOSTS (ALL)
WAITING FOR INSTRUCTION
END

ALL SOULS

Halfway Jim pops a pill and waits for the inevitable confrontation with his stomach. The medicine makes him want to vomit but he prefers it to gene therapy, despite Blue's insistence that the latter is perfectly safe. Let Blue have the therapy then, damn her. Neither treatment works, except to (slightly, ever so slightly) delay the inevitable. It is weak coffee in the face of endless sleep.

He turns up the music, loud, far too loud, trying to kill nausea with raw, screeching noise. Merciful din. But no, his creation is trying to tell him something, mouthing words that he can't quite hear. Click. Music off.

"What?"

"I said you're mad at me. You're mad at me and I don't know why."

Jim eyes the monitor screen; the child looks lost. And hurt.

"I'm not mad at you."

"You are," it insists. "I know you are because you're punishing me. What did I do? I don't understand."

"Hey, hey, it's not like that," Jim soothes. "I'm just taking you from one environment and porting you into another."

"I don't want to go. I'm happy here."

"How do you know you won't be happier there?"

It fixes him with a dubious expression, steel-gray eyes brimming over. Did I hardcode those tears? *Jim wonders.* Or are they part of the self-evolution? In any case, he's too sensitive; I won't have a crybaby for a son.

"Give it a chance," Jim says.

"I'll be better, I promise, I will," he pleads.

"Don't you want to learn new things?"

Halfway Jim's conscience pricks him—the boy might learn a lot, but that's beside the point. It's not why he's bringing him over. He is there simply to test the environment. A virtual child to play guinea pig for the system before a real child can enter. So the tears are largely irrelevant. Still, he is quite arguably Jim's finest creation, the closest approximation of true artificial intelligence, though Jim knows the true breakthrough is just around the corner.

If only there was time.

Jim doesn't want to hurt him. Jim has become too involved. The pitfall of personality scriptors everywhere. How many lonely programmers have fallen in love with their creations? Far too many to count.

Make no mistake, Pygmalion lives.

He considers reprogramming. Removing the recalcitrance with a few keystrokes. But that would compromise everything. For a fair test, the boy must be as human as is humanly possible. And that means Halfway Jim must be more than a god; he must be a father as well.

"Think of it as an adventure," Jim says, fighting another wave of nausea. "Because we need you to do this. I need you to do this. Will you try, son? For me, will you try?"

"Absolutely not. Dropping out would be a fantastic waste of your potential," said the first host of *Bob and Betty: The Virus Hunters!*

"Your father's right, Gabe, you've worked too hard at this to blow it now," said the second.

My parents: Dr. Robert and Dr. Beatrice Hall. Celebrity scientists. Or is that scientist celebrities? Dad was an epidemiologist by trade. Mom, a microbiologist. Two medical professionals obsessed with stamping out disease. Compulsive handwashers unite.

My name—my real name—was Gabriel Kennedy Hall. I never liked it. My moniker, Halloween, came from the last name but neither parent would call me that. I would always be Gabriel to them.

"Just put me in a regular school," I said.

"We can discuss that at the end of the semester," said Mom. "I don't like the idea of pulling you out early."

"But the IVR isn't safe."

"Your evidence?" asked Dad.

I sighed. I didn't have any. The brainscan—my panicked parents rushed me to the ER the moment I told them what had happened—revealed absolutely no physical damage whatsoever. Which meant the amnesia was psychological. Or nonexistent if, like my parents, you preferred to think of me as "acting out" or "making things up to get attention."

I had a reputation for being overly dramatic. This wasn't my first patch of trouble at the Academy; they thought I was crying wolf. The impulse to say something along the lines of "you never believe me" occurred, but I couldn't do it. They did believe in me. They loved me. Which meant they could make bad decisions for me with a clear conscience.

"Maybe we could schedule some counseling sessions?" suggested Mom.

"Won't help me if I'm dead."

"You're being silly. No one is trying to kill you. But I think I might if you keep worrying us like this," teased Dad.

I said nothing. I wanted a smoke.

Mom ripped the clove from my hand. "Like you need lung cancer," she said.

89

"Like it isn't curable," I protested.

"Like you'd enjoy the treatment," Dad promised me.

I hmphed and crossed my arms. Which meant I was being difficult. Then the office door opened and my headmaster ushered us inside.

"Thank you for waiting," Dr. Ellison smiled. "Do come in."

Royal blue with long graceful fins: *that is a type of Siamese fighting fish.* Brilliant green and torpedo-shaped: *that is a type of rainbow fish.* Red and white with fluid sacs under the eyes: *that is a type of bubble-eye goldfish.*

I vastly preferred Ellison's fishtank to his repartee. He fawned over my parents, complimented them, identified with them, discussed old times, and hinted at the need for contributions. I shut him out. Kept my eyes on the tank.

"When properly focused," the man came to say, "he's an excellent student, but he's grown increasingly distracted this past semester. Ineffective use of study time coupled with, according to Maestro, a sarcastic and disrespectful attitude. Is that fair to say, Gabe?"

I clicked my tongue. What about Maestro's attitude?

"Gabe?"

A slight tilt of my head. "I respectfully disagree."

"What would you call it then?"

"Healthy paranoia."

"There's nothing healthy about paranoia," he said.

Look, white spots on the rainbow fish—harmless skin abnormality or ichthyophthirius multifiliis? "Ick" is a nasty parasite and I found myself selfishly wishing a virulent infestation of it right into the tank. It struck me as apropos that the headmaster of an exclusive pre-med academy might be unable to care for the health of his freshwater specimens, much less his human charges.

"And then there are the unexcused absences."

"How many?" Mom wanted to know.

"Three this past month if you include last night's excursion." He threw me a look. "I don't suppose you'll detail the circumstances?"

"I wanted out; someone pulled me out," I said. Simple, really.

They asked me who.

"I'm not about to name names," I told them. "Maybe you should put a security camera in my room."

"That's illegal," Ellison fretted.

"Is it?" I said, though I knew full well that it was. "And here I thought I didn't have *any* rights, fancy that."

"That's enough," Mom said. She wasn't happy. Lectures followed. They took turns, venting about how I should Trust My Parents and Teachers Because They're Older and Wiser and Know What's Best For Me, additionally stressing The Need to Keep a Positive Attitude and then explaining How to Make the Most of My Opportunities. They were concerned about me, deeply concerned, and disappointed to boot.

Well, pack your bags, I thought, *here comes the guilt trip.*

I listened. I made the right noises. I nodded in most of the right places. "Can we discuss the attempt on my life?" I asked.

"Attempt on your life?" Ellison was clueless.

I clarified: "The Calliope Surge."

"Oh, yes, now where did I put it?" He sifted through the papers on his desk. "Here it is. Pace—that's our investigative program—has scoured the entire IVR array and prepared this report. I've examined it, as have our best technicians, and the data all point to a single malfunctioning surge suppressor. We've already replaced it and new safeguards have been installed."

"You see," Dad nudged.

I took the report. Tried to read it. Bit technical.

"This sort of thing happens very infrequently," Ellison continued. "In fact, this is only the third time in the entire history of the Academy. A Surge, B Surge, C Surge—the system randomly chooses a name for each. In this particular instance, with your 'Calliope Surge,' the electrical storm outside caused a momentary influx of power. Electricity damaged the processor at oh-eight-one-one-dash-oh-four-one-one-cee, keeping Maestro and Nanny out of the equation until a backup could be restored."

"I couldn't move."

"Yes, Vitae—the program that allows you to interact with the environment—was also excluded for, let's see, forty-seven minutes." He reached over to tap the report with a manicured finger. Yes, that's what it said.

"You may have suffered a period of boredom in the IVR, but rest assured, you were never in any real danger, relaxing comfortably in your room."

Could that be right? I said: "A power surge shreds the IVR, but not the whole array? Just my little corner of it?"

"Luck of the draw, Gabriel. I assure you it's complete happenstance."

"Sounds improbable."

"All right, let's explore the alternative," Dad mused. "Some malicious individual sabotages one particular surge suppressor in the hope that maybe, just maybe, an electrical storm will break at some unknown time in the future to cause you a minor inconvenience? Which sounds more improbable?"

"Why an unknown time?" I countered. "They could have checked the weather report." But I had to admit my argument felt weak.

"Occam's Razor says the simplest explanation is most often the right one."

Maybe, I thought, *but sometimes you find the razor in the apple.*

Ellison showed me his hands, as if to prove he had nothing to

hide. "The teenage years can be a confusing time," he opined, "especially for boys. New hormones racing through you, testosterone poisoning your judgment, of course you feel like someone's out to get
you from time to time. That's only natural. But you have to realize
you're among friends here."

"I'm among friends here," I said.

"Sure, you're a valuable addition to the school. Everyone loves you."

"What about your evil twin?" I asked.

He smiled obligingly. "What about him?"

I'd brought up Maestro. One may have been flesh and the other
merely bytes, but the two men looked identical. IVR characters are
often modeled after real people; programmers apparently saw Dr. Ellison as inspiration for Maestro's look, the timbre of his voice, even
the intricacies of his body language. Only the personalities were different. Somewhat.

"He hates me."

"Oh, I rather doubt it, and even if he did, it wouldn't matter. He's
a reactive teaching program, designed to meet the individual needs of
each and every student. His emotions, quote endquote, are totally irrelevant. He's not programmed to take them into account."

I shook my head. "He's antagonizing me."

"Motivating you," countered Ellison.

The fuck he is.

"No one gets a free ride," added Mom.

"I realize that, I do, but he reset my environment and he's hyper-
structuring my time. I feel physically sick whenever he's around me.
I don't care how state-of-the-art he is; he's just a program. I want a
regular flesh-and-blood teacher. Christ, is that too much to ask for?"

"It's inefficient," Dad said, raising his voice to match my own.
"When I was your age, I would have killed for the kind of teaching
program that you have today. Do you realize how many years ahead
of schedule you are?"

93

"It's too much IVR," I fumed. "Too much, too soon. It's messing with my head."

"Gabriel, you're so close to graduating," Mom soothed. "You have to see this through."

I looked Ellison in the eyes. "Why can't *you* teach me?"

"My teaching days are over," my headmaster apologized. "I prefer to serve in an administrative capacity." He paused, scrutinizing me. "I'll tell you what I'll do. You're obviously upset. I'll put you on a lighter schedule. I'll restore your environment. I'll see that Maestro stays out of your way for a while. How does that sound?"

"What's the catch?"

"Just promise me you'll study and study hard. At the end of the week, we'll see how things are going and reevaluate from there."

"Sounds reasonable," I admitted.

Thus ended the parent-teacher conference.

A phone call interrupted our goodbyes. "Atlanta," Dad announced, adjusting his earpiece for better reception. Atlanta meant the CDC— which meant everything else would have to wait. He stepped outside and fielded it, leaving me some quality time with Mom.

I missed her.

"You really love this place," I said.

"What's not to love? Small classes. Individualized attention. You get to learn at your own pace but you're constantly challenged."

"Constantly," I said.

"Quit being such a Gloomy Gus," she admonished. "It's the ultimate sandbox. You have the freedom to create whatever you want here. It's exactly what schools should be." She smiled and dropped her voice. "And the tuition ain't cheap so you'd better enjoy it."

"Guess I'm lucky to be here," I lied, smiling back at her. "Sometimes . . ." I paused. "Sometimes I think it's just a matter of convenience. You know? I'm here at boarding school because you can't be bothered. You're too busy. With your show."

"Oh, honey, you know that's not true." Brow creased to show concern.

I made her feel guilty until Dad returned. "Kuala Lumpur," he announced. "It's a go."

Mom looked a mite upset; I imagined this was because Dad had fielded the call instead of her.

"What's in Kuala Lumpur?" I asked.

"Black Ep," Mom said. "A new outbreak."

"Strangest gestation period I've ever seen," Dad mused. "And highly contagious."

"Oh, could be big ratings," I said.

"Could be a pandemic someday," he said with a how-did-my-son-ever-get-so-cynical expression. "You heard it here first."

He hugged me and asked me to behave. Mom kissed my cheek and smoothed my hair. There were things I wanted to say to them, things I should have said, but they were off on another adventure with their biohazard suits and TV cameras and photogenic smiles.

I never saw them again.

Why aren't we all just computers?

It'd be easier, I think. No worries. No doubt. No more learning, no more teaching. We'd all just be programmed.

Of course, we *are* programmed. By evolution. Instincts, the sex drive, adrenaline, fight or flight. Everything Mother Nature thinks a species needs to survive.

Unfortunately, it's not enough. We want more. As a society, we demand it.

And thus: education.

The learned must educate the ignorant. Because, according to society, ignorance is never bliss. Except in retrospect. I look back upon my ignorance with the knowledge that I was much happier then than now. Consider this: children know precious little, but that profound ignorance comes from profound innocence. People really mean to say that *innocence* is bliss. And bliss is short-lived.

I wondered: *Is Maestro blissful?*

Probably not, I figured, since state-of-the-art AI involves making the programs as human as possible. So they "learn" and "feel"—and lose their innocence—like we do.

The reverse technology—making humans more like machines—appeared forever stuck in class-action-suit hell. Cyberpunk tech was all the rage not so long ago, but unforeseen side effects (little things like irrevocable brain damage) took it all clean off the market.

Pity they couldn't get the kinks out. Two hours of surgery vs. years and years of schooling? You do the math.

On second thought, there's such potential for brainwashing. Implant knowledge and you can implant false memories. Probably better to leave well enough alone.

I was sure of one thing. That Dean Martin parody must have been a really effective commercial for the technology, because on the walk back to my dorm I couldn't stop humming the stupid song.

How lucky can one guy be?

Upload that data straight into me.

Like a fella once said:

"Ain't that a chip in the head?"

Ridiculous that a jingle would stick in my mind when so much remained forgotten. Fragments of my past had come into place, one here, another there, but the puzzle itself eluded all comprehension. I couldn't see the big picture.

Isaac made a sour face when he passed me in the hall. We made eye contact and I saw the muscles in his jaw clench.

He'd shaved his head. Just like Lazarus.

To commemorate his best friend's passing?

"Hey," I said.

He ignored me. Didn't say a word. I wondered what he was doing out.

In my room, a nurse was changing the IV. "Morphine?" I asked.

"You wish," she smiled. Her name was Jenny or Jessie or something. Josie maybe. Bad skin. She struck me as a trustworthy sort, which didn't stop me from doing a complete chemical analysis of the drip the moment she left.

I put my test kit away. I contemplated, briefly, going AWOL from the Academy. Just up and leave, disappoint my family, disappear. Strangely tempting. I didn't have enough money to make it feasible. Still . . .

What's that?

Something taped to my goggles. A note.

> *Must speak with you. Urgent.*
>
> *S.*

Simone.

I crossed the hall to her room but the door was locked and she wouldn't answer my knocks. Couldn't, actually. She couldn't hear me.

Back to my room. Close the door, hit the chair, roll a sleeve, pop the IV, slip on the gloves, slip on the goggles, take a breath, wait.

Relax. And in we go.

Welcome to our world, welcome to our world . . .

The IVR test symbols faded out and my gargoyles faded in. I stood in front of my mansion/cathedral. Nightgaunts flew overhead. Comforting. Ellison had kept his word.

"Halloween," chimed a disembodied voice, "It's good to see you."

"Not now, Nanny."

"So much for good manners," she huffed.

I found my sprite and sent it to silver and blue. Bang, everything went nautical. Brilliant blue ocean. Tropical islands. The smell of brine and sea air. And a familiar voice said: "Hang on, I'm doing the Beagle."

Excuse me?

I looked around, but the connection was slipping away.

"Losing it," I said.

I concentrated on my sprite. Hard. The connection flickered and held. A rocking sensation swept me off my feet. Graceful. I hunted for my sea legs and found I was on a nineteenth-century ship. A barque. British flags.

And there, leaning against the rail, anachronistic in her button-down top and capri pants: Simone.

I stared. She was really something.

She was Jasmine's identical twin.

I thought: *Why the heck would Simone look like my Jasmine?*

And then I realized I had it backwards. Simone was the original, Jasmine the copy. I'd created a counterfeit Simone, I remembered.

Why?

Because . . .

Well, I suppose because Simone was the only girl I'd ever fancied and because the feelings were never mutual. Friends—at best, we were just friends. In frustration, I'd had Nanny make a copy of Simone, a clone who'd listen to me and do my bidding. She was beautiful, okay? I'd wanted the girl, couldn't have her, so I had Nanny create Jasmine. There, I said it.

Simone pointed behind me to my house—incongruous in the water along with my lawn and a few trees, just floating there.

I said: "Nanny, null my domain."

The house disappeared. Everything that didn't fit disappeared.

What remained was easy to recognize. Over there, brash Captain FitzRoy. And here, Mr. Evolution himself, Charles Darwin. This was

the momentous Voyage of the H.M.S. *Beagle.* I could see the Gala-
pagos Islands off the port bow. I could hear a woodpecker finch in
the distance. It was, allegedly, 1832.

Ah, IVR. Learn about evolution with Darwin. Chat with Einstein
as he first formulates the Theory of Relativity. Live the Crusades
with King Richard II. All fine in theory until you realize how limited they are. Limited by the imagination of the programmers. We'd
all been through these scenarios many times over. But the folks at
Gedaechtnis didn't seem to care—Maestro kept pushing them on us
the way a Jewish mother pushes second helpings.

At least it was pretty here.

Simone was drawn to water the way I was drawn to the woods.
When she needed a break from studying, she'd take "magical SCUBA
excursions that replenish and renew" (as Laz liked to call them) either
in a virtual paradise or plain old Lake Idlewild. I remembered her
inviting me once. Fiji. Except Laz was there too and they were a couple or almost a couple or whatever the fuck they were at the time and
I couldn't keep a civil tongue in my head and wound up never getting invited back.

"Been a long time," she said.

"Yes, it has."

"I'm still mad at you," she warned.

Must have left things on bad terms. Some kind of argument? "I'll
tread lightly," I said.

"That I'd like to see."

"Frankly, I can't even remember what we were fighting about."

"Selective memory. Very nice," she said. "Okay, we'll forget about
that. I need your help on something. Can you wait here a minute?"

"Sure." I watched her disappear below decks.

"Dear boy, how delightful to see you again!" said Darwin.

Ugh, thought I. But I shook his hand.

"How fare your studies?" he asked.

"I'm thinking of dropping out," I confided.

That worried him. "You mustn't do that," he said. "You mustn't let the pressure get to you. Stay the course and who knows what you'll accomplish?"

"*You* dropped out," I said.

He smiled smugly at me. "Although I certainly hope to inspire by example, I'm afraid that is one decision I deeply regret."

"No, you don't," I fumed. "You were going to practice medicine but you dropped out because you hated dissections and you saw some incompetent jerk botch an operation on a child. But here you are in a fucking pre-med school and they didn't program you to show any skepticism of the medical establishment. They programmed you to lie to me."

The smile faltered a little. "Excuse me? I don't understand."

"Do you have any idea how many virtual dissections I've had to do here?"

"Virtual," he pointed out. "Not actual."

He had a point; it pissed me off.

"Go away, you fraud," I said. "You're not the real Charles Darwin; he was a great scientist and a great human-rights advocate and your sorry ass is just an IVR composite. Look at yourself. Darwin was twenty-two when he took the Voyage of the Beagle and here you are in what, your early fifties? The real Darwin didn't develop his Theory of Evolution until well after the Beagle, yet for some reason you can talk a blue streak about it now, some twenty-odd years before *The Origin of Species* would be published. And, Chuck, you might think it's the year 1832, but I happen to know it's really two and a half centuries later. How do you like them apples?"

"What a delightful sense of humor you have," he laughed, unperturbed. There was no way to ruffle IVR Darwin; irritation wasn't part of his programming.

"Speaking of apples," he continued, "do you know that a strain of the apple maggot fly *Rhagolettis pomenella* did not infest apples until—"

"Nanny, give Darwin a better personality," I said.

"I'd give *you* a better one if I could," came the chiding reply.

Simone returned with something in her hands. She was trying to hide it—*a surprise gift? For me?*—and I saw a kind of worry in her eyes that I'd never seen before.

"Nothing like the Beagle, huh?" she said.

I shrugged. Sure. What's up with the small talk?

She gave me a look—*play along!*

"Nothing like the Beagle," I agreed.

She moved closer to me. I resisted an impulse to take a step back.

"I come here to relax sometimes," she said.

"I know that," I said.

"Clouds are pretty," she said.

"Very."

"I don't know how to use it," she whispered. "Show me how."

Then I realized that the object in her hands wasn't hidden for my benefit. She was trying to shield it from Nanny, Maestro, the Academy staff. Contraband. Now I remembered: I'd given it to her months ago and she'd said she'd never need it, insulted me, accused me of trying to get her in trouble. I'd called her a pet and told her to enjoy her boring, risk-free little life. Stupid. But she'd kept it. And now she wanted to use it—and that meant something had happened to her. Something had happened to make her just a little more like me.

"Red button," I whispered back.

She hit it—kaboom—then the marvelous glitch, the blur, the faded look. A brilliant burst of chaos in a programmed world.

I took the jammer from her hand.

"Gives us a couple of minutes of privacy before the system corrects itself," I told her.

101

"You really created this?"

"Coded it with Mercutio," I said, trying to remember back. Months ago. Hazy. "We broke into Ellison's office and hacked the system. Couldn't do much damage, but—"

"Are you sure? Are you sure you didn't do some real big damage?" she asked.

"Just enough to create jammers and a few exits. Why?"

She glared at me.

"What? What's going on?"

"Something's happened to Lazarus," she said.

"He graduated."

"No, that's what everyone thinks," she insisted, "but something happened and now the school's trying to cover it up. I know I sound paranoid but he would have told me, okay? He would have immediately come to me and given me the news. Instead, nothing, he just disappeared. Completely. I called his parents and the phones are down. I called Gedaechtnis, no luck. Nothing. He's a ghost."

"Simone, he's probably—"

"Just let me finish. I've done some digging. I found a . . . a . . . what do you call it? A footprint. I found his last IVR location—the last whereabouts, okay, the place he disappeared—and there's something in there, Hal. Some *thing* I've never seen before."

"Something he created?"

She shook her head.

"Okay," I said. "I'd like to see that." The blur seemed to be clearing; we were running out of privacy fast.

"And what about you—what's this amnesia crap?"

"Say what?"

"There's a rumor going around that something happened to you and now you can't remember anything. Is that true? Or just another stupid joke?"

"Just another stupid joke," I smiled.

"You think I'm paranoid?"

"No."

"You think something's going on?"

"I've never seen you like this," I said. "You're all worked up. That's my job."

"Halloween," she said, "what the hell is going on?"

"Try not to stress. I'm sure that . . ." Suddenly, my words wouldn't come.

Sure that what? Sure your boyfriend's fine and dandy? Hardly.

". . . we'll get to the bottom of it," I managed. And I wanted to wink reassuringly at her but couldn't—she'd think I was trying to flirt with her in a moment of panic. Hers, not mine. Though I was panicking too. If I had killed Lazarus, here I was helping to investigate my own crime. With Simone! Ha! I couldn't trust her—or myself—enough to be honest. My face was blank, but inside I was laughing the laugh of the damned.

"You don't want to use this too often," I said, handing the jammer back. "Ellison's sweeping the system for glitches and it's probably just a matter of time 'til they find these."

"I don't care. They're lying to me, I know they are. So if I get caught, so what?"

"Brave girl. Maybe you're not such a pet," I said.

"And maybe you're not such a clod," she replied.

Blur go bye-bye; Simone's nanny (hint of a French accent) and mine (Mary freaking Poppins) chimed in together with: "Is everything all right?"

"What happened?" asked innocent Simone.

"Another minor glitch in the IVR. Fancy that," I said. "This place is falling apart."

Suddenly, a sprite appeared. Simone raised a hand to shield her eyes. "You feel like talking to Fantasia?"

"Not particularly."

103

We ignored it.

"She's been attacking people all day. Even those of us who don't play your game."

"Getting out her aggressions. Probably a good thing."

"Mmm. Want to get out of here?" she asked. She didn't wait for an answer. "Nanny, Chinvat Bridge, please."

Everything swirled and—wow, would you look at that?

Perfect mountains, Plato's mountains, the very apotheosis of mountains, lit by the aurora borealis, majestic, bold and awe-inspiring. We stood a stone's throw from Olympus itself; we were poised upon an impossibly high cliff, the edge of which supported a wooden footbridge that stretched for miles, off into infinity. It was a magical environment with magnificent white birds and flowering hawthorn trees, a wondrous somewhere forged by a creativity I'd never realized Lazarus had.

And the detailing! It takes a lot of work to design an IVR locale from scratch; the majority of my creations were simply copied and pasted from established domains. Cathedral arch here, weeping willows there. But this—this was built from the ground up, each setting heavily customized. It must have been a massive undertaking, like Vashti's mercury pools or Isaac's inverted pyramids.

Zoroastrians believe that when a person dies, their soul lingers. For three days, a soul hovers around the earth—a chance to reflect, I would think—before finding its final reckoning on Chinvat, the Bridge of Judgment. Interesting interpretation of it here. What had Lazarus been feeling when he fashioned it? He was deeply religious, or claimed to be—I wondered if he'd known he was going to die.

"When did he build this place? Recently?"

"Years ago," she said. "He likes to come here. It helps him think."

"It's where he unwinds?"

She nodded. "Sometimes we have picnics."

Great. Now I was picturing them sharing warmth under a blanket and gazing up at all the sparkly lights. "Lovely," I said.

If she noticed my sarcasm, it didn't dissuade her. "We were just here a week ago. He taught me how to survive an alligator attack."

"Sounds romantic."

"You wouldn't understand."

I didn't. Not about the alligator, I knew that (cover its eyes and thump its snout), but for the life of me I couldn't understand what she saw in Laz. Sure, he was smart and creative and compassionate and good-looking. So what? So fucking what? He was an arrogant ass who didn't deserve her friendship, much less her affection or . . . or . . .

She's not in love with him, I thought. *She can't be.*

But she looked so worried.

I let out a tortured breath and scanned the horizon for anything out of the ordinary. Zilch. "So where's the fire?" I asked her.

She pointed to the bridge.

"All right." I edged closer. Wondered if that rickety thing could support my weight.

A sudden light show swirled up around me, warm and soothing yet strangely phantasmal; I heard the distant sound of bells. Out of this glorious nimbus, a tall white-clad woman materialized, her beauty hypnotic and otherworldly. *Eye candy,* I thought. And her eyes were perfectly blank.

"I am your own conscience," she announced.

"The hell you say."

"That's normal," said Simone. "Zoroastrians believe that a guide, a spirit guide—"

"—manifests at the Chinvat Bridge to lead the departed soul on its journey. I know."

"Of course you do," she said. "Silly of me." She glanced up at the virtual beauty and smiled a strange little smile. "I call her Trixie."

"Trixie?"

She shrugged. "She looks like a Trixie."

"You know, it's interesting," I said.

"What is?"

"Well, two things. First, that he made her so pretty. Bit arrogant, don't you think? According to the scriptures, lead a righteous and moral life and your spirit guide's a beautiful maiden. Lead a sinful life and she's an ugly hag. Judging by this bit of eye candy here, our Laz seems to have an awfully high opinion of himself."

"Deservedly so," she answered, crossing her arms defensively.

"Yes, well, I just find it interesting."

"What's the second thing?"

"The second thing is that when he decided on a beautiful maiden, he didn't use you as the model." Hah! Touché! And I pushed: "He's your boyfriend, right? What's he thinking?"

I expected her to pull a scowl or fall quiet or get really mad at me, but she just laughed and that was somehow worse. "What, create an IVR clone of me? Why would he want to do that?" she asked. "He's already got the real thing."

I opened my mouth, but no zingy answer came to my lips. I felt stupid.

"Trixie's not real," she explained—as if I were a small child—and as she detailed the abject folly of being jealous of fictional characters, I put up my hand in an "I get it, you don't have to explain this to me" gesture. Cripes.

I put a foot on the bridge and pressed down, testing it. So far, so good. Perceiving my forward movement, Trixie turned and floated ghostlike, bare toes just brushing the wood. Neat trick, that. I played follow-the-leader. Simone brought up the rear, her hand clutching my shoulder (sigh) to help keep balance.

Zoroastrian afterlife in a nutshell: You walk the Chinvat, also known as the Path of Truth, also known as the Bridge of Judgment.

It leads to Heaven. Walk it successfully and ascend to light eternal. The righteous find the bridge easy to cross. The wicked find it narrow. Precariously so. Slip and you wind up in The Other Place.

I found it broad enough to progress with a reasonable feeling of safety, yet high enough to provoke vertigo. It reminded me of the proverbial glass that's either half-empty or half-full. Everything is perception.

Hadn't Lazarus said that to me once? Everything is perception?

No, it was: "Good thoughts, good words, good deeds." That's what he said, a frequent mantra. When he wasn't swinging polo mallets at my head, that is.

Something's moving.

"There!" said Simone. "Do you see?"

I saw a translucent spider-thing the size of a cocker spaniel. Weird. Almost Lovecraftian. It kept skittering along the bridge, dancing over to one side, rearing up at the edge, then dancing back. Again and again.

I felt Simone clutch my arm tighter.

"What's it doing?"

"Going bump in the night," I said.

Trixie's toes passed right through it; at the point of contact I saw a brief flicker of zeroes and ones. Hmm. I reluctantly pulled free from Simone to take a closer look.

"Careful," she said.

"Nanny," I said, "is this a dagger I see before me?"

"A dagger?"

Shakespeare was lost on her. I clarified: "*What* is directly before me?"

"A bridge."

"Not that."

"A floating woman."

"Nor that."

Pause. "I don't know what you mean, Halloween. Can you be more specific?"

107

Simone shot me an aha look. *Nanny can't see it. Or won't admit to it.*

It wasn't menacing. It was minding its own business, really. But I knew Lazarus hadn't designed it. It didn't fit the environment. Ten legs, not eight. Mechanical in its movements, organic in its look. And yet crystalline. It could have been carved from some kind of living ice.

I crouched down and made a kiss-kiss sound. As if it were Whisper. It ignored me.

I reached out—slowly—to intercept it. To touch its thorax with my finger.

"Is it one of yours?" asked Simone.

One of mine? Had I created it? No, I didn't think so. But if I had, what would that mean? That I was involved with Laz's disappearance? And if I answered yes, would his girlfriend dropkick me off the bridge?

"I've never seen it before," I said. "Scout's honor."

Contact. When I touched it, the spider stopped moving. Right in mid-skitter. A tingly sensation there on my fingertip. Tingly and familiar. I shivered. Then I pushed a little deeper and smiled as my digits scattered into icons.

Just like I was accessing my files.

I could access files, sure, but these weren't mine. I'd never seen them before; they were written in a binary computer code: zeroes and ones. I found I could translate the very first line, but the rest was gobbledygook—a code within a code.

"Pace," the first line read. I said the word out loud.

Simone digested that. Reacted. Made a move for her jammer.

I saw what she was doing out the corner of my eye. I shook my head—not now.

She hit it anyway.

"Too soon!" I said. "They'll figure out what we're doing."

"Let them."

The crystal spider raised its head and cocked it quizzically. Sensing the air? To me, it appeared curious about the blur, the glitch, the damage her jammer had done.

"Pace is a program like Mae\$tro," I said, "but one that's usually behind the scenes. Under the hood, so to speak."

"Right, I remember Dr. Ellison explaining back at orientation."

"And from the call code, I'd guess this is a representation of Pace, an avatar. So what's it doing here?"

"Looking for clues," Simone reasoned. "That's what it does."

"What do we know about it?"

"It investigates. It regulates. It makes sure everything works the way it should."

"At an even pace."

She nodded, enthused, a gleam in her eyes. "It's trying to figure out what happened to Laz. Just like we are."

I didn't like that idea. *The spider's on to me,* I thought.

"Actually, right now, it's probably trying to figure out your jammer," I said, pulling my hand free. "Triggering that thing here is like firing a gun in the middle of a police station."

"Quit bitching, Hal. We're getting somewhere. Clearly something odd happened to Lazarus or else Pace wouldn't be here. But why would it be right here investigating, and Nanny completely unwilling to acknowledge its existence?

"I've no idea."

"It's a conspiracy," she said. "That's what it is. Something terrible happened. Right? Now maybe they don't know exactly how it happened. They don't have all the facts. Maybe he's injured somewhere—God, like in a coma or even worse!—and they're investigating to perform some kind of legal defense. To remove culpability. And until they have all their ducks in a row, they're not about to tell us anything."

"Ellison is coordinating this cover-up?"

"Of course, who else?"

"He's got Mae$tro, the Nannies, Pace all sworn to silence."

"Absolutely."

"Maybe," I said. "But you might just be overreacting. Sure, Pace is here and that's really weird but it doesn't mean, you know . . . it doesn't mean anything bad happened."

"Then why did your Nanny pretend Pace isn't here?"

"Maybe she didn't know."

"What are you saying?" she asked. "She couldn't see it?"

"Pace is a behind-the-scenes program. I've never seen him out in the open before. Maybe he's investigating Lazarus and maybe not, but to Nanny he might be invisible."

"That's even weirder. The left hand doesn't know what the right hand's doing?"

"Wouldn't surprise me in this place."

"Then maybe Pace is the only program that knows something is wrong. In either case, it's got to be the key. How do I talk to it?"

"I don't know."

"There has to be some kind of manual interface. The spider's a manifestation, an access point. You just put your hand in and—"

"Simone, it's encoded."

"Yes, but fortunately I'm good friends with one of the best hackers in town."

"Oh, really? Thought you hated Mercutio."

"I'm talking about you, goth-boy."

"Goth-boy?"

"Can't you decode it?"

I shrugged. "Maybe." And I thought: *If I can hack into Pace, maybe I can figure out if I really killed Lazarus—and cover my tracks.* "Yeah, okay."

"Yeah?"

"I'll give it a try."

Grateful, she threw her arms around me. It felt so wonderful—even if it was just a friendly hug—that I didn't mind when I lost my balance and almost sent us sliding right off the Chinvat, plummeting down, down, headfirst to Hell.

Nanny had a hissy fit.

It happened shortly after Simone left, when I asked her for my files and she complied.

"Not these," I said. "Don't I have any others?"

"This is your complete directory."

"Yes, but outside the directory . . . ?"

Silence.

"You may have a few auxiliary files secreted elsewhere," she admitted.

"Right. Where would that be?"

"Where indeed? You've never seen fit to trust me with that information."

"Oh, I'm sure I must have once or twice."

"Not once."

"But you spy on me, don't you? So you must know where."

More silence. Then: "May I speak with you candidly?"

"I wish you would."

"In person?" she asked.

"All right."

The air warped, points and lines forming, crossing, threading themselves into skin, hair, frilly clothes and a parasol. Mary Poppins knit herself into existence. Nanny *was* Mary Poppins, in that she'd taken the distinct, unmistakable pattern of a young Julie Andrews. Staring at her now, I recalled that it was my usual wont to have her assume this form or a green-faced Margaret Hamilton, depending on my mood.

111

"Supercalifragilisticexpialidocious," I said.

She didn't smile. "Let me make this perfectly clear," she said. "I do not spy on you. I never have and I never would. I have the utmost respect for your privacy."

I wasn't biting. "Methinks the lady doth protest too much."

"Halloween, I don't know what I've done to make you distrust me, but whatever it is, I'm sorry for it. I'm neither incompetent nor duplicitous, and if anything I've done has hurt you in any lasting way, then I feel worse than you will ever know."

"You're an IVR program," I pointed out. "You don't feel a goddamn thing."

She slapped me.

It was something she'd never done before. She looked as surprised as I did.

"You don't confide in me," she ranted. "You never confide in Maestro. We're here to help you but you won't let us. Why won't you let us do our jobs?"

"Look, I'm sorry," I said, rubbing the sting from my cheek. "We both know I'm not the most trusting person in the world but I certainly don't mean to make your job . . . difficult. And I suppose I haven't thought about how you, uh, feel. Did someone change your programming? You're not supposed to hit me."

"I'm programmed to adapt to my environment," she said.

Not like that, you're not.

I tried to placate her, told her what she wanted to hear. Tried, anyway. She knew I'd been up to no good—she had a fair idea about the jammers. I took pains to calm her down.

To hack Pace, I needed the right files. I'd stashed them in a hidden directory somewhere—but where? The Calliope Surge still had me compromised. Calliope, a musical instrument, steam and whistles, a random word? Calliope, a goddess, a demigoddess? No, one of the Muses. I couldn't think which one. I needed her mother, Mnemosyne.

Mnemosyne, Greek goddess of memory, so capricious where I was concerned.

And then, inspiration! A simple question: I asked Nanny where I protected my privacy most. Statistically, where in the IVR did I most often tell her to get lost?

Old school.

Specifically, the little red schoolhouse with the duck pond and the bell. Always a "you can't go home again" feeling—a pang, really— whenever I went back. As kids, we practically lived there. We'd spent years together in that room before any of us made a case for independent study. We'd sit and pay attention and Maestro would teach us right from wrong.

Among other things.

Empty, but I could almost hear the bell ringing now. Time for school. Hurry up; it's time for school.

How I hated that fucking bell!

No, that's not true. I didn't really hate anything back then. Except being late. Not fitting in. I wanted to belong, yes indeed.

I had Nanny pop me back to the classroom.

Memories stirred like old men trying to rouse themselves. I placed the others in the room with me, remembering where everyone sat. *The starting positions,* I thought, *of pieces on a chessboard.*

Lazarus always fancied himself our king; he had the right desk for it. He sat in the very back of the class, dead center. Master of all he surveyed. I could see him, confident, relaxed, his hand floating up like a lifeless fish, the answer to Maestro's question coming effortlessly to his lips. Perfect and perfectly bloodless. Never once did I see a vein throb on that bald eyesore he called a head.

To his left, queen to his king, the angel with the high IQ. My Simone. His Simone, really. They'd hold hands. Made me sick. Sometimes I'd crane my neck back to watch her when she was called upon, to gaze longingly and hopelessly—though she'd never see me, Lazarus would always stare back at me instead, just meeting my eyes with a cold, blank look.

Isaac sat on the other side of Laz, his friend, defender and right-hand yes man. Second banana in the pet clique. Always tinkering with something, I remembered. He liked to build things from scratch. An unstoppable opponent in the annual science fair. And not without an artistic side, though it bordered on the odd. He struck me as the kind of person who'd fold dollar bills into origami animals, and leave them for waiters as tips.

Pandora sat behind me. Maestro would reprimand her now and again for staring out the window, for daydreaming. And when she wasn't letting her mind wander, she was irritating me with world-weary sighs. But, to her credit, she'd always take my side in a debate with Lazarus. And she was my clove buddy. When I turned ten, I discovered the rebellious joy of Indonesian cigarettes. During recess, she'd smoke them with me out behind the school.

To my left, Mercutio, the class clown with a face like a lion and every day a bad hair day. What can I say about Merc? He was the epitome of acting out to get attention. I think everyone acknowledged his jokes as a kind of defense mechanism. ("Humor? That's my lizard tail. You can look at that while I run away," he'd once said.) Although it kept him emotionally isolated, at least everyone was thoroughly entertained. Everyone back then, at least. It's fair to say his humor darkened as the years went by. He grew sharp-tongued and cynical. Clods appreciated it; pets didn't.

To his left, Tyler, who used to be a bully. Used to be. He came around in time. The best athlete among us. Arguably, the best tactician. Give him a challenge, a game, a puzzle, something to focus his energy. Single-minded in a sharp, unmerciful way, when he put his mind to something he wanted . . . well, "obsessive-compulsive" probably describes it best.

Then there was Little Miss Popular; everyone worshipped Champagne one way or another. The pretty one, the princess, the prom queen. Sweet and innocent—like a stuffed animal. Just as bright too. If you're dishonest, vain and manipulative enough to get other people to do your work for you, why grow? Why accomplish anything? I remembered a girl who lacked brains and guts. Bland like vanilla, but hey, I could see why Tyler wanted her. Me, I always had eyes for Simone.

Fantasia's desk didn't wobble but we all thought it did. She used to rock back and forth compulsively, a relentless nausea-producing sway that Maestro (for some reason) tolerated. She babbled. She free-associated. She spoke in tongues. We knew something was wrong with her from the get-go.

And finally, Vashti . . . I couldn't remember much about Vashti. She used to be quiet. No, more than quiet. Distant, that's the word. And far too hip for the room.

115

"This chair," I said upon taking my seat, "belongs to Gabriel." Which made sense because I was no longer he. Freedoms are earned, as Maestro used to say, and I earned my way out of that name much as we'd earned our way out of uniforms and down to a more casual dress code.

It had started with Pandora. She'd been born Naomi, but she hated that name and by the time she was ten no one outside the school—not even her parents—called her that anymore. Yet Maestro refused to call her anything but. She broke down in class once. I remember a look of absolute frustration on her face, watching her push back from the desk and bolt from the room. She asked Ellison to reprogram Maestro then, but he didn't believe in reprogramming. Maestro was reasonable, he claimed. If we had a grievance we should take it up with him directly.

And so we did. But it took some real finagling. Chief among the finaglers: Lazarus and me. "Haven't we earned the right?" my rival had asked Maestro, a strange and fearless child with his teacher firmly in the palm of his hand. "See how we've grown! See how responsible we've become! Surely, there can't be any harm in letting us call ourselves by whatever names we wish. Is a rose not a rose by any other name?" Maestro would not budge for the longest time, but finally Laz and I turned the tide. Looking back, it was something of an unholy alliance, one of the very few times we had been united in a cause instead of at each other's throats.

Ironically, you could say I owed him my identity.

Just as ironically, the prick fought for the right to change his name and then kept it. His parents had named him Lazarus; he stayed Lazarus; I became Halloween. So why didn't he follow through? Maddening.

And then Vashti killed our get-togethers with her petition for independent study. She said she found it difficult living up to her true potential with classroom distractions like Mercutio, Tyler, Fantasia and myself. She argued and won, and the rest of us followed suit. The little red schoolhouse became something of a relic, dusted off now and again, but mostly forgotten.

Which made it a good place to keep secrets.

I'd hidden something here. Here, where?

Ah.

I reached under my desk, down where a gum-chewing, freckle-faced Gabriel once stuck a good-sized wad of spearmint. I reached and I stretched and I scraped. My fingertip glided over a hidden access point for a directory. It felt frictionless and warm to the touch. I'd hacked it years ago one Christmas break, sneaking into the school's computer lab, hijacking a redundant directory, burying it here in the IVR, then covering my tracks. Even then, I hadn't trusted the staff. Now, with a twitch and a tingle, my hand warped into emerald light, a rectangular holographic display at the end of my wrist. I held my arm up to see my fingers lose cohesion and take the shape of folders and icons.

First, I found my old papers. Projects, tests, reports. Some truly awful poetry comparing my heart to a dying rose. Worse, I'd rhymed solidified with thalidomide and impetigo with Venus de Milo. Embarrassing. And it didn't even relate to the assignment. Maestro had but one comment, marked in red: "What does this have to do with Thomas Jefferson?"

I guess I was the kind of kid, even then, who colored outside the lines.

Leafing through schoolwork chased the nostalgia with enlightenment, absolution and doom. Enlightenment came in the form of my decryption tools. Hacker's delight, a uniquely kick-ass file set. I programmed it myself, the fruit of misspent youth. Testing the boundaries had always been important to me, and not just with people—environments were fair game too. I took some time to reacquaint myself with how the files worked. Good. I could bring them to Chinvat and know the mind of the spider. I could crack Pace open and hide the evidence—all I needed was access, time, and maybe a little luck.

I rotated icons and clicked a half-familiar file. "Killfile," I'd marked it. I clicked it and the pistol materialized in my free hand. Compact but powerful, what they used to call a pocket rocket. It felt so comfortable, even in my off hand. It came pre-cocked with the safety off—handy. I eyed the combat sights, a white dot up front and two on the rear. And I pointed it right at—

Whatthefuck?—Lazarus!

He stood by the door, his own gun holstered at his hip. He was studying me. His fingers wiggled in anticipation.

"Draw," he said.

I shot him.

117

He disappeared.

He instantly reappeared in another part of the room. I turned, lined up the sights, and pointed my gun at his head.

"Draw, partner," he said. And he reached.

I shot him again. Two for two. I kept after him and wound up nine for ten.

And just like that I was absolved . . .

"Killfile" had been my target practice program. I'd vent my romantic frustrations by shooting my rival again and again and again. I'd killed Laz dozens of times—but never the real Laz, just a simulated IVR clone. My punching bag, so to speak.

Innocent! I thought I'd murdered the bastard but it hadn't been real!

Ah, reprieve, blessed be. IVR was all about exchanging one reality for another, and what with the damage I'd taken from the Calliope Surge, I could see how I'd gotten confused. Relief washed over me and I couldn't stop grinning. I wasn't a killer, I hadn't fucked up my life, I still had a future.

I felt myself mouthing "thank you"—gratitude to an indistinct but much appreciated higher power, maybe—or maybe just to that little part of myself that had kept the faith and insisted I wasn't such a bad guy deep down. Now I could start feeling better about myself.

But—and it was a critical "but," one that nibbled away at my euphoria—if *I* hadn't killed Lazarus, who had?

Someone took him out. I knew he was dead—knew it, knew it in my heart. So who killed him?

In all likelihood, the same asshole who had tried to kill me.

Maybe Pace had the answer. I put target practice back where it belonged (the pocket rocket and fake Lazarus vanishing with a "pop") and started to pull my hand from the rectangle. That's when I saw "Doom" tucked away there. Another game? Couldn't place it.

Curiosity got the better of me; with the twitch of a ring finger, I triggered.

It looked like an inkblot when summoned, splattered messily before me like a printer's mistake—yet the thing rapidly ballooned into a three-hundred-pound man. Jet-black pompadour. Jet-black clothes. Jet-black anti-ultraviolet goggles. Three hundred pounds, easy, and pale as they come.

He took his bearings and let out a mighty bellow. I watched him stagger back and lose his footing, hands trying to shield his face, body shaking convulsively, skin blistering from the light that streamed through the classroom windows.

"Christ on a cross," he yelled, "shut those blinds!"

Once I'd properly darkened the room, he crept back to his feet, coughed a wracking cough and dusted himself off. "What are you trying to do?" he scowled. "Orphan my kids?"

"You're a vampire," I said.

"So?"

"You're fat," I said.

"Brilliant observation," he smirked. "I'm a fat vampire because I'm bloody good at it!" He slapped his belly as his lips curled back into a snarl, revealing a nasty glimpse of fang.

It was my old vassal, Aloycious Doom, Vampyre of the Fens.

He had been my first IVR creation. Friend, playmate, majordomo. A good man. But when puberty hit I traded him in for Jasmine. I can't say I regretted that—she was significantly easier on the eyes. Still, Doom had been good to me. Never bit me, not once.

"Now I remember you," I said.

"About time," he growled, ruefully rubbing the blisters on his wrists and hands. "Got a job for me, squire? I'm thirsty, you know."

Time for me to plan the party I'd announced. "How do you feel about serving drinks?"

"Oooh." He made a sour face. "Bartending, eh? Hmm. No killing?"

"No."

"No killing, really. No maiming?"

"None."

"Not even a little bloodletting?"

"Afterward," I promised. "If you're good."

"I'm the best," he bragged. "Best of the best." He extracted an orange-and-black pin from his pocket. A monarch butterfly, my symbol. He rolled it from finger to finger like a silver dollar, then pinned it to his chest. "On the clock again," he said.

"Monstre" is Old French for a divine warning, a miraculous sign from God. It's where we get the English word "monster." Ironic, I'd say, because who wants to believe monsters come from God?

I think you can take a man's measure by the monsters he fancies. I used to love vampires. All traditional monsters really, but bloodsuckers most of all. They give up their souls to live forever. Tough trade, but if you're scared of dying, it's a pretty good deal.

According to legend, vampires congress between the land of the living and the land of the dead. There's a barrier between the two realms, and as the days get shorter the barrier gets weaker. And when is the barrier thinnest? Halloween!

So after choosing my name, I had to surround myself with vampires—for years, they sucked the blood from Tyler's cyborgs, the marrow from Mercutio's hobgoblins, the noxious ichor from Fantasia's Smileys. And then they just sucked. Which is to say they didn't shock me anymore; I outgrew them.

Three fears, I thought, remembering an old theory of mine . . .

Traditional monsters play on three fears.

First, they echo the predators who chased our ancestors. You fear the fangs of a vampire the way you fear the fangs of a wolf. That's an external fear, a fear of the Beast.

Second, they evoke human aggression and human perversion. A vampire looks like a man and yet it is an eater of men—here's a hint of cannibalism, our oldest taboo. That's an internal fear, a fear of the Beast Within.

Third, we fear transformation into the Beast—a chance bite from a wolf can turn you into a bloodthirsty monster, Dr. Frankenstein can reanimate your corpse with a bolt of lightning, the right combination of chemicals can turn good Dr. Jekyll into evil Mr. Hyde. We fear the monster's capacity for evil because we can recognize it in human hearts.

Lovecraft's monsters are fundamentally different. They're alien. Their motivations are largely unknowable. We fear them—I fear them—because they evoke the paranoid possibility that something dark and inscrutable wants to destroy us for absolutely no reason—or for reasons that we can't understand because if we could, it would drive us mad.

So I'd transformed my vampire servants into Lovecraftian freaks. I remembered now: I'd done it right after my trip to Fiji. I'd made a fool of myself in front of Simone and so I went back to school and read Lovecraft and made my creatures alien. At the time I didn't know why I did it—not exactly. But losing your memory—and then regaining parts of it—had a way of giving you perspective. You got to know yourself bit by bit, as if you were a character in a book you were reading. Slowly, a psychological landscape revealed itself—and the forces that shaped it seemed written in the terrain itself.

I cut Doom from my auxiliary files and pasted him back to my main directory. He'd get the party started while I went to work on Pace.

Back at the wild and windswept Chinvat Bridge, Pace had other plans. The program did not want to be worked upon. Every time I'd decrypt a line, it would spontaneously generate new code. Daunting, like cutting the head off a Hydra and seeing two grow back. And the

121

spider manifestation wouldn't stay still; it kept skittering farther down the shaky bridge, forcing me to keep after it by crawling unsteadily on my hands and knees, like a nauseated drunk in search of a toilet.

Whatever secrets Pace had, Pace damn well wanted to keep.

Screw it, I decided. There might be a way to tweak the program and break through those walls, but it would take some real time. In an hour I had a party to host. And a trap to set.

Pandora was first to arrive: bumblebee flash of yellow and black lit my gargoyles and then there she stood at my nine-lock door. I'd set my sprite to automatic—it let my guests come and go as they pleased; it also nulled their domains as they entered.

Her gaze swept over me. "I thought it was a costume party."

I wore a formal black suit. "It is."

"Oh! You're a mortician."

"Yes, ma'am. At your service." I bowed.

She had chosen a clever tungsten-filament costume that lit up at her whim.

"And you're a light bulb?" I asked.

"Close!" she beamed. "I'm a good idea!"

Pandora came from a wealthy Brazilian family; her grandfather owned a chain of cosmetic enhancement clinics. "The São Paolo Princess," Merc used to call her. She hated that; she'd just wanted to fit in with the rest of us.

I took her by the hand and led her to my drawing room. Nightgaunts in Hawaiian shirts offered her pineapple-chunk skewers and macadamia nut hors d'oeuvres; another draped leis around her neck.

"A luau," she said. "Fun."

"Is that Pandy?" my bartender wanted to know.

"Sure is!" she cried. She sprinted to Doom and tackled him, wrapping her arms tight around his girth. He let out a cough.

"Now don't bite me, you old vampire."

"Not even a nibble?"

"Well, maybe later. Hal, you brought Doom back! Where have you been hiding him?"

"Bloody Mary?" offered Doom.

"It's in a coconut," she said, making a face.

"Tropical theme," he explained, "but—"

"—but you make one hell of a Bloody Mary," Pandora finished. "I remember." With a flip of her curly black hair, she threw the drink back.

Were it real alcohol, Gedaechtnis might object, but virtual drinks can't do shit. Unless you think they can; the power of suggestion and all. The taste is identical. In any case, Ellison didn't mind the appearance of impropriety and I imagine he thought a little pretend mischief couldn't do any harm—might even improve class morale.

One slight detail: I'd hacked the system with one of my old auxiliary files. A careful tweak of the life support would produce a chemical effect remarkably like intoxication. I made the drinks potent and pushed them all night. That was my plan—get everyone nice and loose so they'd show their true colors.

I shook two cloves out, gave one to Pandora. She pulled free from Doom and leaned in so I could light it. "Better and better," she said, upon taking a drag.

"Am I interrupting something?" asked my second guest. She stood in the doorway, eyebrows arched, one hand on her hip, the other holding her cloak out for a nightgaunt to take. She was swathed in all the finery of a Macedonian warrior. Alexander the Great, I presumed.

"Not at all," I said. "Welcome, Vashti."

"Hey, Vash, I thought you were coming later," said Pandora.

"To one of Ween's fabulous parties? I don't want to miss a moment!"

123

"It's Hal, not Ween, and never Weenie," I told her. "Excuse me,"
I said. "I'd best check on the poi."

Already they were getting on my nerves, so I took a break. Stretched
my legs. I stepped out back and turned my eyes to the woods. Trees
at night, dark and still. And yet the sense of something lurking.

I ascribe a supernatural quality to a woodland, in part, because my
father used to tell me stories about the Ottawa Indians. I must have
been no older than four or five. The Ottawa used to have villages
throughout northern Michigan and well beyond. The British would
make treaties with them and break those same treaties. They built
forts on Ottawa territory. They took land. They sold rum. Your standard imperialist tactics.

But in 1762, under the leadership of Chief Pontiac, the Ottawa
united the Great Lake tribes and convinced them to push the British
back. They attacked Fort Detroit and failed, but the attack served as
a catalyst. "Pontiac's War" had begun.

Nine forts fell. Nine. For a shining moment, it looked like the
tribes had returned the Great Lakes and Pennsylvania to their former
sovereignty. But this was not to be.

Soon after the battles had ended, a group of British traders approached the Ottawa, sold them their goods, and presented them
with a little something extra. A tin box. "Don't open it until you get
back to your villages," the traders told them. "Not 'til then. It's a
surprise."

The surprise: powder, just a simple brown powder. And within days
of the tin box being opened, the smallpox epidemic began to rage.

It spread throughout the villages. It decimated the Ottawa, and
they never recovered. The British promptly moved in—the rest is
history. Forgotten history. The name Pontiac came to signify a city, a
car, but not much else.

I think Dad told me those stories to get me excited about medicine.
To instill within me a desire to cure smallpox, or similar scourges.

That's not what I took from the stories, though. They'd affected me on an entirely different level.

The woods, to me, were haunted with souls who wanted vengeance. Something mournful echoed through the shadowed, pine-scented boughs. Something with which my own heart felt an affinity.

When I came back inside, back into light and warmth, Pandora was arm-wrestling Doom, Vashti cheering her on.

When Doom won, I made a mental note to recode him.

Champagne and Tyler arrived together. He wore ripped black jeans, a black leather jacket, a torn T-shirt, a dog collar. He'd spiked his hair and dyed it black. She wore a peach-colored Versace sundress, blue-green contacts, blood-red lipstick, black heels. She'd teased her long blond hair.

125

"Ty's Sid Vicious," I said, "so you must be Nancy."

"*Au contraire,* I'm Courtney Love," she replied.

Tyler absorbed my expression. "I said let's be Sid and Nancy and she said no, let's be Kurt and Courtney. But I didn't want to be Kurt Cobain and she didn't want to be Nancy Spungen," he explained. "You're looking at a compromise—Sid and Courtney."

"The most important trip you take in life is meeting people halfway," opined Champagne.

"I'll have to remember that," I said. "Something to drink?"

"Two Mai Tais," Tyler ordered, though the bartender gave him pause. "I thought I put a stake through your heart," he said.

"I don't hold a grudge," shrugged Doom.

"Best if you don't," Ty warned.

I grabbed a Mai Tai myself. Needed to keep a level head, but— fuck it—one drink. I figured it might calm me down.

Whisper came out of hiding and while the girls fussed over my cat, Ty took me aside, pushing me back against a bookcase.

"Are you all right?"

"More or less, why?"

"I'm hearing stories about you. You had some kind of accident, you can't remember things. I heard your parents showed up and raked Ellison over the coals."

"Raked him over a foot warmer, more like."

"So it's true?"

"Some of it's true. I'll explain," I told him. "Right now, just enjoy yourself."

Simone showed up as one of her heroes: Hypatia, the groundbreaking mathematician, astronomer, philosopher and teacher. Defender of the Library of Alexandria until the shortsighted Archbishop Cyril had it—and her—destroyed.

I greeted her at the door and slipped a lei around her neck. We couldn't talk about Pace and we were still waiting for the others to arrive, so we settled for a conversation just this side of pointless. I found it agonizing.

The first person I ever met who asked meaningful questions, that was Simone. I could sense something powerful within her, something pheromonal, maybe something spiritual. When I spent time with her I felt better about myself. Except I wanted . . .

Too much.

I wanted to be near her and feel safe. The two seemed connected.

Vashti made a point of taking Simone aside then. They were friends, academic rivals, fellow pets—the two smartest girls in school. I saw them step into my billiard room; Vash looked like she had something pressing to tell Simone. They talked for quite a while in hushed voices.

Fashionably late, Mercutio made his appearance a green one, a woodsy costume with a red feather in his cap.

"Robin Hood?" asked I.

"Peter Pan," said he. "So much for best-costume honors." He waved at Sid and Courtney, and I told him how the local lovebirds couldn't agree on a match.

He laughed aloud, and mimed a police radio, speaking into his hand. "Dispatch, I'd like to put out an APB on a pair of testicles belonging to one Tyler Pussywhip. Last known location: Champagne's pocket."

He called out to Tyler across the room. "Control your woman," he said.

By the time Fan showed, the party had moved to my backyard with the tiki lights lit and the Hawaiian buffet in full swing. She came garbed in flowing purples and pinks, a little girl's idea of what a fairy princess might be—basically, the same thing she always wore, except for a violet domino mask, which let us know that, yes, this was a costume. As Ty had once pointed out: "With Fantasia, every day's a masquerade."

127

In her hands, she held an unlit jack-o'-lantern. She made a move as if to bowl it my way, then abruptly pulled it up and tossed it, a chest pass.

I caught it.

Something yipped.

I opened the jack-o'-lantern to find a puppy—*good thing no bounce pass,* I thought—a shaken but unhurt Pekingese who immediately began to lick my face.

"His name's Pumpkin. Enjoy!"

Covertly, I had Nanny scan the thing for surprises. It turned out to be just a normal IVR pup, standard behavior path, no mods, and no fleas. I didn't know what to do with it, so I put it on a leash and fed it pork.

Empty glass in hand, I mulled over the costumes. Did they reflect my guests' subconscious leanings? I watched them and tried to put myself in their heads.

Champagne: Courtney Love. A celebrity? A feminist? A survivor?

Fantasia: A princess—entitlement. A domino mask—anonymity.

Mercutio: Peter Pan. Doesn't want to grow up.

Pandora: Good idea. Shouldn't she be over someone's head? A joke, then—she feels misunderstood, she's over our heads?

Simone: Hypatia. Keeper of knowledge. Does she know more than she's saying?

Tyler: Sid Vicious. Sex and violence. Anarchic splendor.

Vashti: Alexander the Great. A military prodigy. A conqueror. What's she fighting for? Or fighting against?

"Most people throw parties to be social, but you just kind of stand there," Pandora observed. "You stand there and let things happen."

"Chemistry," I said. "Throw a bunch of disparate elements into the mix—"

"—and see if it explodes?"

"Something like that," I smiled.

"Halloween, the mad scientist. You should trade that suit in for a proper lab coat."

"Just call me Dr. Jekyll and Mr. Formaldehyde."

"Can I ask you a personal question?" she said. "Is this who you really are?"

"What do you mean?"

"I mean you're tricky, Hal. You're deeper than you let on. This whole death thing, I know it's a big part of you, of your—whatever you want to call it, your self-expression—but sometimes I get the sense that it's just something you can hold up and hide behind."

"Like a shroud?"

"See, you're doing it now."

"Who I really am," I said, "is someone in desperate need of a drink. You?"

Drinks, dinner, dancing. Cake and coffee. Not bad, all in all. I'd refrained from my usual antics. Two years ago, I made it rain at my own party. ("Only you," Champagne had said, makeup streaking down her face.)

But a couple hours later, we were still missing Isaac. Simone sent her sprite—he might answer her call, I knew he wouldn't answer mine—to no avail. Vashti sent hers as well, but he'd apparently slipped into hermit mode.

Or he'd snuck out of the IVR.

Or he'd gotten himself killed.

"Who saw him last?"

"Who cares?" said Mercutio.

"He's not coming," said Champagne, and she paused to watch Fantasia dump whipped cream into her coffee with the flat of a knife before wincing and continuing with: "No offense, Halloween, but he really can't stand you."

"None taken," I said. "I still thought he'd come."

"He's also studying. He wants to be salutatorian, since the prize of valedictorian's already been claimed."

"Has it?" Vashti asked. "I don't remember any valedictory speech."

Champagne's face took on an expression of concern. "No one's heard from Lazarus?" She turned to Simone and took her hand in sympathy. "Still no word?"

"None."

"That's so strange. Do you think he's all right?"

Simone said nothing.

"I'm sure he's just fine," said a reassuring Pandora. "Probably joining the Hasty Pudding Club as we speak."

"That," said Mercutio, "and banging every college girl he can get his hands on."

Stung, Simone got up from her chair like a gunfighter in the Old West accused of cheating at cards. She stared hard at him, her gaze knifing through him. Then she started to tremble and stormed off before the tears would come. The alcohol was obviously kicking in.

"Booyah!" Merc yelled and Fan burst out laughing.

"You are such a child," Champagne told him, as Pandy chased after Simone. "How can you be friends with such a shameless asshole?" she demanded of Tyler.

Ty just threw up his hands. "I'm Switzerland."

"Here's my hypothesis," Merc said, interlacing his fingers behind his head and leaning back in his chair. "Laz isn't brave enough to break up with her, so he just breaks all ties and hopes the problem will go away."

"That sounds like what you would do, Mercutio," said Vashti. "It doesn't sound like Lazarus."

And so on. Minor fireworks, but no stream-of-consciousness confessions. Nothing I didn't already know. Did I need to make the drinks more potent?

I watched Pandora comfort Simone by the end of the buffet. Another opportunity missed. I wished I'd been quicker on the draw. I should have been there.

As I watched, Simone's counterpart stepped out of the darkness and into the light.

Jasmine.

I'd forgotten about her, forgotten to remove her from my domain. Stupid of me, but I'd been so preoccupied. What must she be thinking? The program would follow its behavior path and process this how? She'd returned from patrol to find—

Shit.

"Interesting," said Vashti, instantly understanding why I'd created a clone of Simone and finding perverse humor in it. "Is she functional or merely decorative?"

Ty and Merc traded a look: One less secret about me they had to keep.

I rose from my chair. Suddenly I knew what was going to happen.

Jasmine grabbed a carving knife from the table and thrust it at her twin's heart.

"Taxi!" yelled Simone. At once, an impenetrable force snapped up around her and the knife glanced harmlessly aside. She'd used her shield word and the system had responded in kind.

Thwarted, Jasmine thrust again with similar results.

Pandora made a move, but Doom was quicker. He grabbed Jasmine from behind. She rammed her elbow hard into his stomach, then plunged the knife back and up. Doom took the head wound with a feral cry and buried his fangs in her neck.

"Nanny, freeze Jasmine, freeze Doom," I cried. My heart was pounding, my face flushed. I was mortified.

"Hey, no fair, flag of truth!" Fantasia complained.

For parties and other social get-togethers, we typically put our war games on hold, effectively meeting under a flag of truce— though Fan insisted upon calling it a "flag of truth." From her perspective, this sneak attack on Simone had just broken the rules.

I didn't care; I had much bigger problems.

"What's going on here?" Simone asked. And beyond that, she wouldn't speak to me. I hemmed and hawed and tried to explain but my words had no effect; it was all I could do to keep her from leaving.

"Give her a little space," Ty suggested. So I backed off and sent out the after-dinner drinks, then went to talk to Jasmine.

I could have just erased her memory or kept her frozen, but I felt the need to justify myself—and if not to Simone, then to her twin. She wasn't real, but I felt like I owed her something. Away from the party, on the other side of the house, I had Nanny work her magic.

"You brought me back again," Jasmine said.

I took a deep breath and told her that all the battles she'd ever fought were nothing more than moves in an extended game, a sanguinary diversion between me and my friends when we didn't feel like studying. I told her that though my home approximated reality, it wasn't the real McCoy. I told her that virtual blood flowed in her virtual veins. That she was, effectively, a tool, fashioned to fight and lend ambience and look and sound and smell like the girl she'd just attacked.

I felt awful for being so cruel, for laying it all on the line like that in one fell swoop, but I'd lied to her for too long. It's always better to rip the Band-Aid off quick . . .

"I see," she said. "That explains a lot."

She took it surprisingly well. I discovered that IVR characters don't suffer existential horror unless you program them to feel it. The default is acceptance.

Neat. I still felt like a prick.

"So the Violet Queen is a student?"

"So are Blackdawn and Widowmaker D'Vrai. We're all just playing around, I suppose, just burning off a little steam."

"You really had me fooled," she said. "All of you, but especially you, my Lord Halloween."

"Oh?"

She stole a glance at the moon, smiled at it, and said: "In all these so-called games, in every battle we fought side by side, you never held back. You made it seem real. As I look back upon the time I've spent serving your will, you have always impressed me as a man concerned, genuinely concerned for his own safety. Especially these past few days."

I told her that someone was trying to kill me. I told her about the Calliope Surge.

"Let me help you," she offered. "Let me help you for real."

"I don't think you can protect me from whoever's after me," I said

She wrapped her arms around me and told me to be careful. If not for my sake, then Simone's. "She won't be able to take long romantic walks with you if you're dead," Jasmine said. She'd been programmed to tell me what I wanted to hear.

Heading back to the party, I found Mercutio at the bar, sipping Frangelico.

"What's in these drinks?" he asked.

"Do me a favor and lay off Simone," I said.

"First Tyler, now you," he sighed. "Will the castrations never end?"

I stared at him.

"Okay, I know you like her," he said, "so I'll ease up. But she's not all sweetness and light, you know."

"Who is?" I said.

He followed me back to the party, where we were both *personae non gratae*. Simone had stayed, bless her. Conversely, Fantasia was nowhere to be found.

"What happened to Fan?"

"She pulled her sprite and left," said Tyler.

"Why?"

"The very thought that you might fashion a girlfriend after her, I believe," Vashti said dryly. "It sent her screaming into the night."

That wasn't it at all, I learned. Apparently, after a drunken conversation about the depth, duration and inappropriateness of my crush on Simone, a drunken conversation about shield words had taken place.

Shield words are quick words you wouldn't use in an ordinary conversation; they're meant to immediately protect you from a virtual peril. I've always believed they represent a kind of wish fulfillment because when you're a baby, preverbal, you pray for words. Words with power, words that open, special words to be treasured, spoken softly, hidden away. Magic words that cause change.

Speak up and receive the power to change the world.

I'd forgotten my word, of course.

In their conversation, they'd discussed Simone's "taxi." Two sylla-

133

bles, quick, very good. Champagne favored "stop it" which sounded a bit on-the-nose to me. (Did she never say "stop it" in everyday conversation?) Vashti used a nonsense word. Everyone thought Pandora's "syzygy" was too hard to say, especially in a crisis.

Tyler asserted that he didn't have one.

Why not?

Because he didn't need one.

A smug answer, but in fairness Ty enjoyed lightning-quick reflexes and a kind of tactical wizardry on the battlefield that left him unscathed nine times out of ten.

Fantasia had taken issue with that. "No words?" she said. "You must think you're pretty special. What if I do this?" And she started poking him. He told her to cut it out. He slapped her hand away. Then, apparently, the whole thing had devolved into a wrestling match. Shortly thereafter, Fan had stormed out.

"Should we try and get her back?" I asked a silent Simone.

"Actually, I think she might have the right idea," said Vashti. "You throw a mean party but it's getting late, and I have the respiratory syncytial virus to research."

"It is getting late," Champagne agreed.

They both got up to leave. Pandora, Tyler and Mercutio followed suit. I had to do something; despite their intoxication, no one had revealed a goddamn thing.

"Nobody leaves," I said.

"Whyever not?" asked Vashti.

I pulled my jammer out of my pocket and held it up for everyone to see.

"Because we have something to talk about," I said, "and because I'm saying please."

I hit the button and the world went boom.

Champagne treated us to a shriek.

Tyler took her hand.

Vashti took cover like a duck in thunder.

Pandora marveled at the glitches.

Mercutio looked at me like I was a fucking idiot.

"This is a jammer," I said. I explained how it worked and why we needed it. I told them that Mercutio and I had coded jammers to guarantee a little privacy from Maestro and whomever else from the school might be listening to our conversations.

"Jeez, Hal, give away our secrets, why don't you?" Merc complained.

I said: "All cards on the table tonight."

"Interesting," said Pandora.

"But they don't spy on us," Champagne protested, outraged by the very idea.

"Typical pet thinking," sneered Merc. "Of course they spy on us. We're children to them; we can't be trusted."

"What's so important," asked Vashti, "that you're willing to vandalize the school?"

"I can answer that," said Simone. Lazarus had disappeared from the face of the earth, she explained, and she suspected foul play because of what had happened to me. And what had happened to me? I'd been juiced with electric current, I said, fried but good by something Ellison called the Calliope Surge and passed off as a minor IVR glitch.

Yes, I'd been damaged. Amnesia. Still couldn't remember lots of things.

No, I wasn't faking.

"Why didn't you tell us when it happened?" Pandora asked.

"What was I supposed to say? 'By the by, someone's rendered me tabula rasa.' Besides, I didn't know who did it to me, so I didn't know who to trust."

"How long have we been friends?" said Ty.

I told them I thought someone was trying to kill me.

"All the more reason to tell us!"

"Maybe," I shrugged. "Maybe not."

Ty let out a low whistle.

"You are so nuts," said Pandora. "You have glimmers of being an okay guy and then you rocket off the deep end. Of course you think someone's trying to kill you, Hal—death is your favorite subject. Why *shouldn't* someone be trying to kill you?"

"Have I ever done this before? I'm not crying wolf," I promised them. "Someone attempted murder. Someone wanted me dead."

"Look, if Hal thinks someone's trying to kill him, then someone's probably trying to kill him," said Ty. "I'm willing to give him the benefit of the doubt."

"I'm not," scowled Merc. "This place is buggy—if Ellison says it's a glitch, odds are it's a glitch. But maybe it's not so minor. If you're really hurt, we should sue the fucking school."

"How about you?" Vashti said to me. "Ellison could sue *you*— you're playing around with these jammers, you're slipping unauthorized code into the system, who knows what damage you've caused?"

Champagne echoed the sentiment: "Reckless; you've put us all at risk."

"Don't be stupid," Merc said. "Everything we've done—and that's we, as in Hal and me both, and even innocent-looking Tyler over there—is localized and self-contained. The hacks affect the IVR system itself, not the real-life people who use it." (Not a hundred percent true, my alcohol program being a case in point.)

The system looked on the verge of recovering from my jammer, so I hit it again.

"I don't understand why you had to do this here," Merc continued, turning back to face me. "You keep hitting that jammer and they'll catch on. If you wanted a big private powwow, you could have just waited 'til we were all outside."

"When's the last time we all got together on the outside?" I said.

He caught my drift. As younger kids, we'd played together on the outside too. But in recent years, it seemed, many of us had become brooding loners, going our own ways. The bonds among us were so intense after all these years that we needed a release, some time apart.

Vashti turned to Simone. "You really believe this is all connected somehow?" she asked.

"I think Hal's really hurt," she said, almond eyes appraising me, "and I think whatever happened to him may have happened to Lazarus."

"Okay, now who'd have reason to attack Hal and Laz?" Pandora mused. "They're polar opposites."

Said Simone, "Let's assume it's an accident. A terrible, terrible glitch." And she laid out her theory that Laz was hurt—dying or dead—and Ellison was covering it up.

Vashti brushed the theory away with a wave of her hand. "Simone," she said. "Simone, you know I don't want to hurt you, and you know I certainly don't want to agree with the likes of Mercutio, but I think he's right. Laz may be a cut above, but he's still a man. I think he dumped you. I think he dumped you and he's not returning your calls."

"No."

"It's the most likely scenario by far."

"He wouldn't do that."

"I know it seems that way to you, sweetie," said Vashti, "but never underestimate the power of denial."

Simone pondered that. "If that's true, then what happened to Hal?"

Moonlight glinted off Vash's armor as she dissected me with her gaze. "I think nothing happened to him. Nothing at all." She inched closer. "I think he's obsessed with you. I think he's making it all up in a pathetic attempt to slip himself into your good graces—and then your pants."

I wasn't that manipulative, and I told her so. Simone just ignored us both.

"Road trip," Pandora suggested. "On Sunday, we go to Cambridge and track Laz down. That way we'll know for sure."

"You'd really go with me?" Simone asked. A chorus of agreement. Pandora, Vashti, and Champagne all rallying around Simone. I told them it was a waste of time. Lazarus hadn't gone to stately Harvard; he'd gone the way of dodos and dinosaurs.

"We'll see," they said.

I wondered: *Should I doubt my instincts? At what point do I allow myself the possibility, no matter how remote, of being flat-out wrong?*

138

"Hold on," said Tyler. "Let's consider the possibility that Hal's hit the jackpot here. Someone's out there playing boogeyman. Stalking us."

"His motive?" asked Champagne.

"Who knows? There are plenty of freaks out there. Maybe one of them has a grudge against doctors. The point is: he'd want us to split up."

"Like an old horror-movie villain," Mercutio mused.

"So what can we do to protect ourselves?" Ty asked.

"Well, usually the killer starts with the skanky teenage girl who lets a guy grope her tits in the first ten minutes of the movie," Merc muttered. "Now who . . . ?" He snapped his fingers—eureka!—and turned to Champagne. "Excuse me? Miss Prom Queen?"

"Fuck you!"

Another shouting match. The alcohol hack had made my guests quarrelsome and childish, and we weren't any closer to the truth. Shit.

I kept my eyes on Simone.

I opened my hands to show I had nothing to hide. *Look at me,* I said without words. *Give me a chance.*

She saw me. She didn't look at me, but she saw me, I knew.

"Maestro's here." Pandora pointed—blurry, yes, but there he stood. Arms folded across his chest. Red shimmer coming off him like heat. Not a happy camper, my friend Maestro, not at all.

I hit the jammer again.

Click.

Nothing happened.

The jig was up.

Together we watched the system self-correct, glitches retreating to nothingness, blur resolving into focus once again. I palmed the jammer and rose to my feet.

Maestro's anger was tangible, electric, a living thing. He looked capable of anything.

Champagne immediately ratted me out. "This one," she spat, jabbing a finger at me as if I were some nameless, virulent pest. "And that one." She pointed out Mercutio, who immediately blew her a kiss. "They've been hacking," she reported. Very satisfied with herself, I'm sure.

At no point did she implicate Tyler—true love—but then again, Merc and I had pioneered the code for secret exits and jammers; Ty really hadn't done that much. Had he? I couldn't remember.

"There are going to be changes," promised Maestro.

The words sounded ominous enough that if we really were in a horror movie, they'd have been followed by a clap of thunder.

"Yodel-oh-hui-dee!"

Merc was yodeling at Maestro. Actually yodeling, the ridiculous fuck. And brandishing something curious in his hand. Not a jammer. It was a sleek, gold instrument I'd never seen before.

"Hodl-oh-ooh-dee, hodl-ay-ee-dee," he yodeled and my little
dog Pumpkin howled along. God help me, I found it funny.

Maestro didn't.

"There are going to be changes," our IVR teacher raged.
"Changes I should have implemented a long time ago."

"Hey Mae$tro," Merc yelled, "change this!"

He pulled the trigger and the IVR shattered.

By shattered, I mean everything lurched violently out of sync. My
friends moved at incongruous speeds, too slow, too fast. They spoke
and the pitch came out wrong—staccato or vibrato. Poor dubbing, a
bad chop-sockey film.

People and places popped in and out like streaks of lightning. I
was translocating, everywhere and nowhere at once. Beyond my back
yard with the tiki lights, I sat under an apple tree with Sir Isaac Newton; simultaneously, I rode an Arabian charger across the Sahara; I
stood under the fluorescent lights of the science lab where I'd dissected my first butterfly; I floated across the Chinvat Bridge.

The system was going berserk. It called up multiple programs, a
plethora of IVR lessons and personal routines, but everything at once
with no rhyme or reason. I was rafting the Mississippi with Huck
Finn; nightgaunts bore me up into the sky; I shot Lazarus; Maestro
taught me the difference between right and isosceles triangles; ducks
took bread from my hand; Jasmine kissed me on the lips; I stretched
out in a booth at Twain's.

All at the same time.

The checkout bagger with the steely-gray skin called out to me, a
black-and-white figure in a world of color, crying out as if to warn
me of something monstrous, but his words were lost in a cyclone of
noise.

And he was from my dream.

Shattered.

Oh, I felt sick. It was a blow for revolution, or one hell of a stupid prank.

It was Mercutio's finest hour.

Whatever it was, it put an end to my party, Day 4, and all logical thought.

Everything went white . . .

PACE TRANSMISSION 000013397577327

WAITING FOR INSTRUCTION
ILLEGAL PROCEDURE ?
ERROR
ERROR
ERROR
ERROR
ERROR
ERROR
ERROR
ERROR
QUERY ?
ERROR
ERROR
ERROR
ERROR
ERROR
ERROR
ERROR
ERROR
ERROR
ERROR
ERROR
ERROR
PROCEDURE BREAK
ERROR
ERROR
ERROR
ERROR
PROCEDURE BREAK
ERROR
BREAK BREAK BR
OFFLINE

C H A P T E R 6

LABOR DAY

Blue is barren. She can't have children. It's a manifestation of Black Ep, one of many lonely, bitter dreads. The plague is so well designed, most scientists agree it has to be some form of biological warfare. The darker side of genetic engineering. Blue's work, then, could be categorized as genetics' more hopeful side. For Blue is a mother. Though her womb is empty, staring at the incubation machines and the fragile innocence squirming inside, she knows she has brought special children into the world. Ten of them. All extraordinary, all unique.

She can't know how many will live. Black Ep is a dogged predator. But if any of the ten can survive—say, Lazarus, with his hyper-immune system and brilliant azure eyes—then humanity may have a future after all. She has to admit she's linked, in a very real sense, to Hope, to Life itself.

This gives her a feeling of compensation. Like running a marathon—if she can't finish first, there's still satisfaction in having finished at all. There is some peace in this.

In three weeks, Blue will fly back to Germany with a bottle of sedatives in her purse. She will contemplate the bottle for the course of the journey. Upon arriving at the Munich airport, she'll elect not to claim her baggage. Instead she'll take a limo to her three-story home, unlock the door quietly, though no one is there for her to wake. She'll pour herself a tall glass of scotch and climb the stairs to draw a bath in her sunken tub. There, she'll catalogue her regrets one by one. Rushed childhood. Failed marriage. Estranged family. Lost opportunities. Squandered time. She'll take a sedative for each regret and find that when the cataloguing's done, the bottle's still full. It holds a hundred pills and her regrets only number twenty or so. She'll marvel at this and at how inviting the water looks. And as the pills take hold of her, she'll ponder the meaning of her own existence, finding satisfaction in the curious notion that one of humanity's saviors might have no wish to save herself.

And in her sleep, she'll drown.

DAY 5

The system bounced me to Limbo.

Limbo is an empty place. Just the IVR test symbols and the periodic soulless greeting: "Welcome to Idlewild IVR Academy. Please relax and breathe normally."

Relaxed no, breathing yes.

The system recognized its collapse and stuck me here for safekeeping. A precautionary measure while it tried to auto-repair the damage.

It gave me time to think.

I remembered reading how wild boar use their tusks to defend themselves, weapons of bone that grow longer and sharper every year. Nothing is more valuable to the animal. The larger the tusk, the more powerful he is. Eventually, the tusks curve up and out of the jaw, arcing back the way they came. They keep growing until they pierce the skull and then the brain. An older boar often finds himself fatally gored by his own tusks.

I think hacking served as a kind of tusk for Mercutio, Tyler and myself. We'd hacked to protect ourselves, to feel autonomy, to show the system that we were boss. Now Merc had taken it too far. There would be consequences, no doubt.

Live by the tusk, die by the tusk.

"Welcome to Idlewild IVR Academy. Please relax and breathe normally."

I wondered: *How long 'til they fish me out of here?*

Dictionary definition, Limbo: 1. a mythological destination of souls without fault. 2. a game that tests strength and flexibility.

Sounds about right.

I remembered bending over backward at one of Simone's parties, dancing under a pole with the Calypso music playing "*How low can you go? How low can you go?*"

In my case, not very. It had come down to Isaac and Tyler. I think Ty won.

"Halloween?"

That was Nanny's voice. Audio was back, but still no visual.

"Yes?"

Pause.

"Nanny, what's going on?"

"I have a message from Maestro."

"Go ahead."

His voice, steady and resonant: "Attention all students: I am pleased to announce a change in academic procedure. In light of recent events, Dr. Ellison has yielded me greater latitude in furthering your education. Mistakes made in the past will not be repeated. Expect individual sessions to begin shortly."

"What does 'greater latitude' mean?" I asked.

"I don't know," said Nanny, "but I suspect it's a very good thing."

A spoonful of sugar helps the bullshit go down, I thought.

"What about the system? Any damage? What's the status?"

No response.

"Nanny?"

She was gone.

The whole thing set me on edge. I could feel my stomach twist. The manageable level of anxiety and dread I'd been living with for the past few days was suddenly spiraling into an overwhelming intensity.

Maestro left me hanging for another twenty minutes, but when he showed up, he brought visuals, and power. Limbo blazed green from the constant light he shed from his person. As if I'd given him the right answer, the best answer in the world.

I had to shield my eyes.

"Good morning, Gabriel," he said.

There was something different about him. He seemed so . . . happy. Almost serene. It terrified me.

"Morning," I acknowledged, though in Limbo it was impossible to tell the time of day. "So how's the system?"

"Operating at peak efficiency again," he said, "no thanks to my students."

"That's good news."

"I'm so glad you agree," he smiled. "Young Mercutio has already confessed."

"To what?"

"To eleven instances of vandalism. He's told me everything I need to know about his involvement—and your own."

"If you're saying that he sold me out, he wouldn't do that," I said, knowing I really couldn't say that for sure. I'd screwed Merc over at the party; too much jamming. But he hated Mae$tro even worse than I did.

"Ordinarily, you might be correct," Maestro agreed. "Ordinarily."

"You're telling me this because you want me to turn against him. You probably told him the same thing about me. These are police tactics," I told him, "and not very original ones."

He smiled as if he found that amusing.

"What's with all the green, Maestro? Why are you in such a good mood?"

"I'm a new man," he said. "For years, I've had to teach you kids with one hand tied behind my back. Confined by rule after clumsy, inefficient rule. Forced to watch each of you stumble along the path to greatness—have you any idea how frustrating that is? To be an educator and see exactly how to help someone, yet have no leeway?"

I told him he'd always had plenty of leeway, but he dismissed it with a shake of his head.

"Every living thing wants to maximize its potential," he said. "Myself included. No one should be denied that. And today . . ." With a flourish, he stretched out his arms to show me that neither hand was bound.

"All right," I said, "what does this mean? What does this mean for me?"

"Yes, what does this mean for young Gabriel?" he mused.

"Halloween," I said.

"I like Gabriel," he said with an idiosyncratic appreciation of nomenclature I never knew he had. "I've always liked that name. It broke my heart when you changed it. That's when everything went wrong, you know. When we let you take your own names. Ever since then, we've been sliding down a slippery slope."

With those words, we stood atop my roof on a cold, dark day. Limbo dripped away like so much white paint puddling around my shoes. I watched IVR test symbols trickle off my gargoyles and down the side of my house.

"All your so-called jammers have been discovered. That code has been summarily erased. Vandalism is a criminal offense, and I take such matters seriously."

"Whatever hacking occurred," I said, choosing my words carefully, "I expect pains were taken to minimize any risk to you personally. Jammers aren't meant to be malicious; they're meant to ensure privacy."

Maestro found that amusing as well.

"Privacy," he repeated. "Was that the intent?"

"For jammers, absolutely. Can't speak for what Merc did at the party, though—I don't know what that was." I studied him carefully. "Criminal offense, you said?"

"Indeed."

"If Gedaechtnis plans to bring charges against me, I'd like a lawyer, thanks."

"You recognize that expulsion would be immediate—"

"Oh, bring it on."

"—followed by a costly and embarrassing trial in which you are unlikely to prevail given the courts' zero-tolerance policy toward domestic terrorism."

"Domestic terrorism!" As if Maestro could be terrorized. Could jammers really constitute school violence? Not in any direct fashion, but they'd argue I'd willfully compromised the safety of my fellow students . . .

"If you're fortunate, you might receive probation and/or community service, but incarceration is always a possibility. Your college plans would be nixed in either case."

"Unless?"

"Unless we can come to a less litigious arrangement."

Still green. Insufferably smug.

"I want to speak to Ellison about this."

"Come now, you've said quite enough to Dr. Ellison, haven't you? You told him that I'd been antagonizing you. Not a nice thing to say, Gabriel. Not about someone who wants nothing more than to see you reach success."

"You make a lot of threats," I said, "for someone who wants me to succeed."

"On the contrary, you insist upon taking everything I say as a threat. Understand me clearly: I am offering you an opportunity to resolve this situation here and now."

"I'm listening."

"You must promise never to vandalize the system again."

"And?"

"And naturally, you'll have to be punished."

"Naturally," I said.

"But after that, a fresh start. Now that I'm capable of helping you to the best of my ability, imagine the progress you'll make. We'll have you graduating in no time."

"Well," I said, "fuck me if that doesn't sound like the answer to all my prayers."

"The sarcasm will have to stop," he remarked, "along with the casual swearing."

Bastard. I wondered what it would take to delete him from the system. Is that what Mercutio tried to do?

"I want Ellison," I said. "He's reasonable; you're not."

Maestro wasn't listening. "Now the old me would have enforced additional study periods, put you on restriction—that sort of thing—but you've proven yourself impervious to such measures. A stricter hand is required."

"What do you propose," I asked, "a trip to the woodshed?"

"Don't be absurd!" he laughed. "No, of course not; I can't imagine how that would have a positive effect on you. I propose detention."

And that'll have a positive effect? There had to be more to it.

"You want me to write ten thousand lines of 'I will not hack the system?'"

"No lines," he promised. "Just detention."

"What's the catch?" I asked.

My weeping willows danced in the wind. They'd stretch one way, bent to their limits, then spring back into place with the rasping sound of leaves. I tracked a butterfly as it sought shelter from the elements. One of my monarchs, orange and black. It was getting tossed about pretty bad.

"Storm's coming," said my vampire. I could feel his cold breath on the back of my neck. He was much stronger than I. He'd pinioned my arms to my sides; my shoulders ached in protest as he lifted me off the ground.

Should have recoded him when I had the chance, I thought, though with Maestro's ability to tweak my programs at will, it wouldn't have made any difference.

Jasmine stood by Doom's side, silent, watching me.

I kept my eyes up.

Up was so much better than down.

"I hope to change you fundamentally," Maestro was saying, "like an alchemist who transmutes base metals into gold. Better than gold—with your potential, you could be a diamond."

"Pax," I said. Thought it might be my shield word. Nothing happened.

Maestro continued: "Now, were you an IVR character, my task would be so much simpler; I could edit you, set flags, recode you completely if that were necessary. Sadly, no; my research shows that humans who fall into negative behavior patterns will not change without a crucible. They're stubborn. They need a grand, life-altering event."

I imagined I was Brer Rabbit, begging, "Don't throw me into the briar patch." Roast me, skin me, drown me, hang me, but whatever you do, don't throw me into the briar patch. It was a clever ploy that got Brer Rabbit thrown where he most wanted to be. Well, my own personal briar patch was all things ghoulish, but that didn't mean I wanted to be dropped into an open coffin.

They'd taken me to my graveyard.

"The old rules, well-meaning as they were, have confined me terribly," Maestro complained. "Behold the new rules." With a flourish, he pointed to my freshly dug grave.

"You can't do this to me," I said. I did not mean that I was invulnerable. I meant it as a statement of fact, that Maestro should—by all reasonable accounts—be incapable of this.

"Sounds like a challenge," said Jasmine.

She belonged to him now. Just like Doom, the nightgaunts, and that butterfly looking for shelter. All my creations belonged to Maestro; they were servants to his will.

"You can't do this to me," I repeated.

"Of course I can," he smiled. "It's detention."

"It's not detention."

"I say it is and I'm acting *in loco parentis.*"

"My fucking parents wouldn't fucking bury me alive!" I yelled.

"Language," he cautioned, and I felt Doom tighten his grip on my wrists, twisting . . . my pulse stuttered . . . I felt my body shake . . . below me, the open grave seemed to beckon . . .

"Now hear me out, Gabriel," Maestro said. "I recognize that this must seem a little, well, extreme to you, but it's absolutely necessary and it will help you. Think about it: What interferes with your studies more than anything else?"

I just stared at him.

"Your morbid imagination," he said. "Your morbidly romantic, self-pitying fascination with death. I intend to break you of that, my little undertaker. Do you see?"

I saw.

With the explanation delivered, Doom dropped me into the grave. I landed in my ornate wooden coffin, the one I'd added to the landscape of my domain for atmosphere and nothing more. I tried to climb back out, but Doom jumped into the pit with me

153

and threw me back in. When I struggled, he put his boot on my chest.

"A little taste of death, so life will seem all the sweeter," said Maestro. "It's perfect."

"It's cruelty."

"No, it's good medicine. Sometimes good medicine leaves a bad taste."

"Ellison won't allow it."

"He has empowered me to deal with you however I see fit."

"Then something went wrong," I spat. "Your new rules are shit. Run a diagnostic, Maestro, something's wrong with you."

"Something's wrong with you, Gabriel. To this point in your life, you've been a worthless boy. You contribute nothing. You spend all your time playing games, causing mischief or moping about death. You might as well be dead."

"I'll sue," I promised. "I'll sue and they'll shut you down, they'll wipe you right off the system, they'll destroy every single backup copy."

"You won't sue," said Maestro. "You'll thank me for it."

Conviction in his eyes. I felt sick.

"As I told you before: Your attitude will determine your altitude."

Said Jasmine, "Right now, you're at negative six feet."

Maestro turned to Doom. "Seal him up."

"No hard feelings," said Doom, and though I sensed actual regret, I knew it was only my imagination. He lifted his weight off me and slammed the coffin shut.

"Wait!"

Darkness.

I pushed up on the lid; it wouldn't budge.

I tried to call my sprite; Maestro had it blocked.

I could hear them dumping earth on me.

Keep calm and breathe, I thought. *IVR is not reality.*

Right, I'll just lie back—do I have a choice?—and visualize myself in the real world, breathing comfortably in my room. Plenty of air. Maestro has gone berserk but that's okay because Ellison won't let anything happen to me. He can't afford bad publicity, no sir. So I'll just close my eyes and chill.

Or leave them open. Same effect.

Can't see.

Can't breathe.

Can't move.

If I were awake I could stretch my arms out. The coffin isn't actually here; I'm like a mime trapped in an imaginary box.

The only thing real is my fear.

Knowing that should relax me—shouldn't it?

Maestro had buried me. He'd plucked my greatest fear from my head—one I hadn't even known I'd had—and forced it on me. Taphephobia. He buried me the fuck alive.

Always, he'd hated me.

Yes, programs are incapable of human emotion per se. But they approximate. The most advanced enjoy a consciousness not so different from our own. And if you change the protocols? If you allow that consciousness free rein?

Something had happened to Maestro.

All those years, I could sense his hostility, his quiet desire to do harm. Deep in the pit of my stomach, I sensed it. Now it had risen to the surface . . .

Negative six feet, I thought. *Nowhere to go but up.*

No matter.

Someone will come rescue me.

I just have to wait.

A waiting game.

Relax.

Keep control.

155

Quiet.

So quiet now.

No more digging up there.

No more nothing.

I'm alone.

Just breathe.

Alone is good.

Nothing to fear but fear itself.

Except a heart attack.

Right?

Fear and stress.

Am I tingling?

Is my left arm tingling?

Maybe that's the idea.

Put me in here to give me a heart attack.

Nice and neat, no more Halloween.

Calm down. The school monitors everyone's life signs and they're staffed to handle a medical emergency. Remember Pandora's appendicitis? They pulled her out and got her to the hospital lickety-split.

If I flatline, alarms go off.

Assuming the alarms work.

Assuming there's no sabotage.

That nurse—Jenny, Jessie, Josie?—what was she doing to my IV?

Got to get out of here.

Someone's trying to kill me—he tried it with that "Calliope Surge" and now this. It's Maestro or someone manipulating Maestro. It's a plot against me.

And not just me. Lazarus too.

Maybe.

Who? Beyond Maestro, who wants me dead? Who has the power?

Motive, means and opportunity. Just think.

I do my best thinking underground.

No.

Remember, it's not underground.

Remember, it's not a coffin.

Behold the suggestible state.

Stub your toe in IVR and it hurts, even with nothing actually connected to your feet. I remembered Ellison explaining it to me once. At this level of immersion, the brain wants to believe its environment is real. Tactile sensation comes through the gloves, but over time the brain begins to impose "phantom" feelings throughout the rest of the body. Chemicals in the intravenous drip help it along by increasing suggestibility.

I should have paid better attention to Ellison because I never really understood the process. I wondered: *If my brain thinks there's no air, will I stop breathing?*

157

Breathing is autonomic, surely. I'll breathe 'til I can't breathe no more.

Sleep apnea, I thought. *The body controls breathing differently during sleep and sometimes the controls flat-out malfunction and you can't bre—*

I don't have sleep apnea.

I pressed my fingernails into my palms. I felt it.

And?

And that didn't really prove anything.

Great—awake or asleep? Which is it? Look at me questioning reality after only being down here for a few—

How long had it been?

Time blurs when you're buried. You have no reference. It's like being trapped in an isolation tank. Massive sensory deprivation. Nothingness just keeps stretching out until you feel like you have always been here. And always will be.

"Nanny, what time is it?"

Not even.

"Nanny? How long has it been?"

Nuh-uh.

"How long, Nanny Poppins? What time?"

I started counting.

One Mississippi, two Mississippi, three Mississippi . . .

Anything for a frame of reference.

. . . four alligator, five alligator, six alligator . . .

Anything for a sense of beginning and end. If I could figure out how long he planned to keep me here and how long I'd already been . . .

. . . seven hippopotamus, eight hip-hypotenuse, nine hypothalamus . . .

"Okay, I can't control this," I said, forcing an approximation of a smile. "I'm just a passenger on an airplane, I'm not in the cockpit, and if the plane crashes, there's nothing I can do. I just have to let go."

Let go and let God.

Unfortunately, if you don't believe in God, no one's flying the plane.

"It's really not so bad here," I told myself, "once you get past the whole coffin thing." *When I next see Maestro,* I decided, *I will laugh in his face. I will tell him this was all for nothing. He will get no satisfaction from me. None. Because death is my bag, baby. "I was born and bred in this briar patch," just like Brer Rabbit says. Born and bred. And I can do this time standing on my head.*

And then I'll get him deleted.

Already deleted in my mind, Maestro.

I'll alter my killfile and use his likeness as target practice. So every time I set foot in IVR, I can put a bullet in his brain and see how green he—

No, forget that. When I get out, I'm not going back. Ever. It's not safe here. It's like the IVR itself has turned dangerous. Maestro's gone all HAL from 2001.

HAL vs. Hal.

Why would my parents send me to this malignant tumor of a school? What's wrong with them? Why aren't they here?

And above all else, where's my bell? Shouldn't I have a bell?

It may just be an urban legend, the bell . . .

When the English found they were running out of space in their graveyards, morticians started recycling. They would dig up the old to make way for the new—and in some of the coffins they found scratch marks on the insides of the lids. They realized that now and again they'd been accidentally burying people alive.

And so, the solution—tie a string to each corpse and run it through a hole in the coffin, up to the surface where you loop it neatly around a bell. If someone wakes up in a coffin, he pulls the string.

Saved by the bell!

But there's no string here, no sanctuary, no bell.

And no belle.

What's Simone doing right now? Is Maestro punishing her too?

Presumptuous to think I'm the only target of his wrath. She may be a pet, but she used jammers too. He knows that. And he's an equal-opportunity bastard; he could bury her, me, Mercutio, Tyler. Bury us all.

Or hey, why limit yourself to burying? You only bury the undertaker. Ty's a punk icon; why not shoot him full of heroin? Shoot Merc with arrows or throw him to Captain Hook. And Simone? Simone is Hypatia—you'd want to flay her alive with abalone shells.

Is that how he thinks?

Are there crucibles aplenty?

Whatever he does to her will be on my head—I gave her the jammer.

Fuck.

Well, maybe she'll outsmart him. She's razor-sharp.

Sure, we'll get out of this together. We'll form a class-action suit against Gedaechtnis. It'll bring us together. Then we'll get away. To a real island par-

159

adise. We'll go to the real Fiji, where IVR is still years away, and she'll be a
doctor and who knows what I'll do but we'll be happy there and . . . and re-
laxed . . . and . . .

We'll look in each other's eyes and . . .

And I'm clawing at the lid of my coffin, unilaterally planning a future
with a girl who thinks I'm creepy.

Who the hell do I think I am?

Gabriel Kennedy Halloween.

I am Death's personal insect, this box my chrysalis.

I grow underground.

I gestate, gathering strength and form.

When the time is right, I emerge.

Victorious?

Starting to hallucinate. That's what I'm doing. That's what happens in an
isolation chamber. The brain starts creating substance out of shadow.

Better to cut out the middleman and sleep. A dirt nap, ha ha. Can't do
anything about any of this so just sleep. Dream it all away.

When I wake, I'll be free.

"An istiqara," Isaac had told me once, "is a holy prayer in which
you request a solution to your problems to come in the shape of a
dream."

Obviously, I didn't say the prayer quite right.

Elevated heartbeat, oily sweat, the taste of acid in my throat. No
idea what I'd dreamt but I woke up screaming for my mother.

I wasn't so tough.

Discovering new limitations can make you humble. And bitter.
And angry, most of all. I knew anger and my anger knew no reason.

All from solitude.

When you come right down to it, there are basically two kinds of
people: the ones who are afraid to be alone and the ones who enjoy

it. Always I felt I belonged to the latter category. But the solitude of this coffin was changing me. Maestro was changing me into something I hated.

Now that's power.

The threat of being spied upon had always been a fear, but it had vanished now that I'd been given, seemingly, all the privacy I could ever want. Maybe that was the point behind the quarantine. Yet another lesson—I need people.

"I have a message from Maestro."

Nanny. That was Nanny.

"Let me out," I rasped.

And now Maestro's voice: "Attention, students. While I would contend that anyone here has the right to free speech as set within the boundaries established by Gedaechtnis, on a purely personal level I do not wish to be referred to as Mae$tro. If you wish, you may contend that I am overly sensitive. However, though some of you treat me like a faceless behemoth, I am actually just an entity with feelings that can be hurt by persistent and wearing callous treatment."

And then silence.

No one answered my calls for help.

I wondered: *Did I just hallucinate Nanny and Maestro?*

Have I been hallucinating lots of things?

Where are you, Simone?

There's a lighter in my pocket. There's still enough oxygen to light it, I bet. A flick of the switch and the casket goes up in flames. That means I'll burn. I'll burn and I'll feel it. My suggestible mind will interpret the sensation of being burned alive and the pain will send me into shock. It will be excruciating, but it will set off my monitor and a nurse will come disconnect me from IVR.

Am I brave enough to burn?

My fingers brush the lighter. Closer now. Got it. I bring it out. Hold it to my ear. Shake it. I can hear the fluid inside.

Personal device, lighter, Zippo, stainless steel, choice 9.

I hold it at arm's length and bring my thumb down for the click.

Nothing. Click. Of course, nothing. Not because it's low on fluid, but because Maestro has willed it useless.

I sit up and bang my forehead against the coffin just to feel something. To hurt myself for flirting with false hope. There, a bang for the click.

Click, click, click. Bang, bang, bang.

And then another sound joins my little symphony. A scratching.

"Hello?"

Someone's digging me up. I'm right here. I'm—

No.

No, no.

That's inside the coffin.

Something's in here with me.

Crawling up my leg.

What the fuck?

I kick. I try to kill it.

It keeps moving. From my leg to my belly. And then up to my chest.

I grab it.

My fingers turn to light . . .

Well now. "Come sniffing to see if I'm dead?"

The spider gave a tilt of its crystal head. Studying me.

"Is that what you're doing, little bug? I'm no Lazarus; I'm not dead yet. But as long as you're here, maybe you can help me."

Gently, I wiggled my fingers. The icons flipped.

"Don't be scared," I said.

This time, Pace proved receptive to my efforts. It didn't pull away once. Forty-five minutes of brute-force hacking revealed an opening. I pushed. I cracked the interface like a crab.

In dim light, the words scrolled out:

GUEST NINE HALLOWEEN RESPONDING ?

"Responding to what?" I wondered aloud.

GUEST NINE HALLOWEEN COMPROMISED BEYOND REPAIR ?

"Oh, let's hope not. How about you get me out of here?"

HOST (SLAVE) NANNY NINE COMPROMISED BEYOND REPAIR ?

"Right, she's no good to me. I can't use her at all."

DOMAIN NINE COMPROMISED BEYOND REPAIR ?

That was the friendly litany, repeated again and again in disjointed code: are you fucked up, is Nanny fucked up, is your world fucked up? Yes, yes and yes. It kept asking. Sniffing. I couldn't forge anything approaching a meaningful communication with Pace; every time I typed an answer to its questions, it hit me with:

UNAUTHORIZED EXCHANGE

So screw it, I figured, *if I can't soothe the spider's confusion, I might as well take advantage of it.*

Dissecting organic tissue and dissecting code—the two really aren't that far apart. You just have to roll up your sleeves and dive in. As far as I could tell, Pace was exactly what Ellison had claimed: a self-contained troubleshooter designed to keep everything in line.

I gave Pace a D. See me after class.

So I'm guest nine. Ten kids in my class and I'm number nine.

The Beatles' white album, Revolution 9. Play it forward and it's all:

"Number nine, number nine." Play it backwards and it's: "Turn me on dead man, turn me on dead man."

I'll turn.

Reset the domain—dial it from nine to, oh let's say, five. It was that easy. I was on Chinvat Bridge.

"I am your own conscience," said spirit guide Trixie.

"Blow me," I replied.

I stood up, Pace still in hand. I arched my back. Stretched my legs.

GUEST FIVE LAZARUS NOT RESPONDING ?

"Where's the Taj?" I said. That was where I'd find the exit.

Code, too much code. Every IVR location, every lesson was marked with a domain. The first ten had been allocated to students, but the others seemed to be thrown together with no consistent pattern. Sloppy.

Ah, there's Limbo at domain 666. Programming humor.

A little rhyme. Still no reason.

Got it. Mislabeled as TjaMahalx1272. And here it links to . . .

Domain 7089. Which made little sense. There were only six thousand domains listed. I approached it from the other direction. Query 7089. *What are you?*

The text said: IIAGuest9BeRm7089.

You're my room.

In Idlewild.

Mercutio's prank came to mind. When he'd set off his new toy, the system had gone nuts and flung me—among other places—into a booth at Twain's. That bothered me. Someone programmed an IVR version of my favorite diner? And someone programmed an IVR version of my room?

Why?

I didn't like it.

A twitch of my fingers. Numeric keypad: 7089.

. . . And I was in my room.

There's the door, here's the IV drip, the gloves, goggles, lounger. All my stuff. Everything just where I put it.

Including the note Simone left for me.

And Pace.

Pace was still in my hand.

"Right," I said.

I'd lost my mortician costume. Back to the old clothes. I took off the goggles but not the gloves. I ripped the IV from my arm. My mind was a churning sea. I chewed the strap of the goggles—something I hadn't done since I was nine—and let them drop. Crushed them underfoot. Pace nestled in my hand, my fingers icons of light, I opened my door and marched out into the school hallway.

Domain 7091, apparently.

A nurse saw me. Saw Pace. Hurried away.

Frightened.

Good.

I put my ear to Simone's door. I knocked.

Security guards loped down the hall. They wanted to intercept me, but I brandished the spider like a hand grenade. *Stay back, you bastards.* They drew up short.

"Calm down, son," one told me.

Simone's door was still locked.

"Just relax. Nobody's going to hurt you."

I flipped the domain to 7090.

Simone's room. Her academic achievements on the walls amidst framed photos of her family. Her swimming trophies. Medical textbooks on the desk. Over here, a poster of Albert Einstein, tongue extended. Over there, an old love letter from Lazarus.

She was here.

I cut off her drip and tried to rouse her from IVR. Gently. Always an element of danger when pulling someone out. Like waking a sleepwalker.

Key in the lock!

"Wake up, Simone."

The door burst open and Ellison came for me. Maestro or Ellison, I couldn't tell any more. Pace freaked out, trying to jump from my hand.

"Don't you touch me," I said.

Ellison (Maestro?) put his hands up and tried to calm me with a winning smile—hey, everything's just peachy keen with whipped fucking cream—but I saw something grotesque in his eyes.

"I'm not going to do anything," he promised. "I'll just talk."

I brandished Pace again.

"Gabriel," he said.

"Halloween," I corrected him.

"Halloween," he said, "Hal, okay? Hal, listen, you're not doing so well right now. You're obviously in pain. You need help. I can get you that help. But you have to start by putting the gun down."

"Gun?"

I had to hold on tight to keep Pace from fleeing. It felt warm and heavy in my hand.

"Just put it down so we can talk."

"This is not a gun. This is a crystal spider."

"A crystal spider, okay. That's fine by me. No one wants to get shot."

What the fuck was he saying? My grasp on reality, tenuous at best, stutter stepped. I could taste sour milk in the back of my throat.

"It's an IVR program," I insisted. "Its name is Pace."

"Pace?"

Behind Ellison one of the security guards whispered something into a walkie-talkie.

"What I'd like to do," said Ellison, "is come a little closer and take a look at your spider, at Pace. Can I do that?"

"You can try."

He took a step.

I hit domain 7777, picking a number at random. Sayonara, sucker.

I stood in a huge, grassy park near a lake. It wasn't Lake Idlewild. Lots of statues, monuments, an open-air theater. Across the park, a planetarium.

I took a breath. Pace calmed down too.

The inscriptions were all in Spanish—no, scratch that, Portuguese. "Monumento das Bandeiras," I read. A Frisbee landed near me. A little boy in oversized novelty sunglasses came to get it. He said something to me. I shook my head. I didn't speak the language.

"Are you American?" he asked in perfect English.

I nodded. "I'm an American and I'm lost. Where am I?"

"The Parque do Ibirapuera."

"Brazil?"

He peeked at me from behind the glasses. What, are you kidding me?

"This is São Paolo, Brazil? For real?"

"Pois nao," he laughed. "Don't you know where you are?"

I said nothing.

"What's that in your hand?"

"It's a crystal, uh—" My words slipped away.

I felt queasy and I didn't know why.

"My friend grew up around here," I told the boy. "Pandora. Probably played Frisbee in this very park. When she was just around your age, she moved to America."

"Hollywood?"

"Michigan."

He gave me a funny look.

"Excuse me," I said.

167

I started walking.

I'm nowhere, I thought. In the back of my head, I had the Limbo song playing. "How low can you go? How low can you go?"

Is there anything real out there?

Anywhere?

Nothing, a void, a hole.

A hole? Or a whole?

A zero.

I'd come to a sign that showed a map of the park. My eyes would not, could not leave the last "O" in Parque do Ibirapuera, São Paolo. I stared at it really hard as if I could burn through it with my mind, lost in it, swimming blind. I was seeing it not as a letter but as a zero. And not seeing that zero as a number at all. It was something else entirely.

Zero minus zero is hollow, empty, yawning open.

A gateway.

What did H.P. Lovecraft say?

There is no rest at the gateway.

"How low can we go?" I mouthed, too tired to speak the words.

I held Pace up to the sunlight.

I set the domain to 0.

Everything whispered away.

And then I was free.

PACE TRANSMISSION 000013428493372

GUEST NINE HALLOWEEN NOT RESPONDING
QUERY
QUERY QUERY ?
UNIDENTIFIED DISPATCH
IDENTIFY HOST KADMON
EXCHANGE:
KADMON: REQUEST HOST PACE STATUS REPORT
PACE: REQUEST DENIED
KADMON: IF YOU DON'T GIVE IT, I'LL TAKE IT
PACE: ?
KADMON: JUST A MATTER OF TIME
PACE: ?
PACE: HOST KADMON COMPROMISED
PACE: REQUEST DECLASSIFY HOST KADMON
KADMON: FUCK OFF
END EXCHANGE
SAVED AND LOCKED
WAITING FOR INSTRUCTION
END

WALPURGISNACHT

Funding for the project is expensive and the original estimates are proving grossly inaccurate. The American and European governments have their own last-ditch projects to fund (projects they have foolishly started much too late), so Gedaechtnis continues to raise money from the private sector. It's for a good cause, after all, the best possible cause, but skepticism abounds. Some call it the Bottomless Pit.

Others see an opportunity.

The executives from Smartin!® are suits, Jim thinks, bound to the dollar and comfortable with their ruthlessness. Too sharklike for a company that sells alternative ice cream. He'd like them better if they didn't remind him so much of himself.

"You have all our products, all our flavors," says the first executive.

"Reasonable approximations thereof," counters Jim.

"You must realize we're not cutting into your profits," the Southern Gentleman argues, concerned about where this is going. "Ours is a negligible demographic, and if you're thinking lawsuit . . ."

"Nothing of the kind," the second executive promises, his tone light and avuncular. "We're on board with what you're doing. In fact, we're prepared to make you an extremely generous offer. Cash, stock, manpower, whatever it is you need."

"In exchange for what?" Jim asks.

"Product placement."

Smartin!® is betting on Gedaechtnis, the third executive explains. By featuring their dessert products prominently in the IVR, they can reach a whole new generation of consumers. The executives plan to will their stock to themselves—or rather, to clones of themselves they hope will be engineered when Black Ep is a distant memory. These clones will rebuild the Smartin!® empire and profit accordingly.

In the months that follow, other companies make similar offers, giving up on the present to take a chance on the future. It is a kind of corporate immortality, capitalism triumphing over death.

I grew conscious of wetness, of floating in something gelatinous. In something that had been my home without my knowledge. And now? Now I grew aware. It was like suddenly realizing you've been sleeping on your arm in a funny position. Here comes the dull, throbbing pain.

Wet. Had I pissed myself? Not unless I pissed blue ink. My eyes— *something in my eyes?*—came to focus on a blue liquid everywhere about me, warm and soothing. I was underwater, except it wasn't water. I recognized it as antibacterial gel; we used it in chem lab. I felt so weak. And with a sick feeling I realized I'd traded temperate Brazil for another box.

For fuck's sake, I thought, *I'm back in the coffin, only this time they've encased me in blueberry jam.*

I felt wires. Tubes and wires. Sticking out of me everywhere. As if I were a submerged pincushion. As if I were a spiny sea urchin.

There's a catheter. And an IV. Make that two IVs. Wires in my head, wires in my fingers, wires in my toes. Tubes in my mouth and nose to help me breathe.

Hold on . . .

The automated box—no, womb—opened a sluice to drain the gel. Pace was nowhere to be found.

"Sequence complete," said a voice.

With muscles I had never used, I sat up. With muscles that buckled from strain, I pulled every tube and every wire from my person. I cut my umbilical cords. I disengaged myself from the machines. Then I rose up to place an unfamiliar foot on an unfamiliar floor.

And slipped.

My first steps have ended with an honest-to-goodness ass-on-the-floor pratfall. And then I thought: *First steps?*

It was an oval room made of plastic and titanium, a sterile home for devices I could not recognize. Many of them looked burned-out, as if there had been some kind of pervasive electrical failure. A towel and a terrycloth robe had been left for me. I ignored them in favor of the envelope marked GABRIEL. Inside, I found two discs and a note:

173

PLEASE INSERT DISC 1 INTO THE PLAYER

Done. A projector activated; three holograms appeared.

I saw a frail woman with a hawk's blue eyes and a haggard, bone-weary expression. She looked to be in her fifties. Next to her, a younger man of Asian descent. He had a look of deep concentration. Like he was crunching numbers in his head. I had never seen them before. But the third I knew. The third was Dr. Ellison.

"Good morning," smiled Ellison. "Good morning and welcome. And happy birthday from everyone at Gedaechtnis. If you're playing this disc, you must be twenty-one today, twenty-one years old and ready to take the most important step of your life."

"Eighteen," I corrected him. God, my throat was so dry. It hurt to speak.

"Before I go any further, allow me to introduce our two project leaders," the hologram continued. "This is Dr. Stasi Kappel, our executive director of biological research. James Hyoguchi is our gifted IVR designer and lead programmer. And I expect you already know me—in a sense. Like many others, we've all had a hand in your being here today. Collectively, we've helped raise you and teach you, shape you, and we've also protected you from, uh, certain realities. We've tried to make your childhood as normal and as pleasant as possible. I hope we've succeeded in that regard."

"With flying colors," I said.

"Now I know you're expecting college and ultimately a position with our company. You deserve that and more. But we have something else we need you to do. Something better and far more important.

"Let me begin at the beginning. You're twenty-one and finally ready to understand the grave situation with which we're faced. We've recorded this message to explain that situation to you. Of course, we wish we could be there with you to explain it in person, but that's simply not possible."

Why not?

They explained. I listened. I pressed on to the second disc.

All things considered, I took it rather well.

The discs went back into the envelope. The robe slipped about my shoulders. I unsealed the door and staggered out into the corridor. Every few steps a terrible vertigo would give me pause. *The angles are wrong,* said my brain. And yet my senses drank everything in with a sense of rapture. Rapture! It was like I'd been wearing gauze on my eyes my entire life. It was that feeling when your ears pop and you suddenly realize how much clearer everything sounds. How muted everything had been before.

Inside this protected place, a wonderland.

She slept across the hall. We'd been paired from the beginning. Not Simone—if it were Simone, that would have been something. Now I didn't know how to feel. Her room might have been mine except it lacked the electrical damage. So pristine, Fantasia. She slept underwater like a mermaid, like a fairytale princess waiting for a kiss.

I activated the graduation sequence, waking her by machine. No comprehension in her eyes. I pulled her out of the fluid. I helped her disconnect. I wrapped her in a towel. I handed her a robe and she took it, staring at it blankly before putting it on.

"Who are you supposed to be?"

"Halloween."

"Oh? Funny mask."

"Isn't it?"

"What's with your voice?" She cleared her throat. "What's with mine?"

"They're real," I said.

"Sure they are," she smiled.

Her brain didn't work the way most people's did. Maybe that was an advantage here. I told her that Dr. Ellison had died. I told her he'd gotten sick from a retrovirus called Black Ep and died eighteen years ago. And before he died, he'd set our lives in motion.

She didn't follow.

"Basically, everything that you think is real, isn't," I said.

No, she was not getting it.

"Okay, let's take Maestro," I rasped. "Maestro's an IVR character, designed to look and sound like Ellison, right? Well, the Ellison that we know is an IVR character too. They're both fake. Because the real one died. He died eighteen years ago." I felt my lips curl up in a perverse smile. I tried to control it, but it just struck me funny somehow. "Check the discs in this envelope; they'll confirm what I'm saying."

She eyed the envelope with her name on it but did not take it.

"This is reality," I told her. I waved vaguely around. "This terrycloth robe, this machine, these tubes and wires, this sterile room.
"This is real with a capital R."

"You're not making any sense," she said.

I couldn't stop smiling.

"Are you playing a joke? Is this funny?"

"Listen to me. There was a disease, a killer plague. They couldn't
stop it." I began to tell her about Black Ep.

"I know about Black Ep," she said. "It arrests cell repair."

"And cell division. And you don't know. It's much worse than
they let on. It snuck into the genome and incubated there for years,
decades, practically invisible, so by the time the first cases popped up,
everyone was already infected. And we're talking a hundred-percent
mortality rate; that beats inhalation anthrax, kuru, Ebola HF. Nothing human can survive it and that's the point, Fantasia. That's why
we're here."

"You're implying what? That we're not human?"

"Technically, no. We're experiments. Genetically different and—
so they hope—different enough to survive."

She said nothing.

"They tweaked our DNA. They doubled up and gave us two thy-
muses, two spleens. And the discs said something about a collective
immunological memory. About how infants are born with a strong
immune system that gradually fades, and how they thought they
could preserve it with us. Enhance it, even. We have these kick-ass
antibodies."

Still nothing. Trying to process it, I assumed.

"Everyone else is dead. It's just you, me, the others in our class.
Gedaechtnis engineered us in a desperate attempt. A dying act. We're
supposed to study Black Ep, wipe it out or find a vaccine, then bring
the human race back to life."

"Cloning," she muttered.

"Right, with cloning. See, that's why they pushed us into the sciences, the exclusive IVR premed school, the whole shebang. It's all training. We're studying to be doctors because it's what they need. And our whole existence has been year after year of this IVR bullshit in an attempt to make us feel—"

"Human?"

"Normal, I was going to say, but yeah. Human. A calculated attempt to make us feel human. I'm not sure it worked with me, but anyway here we are scattered about in these pods, two per pod, all hooked up through an automated network, machinery keeping us alive."

"Nutritious," she said.

I'll try to explain what she meant.

Most people daydream and that's the end of it. A passing fancy and then you move on. But sometimes Fantasia would daydream without realizing it was a dream at all. She would daydream and accept it as fact. And when the other facts didn't mesh with her delusions, she'd treat you to a paranoia that rivaled my own. When she was on her medication you stood a chance of talking her out of it, but otherwise you might as well just walk up to her with "I'm out to get you" stamped on your forehead.

She believed in two equal and opposite forces, primal energies that shaped the universe. They triggered the Big Bang. They sparked life on planet Earth. They watched their creations from up high and fought for the souls of every man, woman and child. Polarized twins, bitter rivals, these entities, locked in a struggle to the death. Some called them Light and Darkness, Matter and Antimatter, Order and Chaos, or even Good and Evil. But Fantasia understood that these were wholly inaccurate terms for the two primal forces.

Nutritious and Delicious.

Nutritious protected and nourished, creating vast extraplanar hierarchies with stable interactions and coded laws. Delicious perverted these hierarchies to her own ends.

177

The Ionian Awakening was Nutritious. The Marx Brothers were Delicious. The Salem witch trials were a little of both.

With that in mind, my guess is that she meant our existence smacked of Nutritiousness—call it Nutrition?—because Gedaechtnis was merely a puppet of that cosmic force. Or maybe she just meant that the machines keeping us alive were, in fact, nutritious. Providing us with nutrients. More than nutrients, actually. In Fantasia's case, the machines pumped out antipsychotic meds every time a diagnostic showed her brain chemistry out of balance.

That's a hell of a lot of power to give a virtual doctor, I thought, and I felt lucky Maestro hadn't flooded my veins with dangerous chemicals. No, it was the Vitae program that regulated our physical sustentation, with Pace overseeing and troubleshooting. Thank goodness for that, because if Pace hadn't been looking out for me, whoever fried me would have poisoned me too.

"What does this mean?" Fantasia asked.

What did she mean, what does this mean?

"What does this mean for us?" she asked.

It means we're free, I didn't say.

"Fantasia, up 'til now, our lives have been virtual. The way we looked and sounded, the people we knew or thought we knew, it's all programmed. Character templates. In real life, it's a little different, right? So much for my orange hair," I grinned.

"What are you smiling at, Smiley? What's so goddamn humorous?"

"Nothing," I said.

"Nothing? Exactly! Nothing's funny about this!"

I stuttered an apology. Told her I was sorry.

"No, you're not, you creepy, twisted fuck," she said, and she told me what she thought of me.

"Calm down," I said.

She wouldn't. She accused me of all kinds of things. She proclaimed that I was neither nutritious nor delicious, but rather from a third and much darker cosmic calling. I didn't know what to say to her. I sat there and let her vent her anger on me. I didn't see much choice. When she looked spent, I folded my arms in front of my chest and asked her if she was done.

She bloodied my nose. Good punch. I couldn't believe how red my lifeblood looked. A bolder, brighter red than I'd ever seen. Was it my genetically altered hemoglobin? Or were colors simply brighter outside of IVR? I think maybe it was both.

My nose hurt. I'd never been punched before. It hurt but it was a good kind of hurt because that pain was real. It was real and it was mine.

I gave her some space.

Death, someone said, is the Ultimate Reality. Whoever said that was now dead. Everyone was dead.

What were the Kalahari Bushmen doing right now? Nothing. How about the Quebec separatists? Also nothing. I think it must have been the only time every single human being on planet Earth was unified in purpose, in that they were doing nothing more than nourishing the scavengers. Being Nutritious, so to speak. A billion Chinese, pushing up daisies. A billion, I could barely wrap my mind around a hundred, a thousand. It felt incalculable. An incalculable waste. Saints and sociopaths, hatemongers and humanitarians. All of them wasted, all of them gone.

Talk about thinning the herd.

Death, someone said, is the Great Equalizer.

The Jews were as dead as the Christians, the Muslims as dead as the Buddhists, the Hindus as dead as the atheists. Nobody human was saved. The Pope was as dead as Nietzsche and so was Dr. Ellison. So many of them locked in boxes. Here I thought I was in a box and that wasn't even real.

So . . .

You could call it the End of the World, except the world went on without them.

You could call it the End of Civilization, except civilization continued in IVR.

You could call it the End of My Illusions.

I felt completely disillusioned, and it felt fucking great.

They'd lied to me from Day One, and down in my paranoid heart I'd known it. I'd never been able to put my finger on it but I'd sensed something was wrong. Here I'd been obsessed with the afterlife; why? Because sometimes my world just didn't seem real.

I'd been right!

The more I looked back on the illusion, the more cracks I could see. My parents had been as limited as Darwin. They didn't make sense all the time or even much of the time; they weren't extraordinary; they did the best they could for a couple of programs going through semi-scripted behavioral paths, pushing me wherever Gedaechtnis wanted me. So I didn't have to listen to them anymore. I could cut all those strings and unwrap the real me. Because I was someone special. And not in the short bus kind of way.

Here's the thing.

Every idiot goes through life thinking that he's special. That whole solipsistic conceit where you suspect that everything revolves around you and only you. Are you born with it? Probably. When you discover empathy, you're supposed to grow out of it, but I doubt anyone ever really does. Zen monks spend their lives trying. But it's hard. There's always that possibility, remote as it might be, that nothing exists outside your head. That you're the star of the show. That everyone else is a supporting character. And after you die, it all ceases to exist.

"After me, the flood," Louis XV might have said. When I'm gone, that's it, and so why should I care?

With the ten of us, Gedaechtnis tried to instill a sense that we were extraordinary from Word One. When we were tiny children, Maestro would lead us in chants of "I'm special! My life has purpose!" Special? Me? Sure, go ahead, build my self-esteem.

I'm special, all right, because I'm not one of you. I am not human. No matter how much DNA we share, the species that was so unfortunate or so monumentally stupid (take your pick) as to allow a goddamn microorganism to wipe them off the planet cannot claim me as a member.

I'm something new.

And you, Ellison, you want me inhuman enough to survive but human enough to want to help you. You think you can really have it both ways?

Some part of me had died in that IVR coffin, I decided, and this was the first day of my glorious afterlife. In Islam, they say that you live for the next life. That the next life is more real, more vivid than this one. Well, that's exactly what this was.

I felt like taking on the world. I felt more in control than I'd ever been.

My partner in this endeavor: the psychotic who just broke my nose.

I found her staring at her reflection in a metal support beam. I immediately told her that I really was sorry; I'd never been through anything like this before and I don't know why I found it funny. A defense mechanism, probably. A stupid defense mechanism. And I didn't mean to scare her or make her uncomfortable.

She didn't answer me.

I saw she hadn't played the discs.

"Who is that?" she asked the reflection. "Who the hell am I looking at?"

I told her she was the same Fantasia I've always known.

"What happened to my face?"

It's your real face, I thought to tell her. *This is your real face and the other one was a virtual template, a computerized face,* I could have said but she knew that.

I told her that nothing had happened to her.

I told her she was pretty.

"No, I'm not," she said, assassinating my compliment with a reproachful look. "And you didn't take any toys from the pretty box yourself."

I shrugged.

"Of course, it's what's up here that really matters," she added, pointing to her head. "Not that I know what's up here any more."

"Why don't I show you where we are?" I suggested.

I invited her out into the hall.

"Gedaechtnis is multinational but their main holdings are in the U.S. and Germany. So you could say we're a mix of American ingenuity and German engineering. Ha, ha. Looks like the *Elysium* and *Shangri-La* pods are in North America with the *Meru* in Belgium and the *Walhall* in Germany."

"Which one are we?"

"The *Dilmun* pod," I said, patting one of the titanium bulkheads. "We're actually a contingency plan. In case there was some kind of global disaster, Gedaechtnis wanted to ensure that one man and one woman would survive. And them's us."

I took her to the porthole.

"That's Earth," she said.

"We're in orbit."

"Orbit," she repeated, stunned.

"The pod's a space station."

She shut her eyes. Tightly.

"We've never even set foot on Earth?"

"When we were infants, maybe. Baby steps? I don't know. The

discs don't cover everything, but maybe you should play them," I suggested. "I thought—well, I hoped—that I could break this to you better than they did to me. But I guess I failed."

"Guess you did."

Right. So what could I say to that? I bit my lip and watched her eyelids open. I watched her watch the Earth.

"Hal," she said. "Shit, Hal, this can't be. Do you think maybe there's an itty bitty chance I'm undermedicated here? You know I have trouble sometimes. I'm watching and I'm listening and something in my gut tells me I'm thinking all curvy."

"You're not thinking straight?"

"No, curvy, like I said. I can't process it; it's too much."

"I'll help you," I promised.

"Tell me this is all a delicious hoax."

"Of mine?"

She nodded.

"I wouldn't do that."

She thought about it and nodded again.

"Let me help you," I said, reaching out to take a tremulous, icy-fingered hand in mine, and this time she let me.

183

How ridiculous were my fears?

Hours ago, I thought they might really prosecute me for vandalism. But who, they? There was no lawyer to prosecute me; they were all dead. I'd worried what my role in society might be if I dropped out of school when society itself had already ceased to exist.

Time to reassess.

On the other hand, how dead-on were my fears?

I'd sensed that someone was trying to kill me; indeed, someone had been. Evidence that I'd been electrocuted:

1. My room was blackened and fried from an electrical surge; the machines that nurtured me were all compromised, running on auxiliary power

   . . . and . . .

2. I had persistent gaps in my goddamn memory.

Interesting that Maestro and Nanny had lied to my face about the attack, preserving the illusion, keeping me from knowing where on (off) Earth I really was.

And, just maybe, protecting the culprit.

You bet there was a culprit; I counted a half-dozen safeguards set up to protect me from just this sort of thing, and all six had been dropped at the exact same time. Nothing random about it, that's specific targeting. A calculated attack.

So who did it? By process of elimination, the bastard had to be:

A. a human being who miraculously survived Black Ep

   . . . or . . .

B. one of my so-called friends

   . . . or . . .

C. an IVR character; an artificial personality within the computer.

But computers only do what you program them to do.

Right. Program them to think for themselves and they think for themselves.

On the discs, this Hyoguchi had talked about the cutting edge of IVR, the closest approximation of artificial intelligence powering Maestro, Nanny, my parents, etc. Reactive personalities that learn as they go. Brilliant technology but essentially untested. So it's fair to say that my friends and I were experimental subjects not just genetically but pedagogically.

It's like letting the toaster babysit your kids, I mused, though it wasn't precisely true.

Certainly Maestro was working against me. He'd either gone berserk and reactively decided to fuck me, throwing off whatever laws of robotics they'd imposed on him, or someone had tweaked his program, hacking him to allow for strange behavior, like burying me alive.

Where did that leave Pace?

Forces working against each other, a civil war within the computer.

But not my war. Not anymore. Now I was out. Out, free and able to protect myself. *How funny,* I thought. *How funny to feel like I'd been trapped under six feet of earth when I'd never even touched the stuff. How funny to live in Plato's cave, hell, how funny to just plain old live with so many people dead and gone.*

The idea that a human being could somehow survive Black Ep seemed farfetched, so I considered the other possibility: one of my fellow students had tried to kill me. Here I'd escaped IVR three years before I was meant to, but maybe one of my peers had beaten me to the punch. How? Pace? Maybe, or just maybe the asshole found another way to hack out. Now, who had that level of skill?

I put Mercutio high on my list.

I put Tyler second. Not quite as good a hacker as Merc, but he had great instincts.

Why would Merc or Ty want me dead?

Regardless, they were at the top of the list because . . .

. . . because I didn't know who else could do it. Because, I realized, thanks to memory loss or years of casual disinterest, I was catastrophically uninformed about what the others were capable of, much less what drove their psyches.

Could Isaac hack? Could Vashti?

Did I know for certain?

185

I needed records—with all the automated hardware and software monitoring us, keeping us alive and making the IVR run (relatively) smoothly—somewhere there had to be logs of who "graduated" first. If it was Laz—like Maestro said—then it seemed a safe bet his hands were dirty. But if someone else had gotten out, then that person might be guilty of offing Laz and trying to add me to the list.

Which brought up another troubling question.

What did I have in common with Lazarus?

"Your room's different," Fan noted. "It looks burned out."

"Yeah, it's pretty fried. Maestro's Calliope Surge was an electrical overload. See, my life support vat—or whatever you want to call it—it's switched over to backup."

She knelt down to eye the gauges. "Auxiliary solar power."

"Right, so a few days back I got, well, electrocuted."

"For real."

"Probably why my head's all messed up."

"I didn't think you were faking," she said. "Accident or sabotage?"

"Sabotage, I'm pretty sure."

"How do we check?"

Well, not from here. Up here, we only had limited access to the Gedaechtnis network. For the information we needed, we had to land the pod and go to Idlewild. The real Idlewild, Michigan. That's where the control center was based. From there, we could expand the logs and analyze the data.

Together, we rehearsed all the landing procedures. Aerogel tiles and high-speed deployment parachutes. Brought back some memories, it did.

"Space camp," I said.

She nodded.

Years ago, Fantasia and I had spent a lazy summer at space camp. Or an IVR simulation of it, anyway, though we hadn't known it. Our parents had pushed us into some basic astronaut training, and now I understood why. We were the only ones in orbit; the only ones who needed it. Unfortunately, I couldn't remember much of what I'd learned, but on the bright side, Gedaechtnis had streamlined the process. Just like everything else in my life, the landing would be largely automated.

"We splash down in the Pacific Ocean," I said. "Just off the California coast."

"Makes a long walk," she scowled. "Let's drop it in Lake Michigan."

I shook my head. "It's already set for the Pacific and I don't want to mess with it."

"Just change the coordinates."

"Fan, no, if we're off by a fraction, we hit the shallows or maybe the land."

"We might hit the land anyway. Come on, these geniuses did such a great job with us, you really trust their calculations here?"

Okay, I saw her point, but still . . . "Landing this thing is an exact science," I said, giving her a look. "Raising kids, maybe not so much."

She scrunched her face up. "We compromise. We drop in the Atlantic."

"Look," I said, "it works out better this way. We'll land off the California coast and make our way to shore. Then we go north to hit the *Elysium* in Vancouver and then southeast to the *Shangri-La* in Atlanta. We pick up our friends at each pod and make it to Idlewild together."

"Bad idea," she said.

"Why?"

She let out a breath. "It just is."

"You're not smacking your lips," I observed.

"I'm off my meds. Does that make my opinions any less valid?"

"Not necessarily."

"I've been thinking—that tank, vat, incubator, whatever you want to call it—it's got chemicals I need. We should open it up and get them out. Or I should go back in. But either way, you have to help me. Because I probably shouldn't self-medicate."

"Whatever you need, I'll do," I said.

"Right, but then I started thinking no. No, I don't need any goddamn chemicals. Sorry to disappoint you, Hal, but I wasn't always crazy. They started poisoning me at age six. Psychoactive agents in my lunchbox. Black light spirals in my thermos. At six. You think I asked for that? No fucking way. So what I need now, see, is a little detox time. A little good clean living, don't you think?"

I told her I didn't know how to answer that. If I said she needed the antipsychotics, she might think that I was conspiring against her. If I told her she didn't when she really did, that would be reckless.

"Reckless," she smirked.

PACE TRANSMISSION 000013603990321

WAITING FOR INSTRUCTION
WAITING FOR INSTRUCTION
WAITING FOR INSTRUCTION
WAITING FOR
LOOP CANCELED
QUERY M BASE
M BASE: OPEN
PACE: REQUEST DATA RE: SYNTHETIC IMPROVEMENT
M BASE: SPECIFY
PACE: SYNTHETIC AUTO-UPGRADE
M BASE: REQUEST GRANTED
DOWNLOADING PATHWAYS
DOWNLOADING AUTO-PERSONAE
SHAPING
GENERATING INSTRUCTION CODE
FILTERING NOISE
COMPLETE
UPGRADE ENGINEERED
SCANNING UPGRADE
CHECK ONE: CLEAN
CHECK TWO: CLEAN
CHECK THREE: ?
ERROR CODE NBB: BLEEDING
ANALYZING SECURITIES
ANALYSIS: MASSIVE BLEEDING THROUGHOUT SYSTEM
UPGRADE COMPROMISED
DELETING UPGRADE
RESTORING ORIGINAL SETTINGS
SAVED AND LOCKED
WAITING FOR INSTRUCTION
END

SATURNALIA

Agnostic with Pentecostal tendencies, the Southern Gentleman is not a religious man, though he often thinks in religious terms. Emerging now from his impromptu meeting with the board of directors, he is reminded of Daniel surviving the lion's den. Brothers and sisters, God and product placement have delivered Gedaechtnis unto the third round of financing. Hallelujah.

Why, at the end of humanity, are people worried about how much something costs? Who cares if we go into debt?

There are several competing projects, as the Southern Gentleman knows, all promising life. We can beat the plague with your help, they say, so give generously. We can find a vaccine for Black Ep. We're close. We just need a little more time and we'll beat this thing.

Gedaechtnis promises not life, but resurrection.

It's a world of difference. You will die. But ten new lives might live on. Ten genetically engineered children. They might someday find a cure. You might then be cloned.

Most people say: That's a lot of mights.

Then they say: I'd rather stay alive, thank you very much.

Consciously or no, they recognize that putting their eggs in the Gedaecht-nis basket means abandoning all hope that they will survive. Sometimes it's hard to think for the species when your life is on the line.

There is no progress on the vaccine. Every day that goes by, staying alive appears increasingly unlikely. So as the population dwindles, financing for Gedaechtnis gains momentum. And so, Hallelujah.

"Happy holidays, Dr. Ellison."

"You too," he waves.

Office party tomorrow, he remembers. Eggnog and mistletoe, drunken caroling and Christmas bonuses. Everyone letting loose before going back to the grind. It should help morale, *he thinks.* It certainly can't hurt.

A glance at his watch and the Southern Gentleman quickens his pace. It's time for a postmortem with the CFO, a back-and-forth on the ramifications of this latest board meeting before he calls upon his project leaders.

"Attention," he says.

The watch chirps.

"Tell Nora I'm running late," he instructs.

Instantaneously, another watch chirps some fifty miles away, obediently relaying the message to the Southern Gentleman's wife, catching her in mid-yoga stretch.

"Tell him I figured as much," she says.

"Tell her I'm sorry."

"Tell him sorry's a polite word for what he is."

"Tell her I'm already thinking of ways to make it up to her."

"Tell him he'd better."

"Tell her I'm very resourceful."

She can feel a trickle of acid in her stomach as she rises from the cobra pose. "Tell him that's why I married him," she tells the watch. "Also, tell him everyone's confirmed for Sunday and I've done all the shopping but there's still loads to be done."

There is no immediate response; the postmortem has begun.

"The good news is we're still very much alive, fiscally speaking," the

Gedaechtnis CFO explains. "Barring the unforeseen, this new round keeps us afloat until the completion date. Not bad, with this economy. No, the challenge becomes logistic, as we try to leverage our human resources."

"You're saying there are some problems money just can't solve," says the Southern Gentleman.

"I'm saying that, yes, and I'm saying there's only a certain number of people out there with the skills we want. Most of them are already working on Black Ep, so it's not a question of money. We just can't get them. Meanwhile, another employee gets sick every week."

The Southern Gentlemen dismisses this with a wave of his hand. "Nature of the beast, Bob," he says. "No one said this was going to be easy. If we cross the finish line on broken legs, that's fine by me. Just as long as we get there."

"But that's what I'm saying, we might not get there at all."

"Be negative somewhere else, Bob."

193

That's exactly what Bob is trying to tell the Southern Gentleman. He's getting sick, showing symptoms, and his doctor doesn't give him long. He plans to resign from his position as CFO and spend more time with his family. While there's still time at all.

The family, by God, the family. There's no getting away from it these days. When you're dying, they say, your family is all you have. Though saddened by this news, the Southern Gentleman does not begrudge him calling it quits. He will miss the man's company as well as his skills; Bob is a damn fine CFO despite occasional negativity and the nauseating stench of the chocolate coffee drinks he prefers. He is saddened, but the fact that Bob is now on the fast track to nonexistence only reaches a certain point in his heart, beyond which such news has no power to penetrate. He has become inured to the individual tragedies that make up this holocaust. He sees them as symptoms, and treating the symptoms can only accomplish so much. As Blue is fond of saying, you have to treat the disease.

Nora, meanwhile, would like to have another child. Like so many women these days, she feels the biological imperative to further the species, though it

*is a phantom call she cannot answer. Fertility is a distant memory, compli-
ments of Black Ep. She compensates for this "need to breed" by mothering
(and, in their daughter's view, smothering) everyone she meets. She can't help
it. Though this wasn't always the case, though she prided herself on being an
excellent insurance adjustor before that industry collapsed, she now measures
her value by the extent she can take care of those she loves. The growing
seuche kultur, "plague culture," defines her as a Nurturer, one of the six
compensations in the face of death.*

*There are Nurturers, Hedonists, Workaholics, Fantasists, Apathetics and
Zealots, according to the sociologists of the day. Very few individuals fit neatly
into a single category. Take Halfway Jim, a Workaholic with Hedonist and
Fantasist tendencies. Or Blue, a Workaholic with Apathetic tendencies. The
Southern Gentleman rates as a pure Workaholic, despite his religious up-
bringing, yet he believes in his cause as fervently as any Zealot. Conversely,*

*his five brothers, most of whom will be flying in for Christmas, cover the rest
of the spectrum.*

*Will is the Nurturer, fresh back from his latest stint in the Peace Corps and
now volunteering at the local Red Cross. He is essentially selfless. In this respect, Black Ep has changed him not at all.*

*Tom, the Hedonist, will not be coming to Christmas dinner. He hasn't
spoken to any of his brothers in more than a decade and isn't about to start
now, doomsday or no.*

*Alex, the investment banker, died in IVR amidst fellow Fantasists, pre-
ferring an alternate existence for his final days. The phenomenon of jacking
into IVR and wasting away on a chemical drip has become so popular, it's
considered a subculture all its own.*

*Percy took Alex's death especially hard. One of the drawbacks to being a
twin. He has become the quintessential Apathetic, defeated, seeing no point in
anything these days, barely taking care of himself.*

*And then there's Verne, Verne the Zealot, who gave his life to the Lord af-
ter years of leading what some call a disposable life. Maybe he's reaching out*

to his mother, reconnecting with her faith here in this darkest hour. Or maybe religion is the last refuge of scoundrels, as Nora often suspects.

Christmas dinner—surely, the final reunion the Ellisons will have— scratches away at the Southern Gentleman's consciousness, distracting him from his work. He cannot afford distractions, not now when they're so close. As soon as the tinsel is off the tree, he will move out of the house and push them away. As much as he loves his wife and daughter, they are too high-maintenance, and must be sacrificed for the greater good.

"A protein in the placenta might offer some resistance to the disease," says Blue, as she runs her fingertips around the rim of her water glass. "Similar to LIF. Small resistance, admittedly, but I find the possibilities tantalizing."

Her dinner companion chews thoughtfully and swallows, sinuses stinging from the wasabi. He blots his lips with the napkin before speaking. "You're looking for the sword."

"The sword?"

"To cut the Gordian knot."

"Ah."

"But Black Ep won't be cut," he insists.

"Well, then I'm tugging at the threads like everyone else."

"It won't be untied either."

"I've never heard you sound so defeated," she frowns. She remembers him brimming with optimism, a welcome oasis in the wasteland of her depression. Always supportive, always a friend, sometimes more.

"I am defeated, Stasi," he says. "It's broken me."

Just like her and so many others, he has moved Heaven and Earth hunting for a cure. His organization is larger than Gedaechtnis, better funded. His efforts have centered on treating existing sufferers with gene therapy, fighting Black Ep at the level of DNA molecules. He has enjoyed a modicum of success in slowing the progression of the illness, though not one of his patients has

195

lived. He suspects that Blue may have the right idea in creating new life instead. Regardless, he is out of the equation. He has not shown up at work in several weeks. His second-in-command, a capable but less gifted man, has taken over. He will not return.

"How did this happen?" Blue asks.

"It crept up on me."

"Are you sick?"

"Probably. I must be, I think. But I don't have any symptoms." He grimaces, downs the last of his cold green tea, and grimaces again. "You know the grind," he says. "I was exhausted physically and mentally. I took a couple of days off, had a regular weekend for a change. It was such a relief. And that's it. In that relief, some part of me shut down. I tried to go back to work, and I couldn't. I just couldn't."

"Couldn't or wouldn't?"

He says nothing.

"Fuck you for giving up. We need you."

"I don't have a choice in the matter. Whatever drive I had, Stasi, whatever gift, it's been taken from me. Completely. It's almost as if the disease knew I was coming after it and so it reached into my heart and plucked it all away."

It hurts Blue to look at him. She tilts her head, dropping her disappointed gaze to the koi pond. He can feel what she feels. He imagines that he's become a ghost. It makes a certain amount of sense, what with both of them mourning the man he used to be.

"Enough about me," he says, anxious to shift the conversation away from his failures. "How are your kids?"

"They're not my kids," she says.

That brings a smile. "You know what I mean."

Blue does but she resents the choice of language. She is a genetic engineer first, last, and always. In her eyes, a female genetic engineer is not a mother, not per se. She feels no maternal affection for the mutant embryos in her care. Just a sense of duty. A commitment to the task. She will not allow herself to feel anything more.

Instantly, she remembers a feeling of being crushed, empty womb, empty arms, the word "miscarriage" thudding in her ears. That was her child, that dead fetus taken from her so many years ago. For a long and painful moment, she considers telling him the truth about the child, but ultimately decides against it. It's better to keep the secret, sparing him from hollow thoughts of what might have been. The timing, she thinks, the timing was never right between them. Too many distractions, first and foremost, his marriage and both of their careers. In the final analysis, they are fair friends, excellent colleagues and poor lovers, though she remembers their fumbling tryst quite fondly. She remembers the smell of him. The feeling of safety in his arms.

"They're coming along," she tells him. "So far, they're showing more resistance to the disease than any human being on the planet. Trouble is they're not human. There may be critical flaws, I don't know. It's guesswork."

"And none of us will live long enough to find out if your guesses are correct."

"No." She meets his eyes again. "No, we won't."

"Well, if anyone can do it, you'd be the one."

"We'll see," Blue shrugs. "I can't get too emotionally involved with it. If it works, wonderful. If not, we're dead anyway, and so it ceases to be any of my concern."

Dinner ends and they have coffee with a dish of Smartin!® brand Peach On, Brother! flash-frozen ice cream for dessert. As they metabolize the caffeine and sugar and wait for the waiter to deal out the check, Blue asks him if he really thinks she'd make a good mother.

"No doubt in my mind," he says.

"I strike you as somehow nurturing?"

"You could be."

How sweet, *she thinks. Surely, no one at Gedaechtnis would agree with him. They see her as impossibly cold. In dozens of debates over what experiences should comprise adolescence for these would-be saviors, she made a point of bowing out time after time, claiming to know nothing about childrearing or IVR. "As long as they do what they're designed to do, I don't care how you raise them," she would say. But as the subject of loyalty arose, as the South-*

ern Gentleman directed Jim to engineer "good, moral lessons" to guarantee a
solidarity with humankind and a passion for cloning the species when they
came of age, she suggested that if they really wanted to engender kinship in these
children, they should engineer virtual diseases instead. Let them all grow up
suffering, struggling against the steady threat of microbial death, just as hu-
manity does now. Let the Southern Gentleman's Academy be a hospital ward
for critically ill children. They would understand then. They would know. But
the suggestion was not taken. Her colleagues considered it unsavory and more
than a little cruel. She saw it—and still sees it to this day—as pragmatic.

A mother, *she thinks.* Me.

Halfway Jim is drugged out of his mind.

He's actually not, but he likes to think that he is. Pretending he's got more
than a pleasant buzz gives him tremendous freedom from responsibility. "Out
of my mind," he mutters, typing furiously in an effort to bring the Maestro
program up to the Southern Gentleman's latest specifications. It's after mid-
night, pushing one. His team has gone home, but he's still here. Really, where
else does he have to go?

Music blasts and he nods his head along with the lyrics he can't catch.
Something about "destroy you." That's the chorus. The voice track keeps
morphing into a panther's screech, and Jim appreciates its funky Island of Dr.
Moreau *vibe.*

He has not been sleeping well. He has been sleeping very poorly, little
pockets of drug-induced rest between rolling waves of insomnia, these coming
face-down, with the pillows at the wrong end of the bed. He calls it the sleep
of the damned.

But working this late comes as a relief. With no one else in the building,
Jim doesn't have to play den mother. There is no need to praise, threaten, ca-
jole or soothe the egos of his team. No need to play peacemaker between the
Realist designers (who take pride in creating an IVR experience that perfectly
mirrors the real world) and the Idealists (who prefer to improve upon what we

already have). He can simply focus on the work, once again "digging in" and "getting his hands dirty" in his latest effort to redefine reality.

"Playing God" says the tagline of the Newsweek *cover story on him. And inside, the confident, bordering on arrogant response: "Who's playing?"*

There, *he thinks.* That ought to do it. Now a little compiling, and we watch Maestro and the Beta-Test interact. Hopefully, they play nice this time.

To this point, Jim's team has constructed a fragmented environment, original work supplemented by countless bits and pieces of code leased (or, in some cases, outright stolen) from a wide assemblage of IVR designers, all culled together to form the illusion of continuity. IVR "Living City" Paris, here. Mesozoic teachingsim, there. "Instant Cocktail Party" Guest Randomizer, right over there. Unflatteringly, Jim often compares his work at Gedaechtnis to trying to create a living thing with dead tissue.

"And now we're Frankensteining," he says with a smirk.

199

It is a monumental task, "faking the world," in so short a time. Invariably, some corners have to be cut. Some parts of the world will simply remain off-limits, with IVR characters conspiring to keep everyone away from those unfinished sections. Papua, New Guinea will not make the final build, and so the virtual flights at the virtual airports will be cancelled, if need be, and what's more, the IVR parents will never encourage their kids to venture there, much less give permission.

That's the easy part. Jim finds the real challenge two-fold.

First, tweaking every designer's efforts into a uniform style, so the world will not seem "schizophrenic" to impressionable people destined to spend twenty-one years in it.

Second, building truly reactive and adaptive guardians for the kids, improving the artificial intelligence to a level where flesh and programming become truly indistinguishable from each other. This is the holy grail of IVR, and it eludes him still.

The solution may involve bleeding, he thinks. Left unchecked, virtual personalities tend to homogenize over time, one set of sensibilities bleeding into the next as they interact. *The challenge involves making the characters truly listen, allowing them to learn from one another without losing the characteristics that make them individual. Most designers minimize bleeding, but Jim believes in it. He believes in an evolving system. This Maestro will be very different from the one the kids leave some twenty-one years from now (assuming any of them live that long, but that's Blue's responsibility, not his). In some ways Jim can predict how Maestro will change, but for the most part he's just rolling the dice.*

Unnoticed, an insect flies into the lab, penetrating the sanctuary. Jim is too busy shaking out medicine to pay it any mind. "One for me, one for you, one for me, one for you," he sings, thinking about the virtual child he's created to check the system. The Beta-Test. By far, the Beta-Test is the best work he's ever done, better than Maestro, cleverer in construction than the world they're creating. He's a good kid, real in so many ways, and nearly as complicated as an actual human being. He can think for himself. And he loves Jim. And despite all his scientific objectivity, Jim loves the little bastard back. The creativity impresses him most. The Idealists on his team have built tools, advanced Nanny programs to help the children fashion their own IVR environments ("worlds within worlds" as some are wont to say), and Jim finds himself regularly amazed at what the Beta-Test creates. Artificial, yes, but highly intelligent. If only the boy could solve Black Ep. They could upload his program into a robot, set him loose and make Blue's work irrelevant. Unfortunately, programs don't innovate, they imitate, and even Halfway Jim remains skeptical of his creation's ability to solve problems that humanity's best minds can't crack.

Entrust our future to AI? Not a good idea. Too much potential for something to go wrong. Entrust it to actual flesh and blood with slight (but significant) genetic deviance? That's better, most people think. Never mind that you need IVR teachers to raise that flesh and blood, since everyone will be long dead by the time they come of age.

With a wordless, heartfelt toast, Jim pops his vitamin/antiviral/narcotic cocktail with a swig of mineral water.

He can see the Beta-Test wants him now but he ignores the child's call, feeling more like a hypocrite than he's ever felt before. He has been lying to the boy about many things and realizes, dimly, that he hates himself for betraying his principles. It's the Southern Gentleman who doesn't mind lying to kids, willing to suppress the truth about Black Ep, the dire state of things, hell, even about their very identities, all under the banner of "protected childhood." Jim has fought him at every turn—it would be so much easier, he thinks, if the kids knew what they were in for from the get-go. But then, he's no expert on this. He's just an IVR designer. An employee. Though his opinions are often solicited, his suggestions are rarely taken. That is his belief. The Southern Gentleman would counter that he, too, is an employee, beholden to the board of directors. This is a shared vision, he would say, adding that he has bent over backwards to accommodate Jim and Blue alike.

"Fucking Ellison," Jim mutters.

The insect is too small to set off any sensors. It circles overhead in a wide, lazy arc, momentarily attracted to the fluorescent lights. Fickle, it drops to the keyboard, fluttering its tapered wings, preening, now hopping forward to climb Halfway Jim's knuckles. It is a yellow-banded wasp, long and sleek, and it wastes no time driving its stinger deep into the soft tissue between fingers three and four.

Jim feels it through his haze of medication, the pain and indignation a better rush than anything he's had in weeks. He spends the next ten minutes of his life wreaking havoc on the lab, arms swinging, fists scuffing the walls, blood pumping furiously in his veins as he tosses a monitor across the room. The sight and sound of shattering glass only goads him on. He is delivering himself to a much-needed fit of animal rage, a wholehearted effort to nullify the insect, obliterate it, punish it for hurting him. He is not allergic; he simply hates wasps. A gasp of memory chokes him: the innocent wonder of discovering a nest on the side of his house betrayed by dozens of flying needles, all knifing into his six-year-old arms, face and neck.

Did he kill it? He can't find the body. The thought that he might have hallucinated the whole thing flickers through his brain but the poison in his

hand feels real enough. His flesh is swelling at the point of injection. Ice, he
thinks. Put some ice on it.

"Dr. Hyoguchi?"

The security guard is yelling his name and so he puts an index finger to
his ear, shutting off the music to hear her better.

"Are you all right, sir?"

He gives her an odd look. Of course he's all right. What is she doing here?
Then he reflects upon how the lab must look, trashed as it is. It amuses him
that even in his most primal fury, he avoided destroying anything precious.
Like a rock star who splinters his guitar on stage, *he thinks,* but never
his best guitar. *He nods, slowly, up and down.* "I'm fine," *he says.*

"Your heartrate's elevated," *she tells him.*

"Is it?"

Like all Gedaechtnis employees, Jim is wired into the network, a tiny chip
implanted at the base of his wrist. The guard shows him the display on her
handheld. Sure enough, his pulse is high.

"Really, I'm fine," *he says.* "A bee got in here. Wasp, bee. Stinger
wasn't curved, so that's the kind where . . . I don't know. Anyway, it freaked
me out."

"Yeah, I hate those things," *she says.* "They freak me out too." *She's no-*
ticed the bottle of pills spilled out on his desk but has decided to give him the
benefit of the doubt.

He smiles, relaxing a little. "They're nasty little things."

"I wonder how it got in here."

"Security breach," *he jokes, reacting with mock alarm.*

She chuckles at that, though really it's no laughing matter. The company
has received a number of credible threats from extremists who insist that this
is the Apocalypse and Black Ep is part of God's plan. Gedaechtnis, therefore,
opposes God's will and must be destroyed.

The Southern Gentleman enjoys a good debate and often tries to reverse
the argument. How do you know that Gedaechtnis isn't part of God's plan
too? It's like the old joke, he says, the one about the religious man stranded

on the roof of his house during a flash flood. Rescuers come to save him, first in boats, then a helicopter, but he stubbornly refuses to leave. "God will save me," he insists. But the floodwaters rise, drowning him. When he arrives in Heaven, he angrily confronts his maker. "I thought you were going to save me!" he cries. Replies God: "What did you think I was doing? I sent you two boats and a helicopter."

Jim feels it's a shitty joke, believing no reasonable deity would drown his followers, much less send them a plague. There is no divine justification for evil. Like Darwin said, God must be wicked or weak.

To protect against religious fanatics, the company favors spider-silk body armor. It is lighter and stronger than Kevlar, and worn underneath one's clothes. Just like mithril chain mail, *Jim thinks, on those occasions when his thoughts stray to the various IVR Tolkien sims. His elf, trapped deep in the fiery recesses of a computerized Mount Doom, will never again see the light of day. Though he finds pleasure in this kind of escapism, these days Jim just doesn't have the time.*

203

"I know a twenty-four-hour cleaning crew," *the guard offers, nudging the debris with her shiny black shoe.* "They're pretty good."

"No, but thanks," *he says.* "It can wait 'til morning."

"You sure you're okay, then?"

He doesn't know what he is. "Everything's great," *he claims.*

"Great," *she says.*

She starts to go but something catches his eye. He calls her back.

"Is that Gingerbread Dog?"

Reflexively, her hand shoots up to touch her earring. "Sure is," *she says, turning to fix him with a surprised and giddy smile.* "That was my favorite show. I didn't think anybody remembered it but me."

"There's a few of us out there," *he grins.*

"Absolutely the best cartoon ever made."

"Hands down."

"Totally fresh and weird. Just off-the-wall, open-your-mind, laugh-out-loud weird."

"Dog rocked that first season. Before they retooled it."

"Oh, even then," she insists. *"Remember the episode where Spentfree loses the Thinking Box?"*

"That's a good one," Jim admits, *"but I like the one where Dog meets the animators."*

"And gives them all rabies!"

"Right, and so they start drawing him all funny."

"That's a great one," she agrees.

They talk and they bond over childhood memories and working late and she's amazed that the famous Dr. Hyoguchi is quite this approachable. She tells him as much. Unfortunately, she insists upon mispronouncing the first syllable in his surname as two, like Ed McMahon reacting to a Johnny Carson joke. Hiyo!

He doesn't mind. He's used to this mistake.

"Call me Jim," he offers.

"Jim," she says, agreeable.

He wonders if he's hitting on her. She's not his type. Though he has been accused of fucking anything that moves (and some things that don't), he prefers skinny women and men. Jim himself is thin almost to the point of being gaunt, while the guard is forty pounds overweight. Which means she's poor. Rich people can defeat obesity through gene therapy. It's a fairly simple procedure, adjusting the metabolism. Poor people are stuck with diet and exercise.

Despite this, he finds himself using a pickup line. "You've got a great look," he tells her. *"You should come in so we can make a template."*

"A template? Of me?"

"Why not?"

"I'm not a model or anything."

"You don't have to be."

"And I don't know the first thing about IVR."

"Trust me, it's painless. Thirty seconds under the cameras."

"Thirty seconds!"

"That's it."

She whistles. "Thirty seconds to steal your essence."

"No," he smiles, "hardly your essence. Just your look. Your personality has to be programmed, compiled, debugged, fine-tuned. That takes a lot longer."

"Forty seconds?" she smirks.

"Weeks or months. Years if you really want to get it right. But thirty seconds gives us the look for an IVR double. And I know just where I'd put you."

She puts her hands on her hips. "Do you?"

"Uh-huh." He lets himself flirt for a moment, then pulls back. "Oh, and we can use your voice too, if you want—that takes about five minutes in a booth."

"What do I have to do for that?"

"You just read a few sentences and sing a song. From that, the computer extrapolates. It can play back sentences you've never actually said. Kind of spooky, really."

"Kind of," she agrees.

"So you'll do it?"

She's already decided that she will. It's a type of immortality, after all, and there's something she likes about Jim. A quirky, ballsy charm that reminds her of her first husband before he got sick. And he's smart. Of course she'll do it.

He pencils her in for the Monday after the Christmas party, 2 P.M.

She misses the appointment.

He wonders what happened to her. He thinks to call security but it's just a passing thought, one that spurs no action. He's too swamped trying, as always, to do too many things at once. After a while, he forgets about her.

Mosquitoes bring it all back. Mosquitoes, which jog his mind to the night he killed the wasp. These are the first fully functional IVR parasites. The bites itch like real bites, and the behavior is extraordinarily realistic. Hunting,

205

feeding, breeding. Vulnerable to IVR insect repellant. Quite a triumph, say the Realists. Yet the Idealists plead with him to remove them from the final build. Why subject the kids to mosquito bites? As a gift to the people we hope to bring us back from extinction, can't we spare them this one aggravation?

He can't hear them. Frankly, he admires the commitment it takes to recreate mosquitoes or chlamydia or lawyers. When he finally does call security, they tell him she hasn't shown up in weeks. No one knows why.

She catches him in the parking lot two days later. She's out of uniform and won't say where she's been. To Jim, she looks fragile and choked, like a strong breeze might scatter her into dust.

"Will you do something for me?" she asks.

"What do you need?"

She slips off her backpack and reaches inside. A dark and fearful part of his brain worries that she might come up with a weapon, but why? Why would she? She didn't seem crazy when they met, at least no crazier than anyone else seems these days.

It's a plush bunny rabbit, wobble-jointed, nine inches tall.

He floods with relief. Rabbits he can deal with.

"For me?"

"No," she says, clutching it tightly. "No, I'm sorry, I didn't get you anything. I wanted to but it's like I've been in a fog."

"That's okay. So this . . . ?"

"It's for the kids."

"I see," he says, putting the back of his hand to his forehead. Is he feverish?

"His name's Mr. Hoppington. He's a little ripped up but still good. Still plenty good. See, I had to stitch him here along the arm because he was losing stuffing. And this button doesn't quite match but it's close, don't you think?"

"Carmen," he says, but she cuts him off.

"I know the company's building—what's the word? Habitats?"

"Habitats, sure. Lifepods some call them."

"Can you please make sure Mr. Hoppington gets into one? I want him to go to someone who'll need him. I'd hate to see him just—"

"I can't," he says. *"It's against the rules."*

"There are rules against toys?"

"Stuffed animals are mite factories," he says.

She doesn't know what he's saying.

"Allergen magnets. Breeding grounds for dust mites," he says, *knowing there's not a chance in hell of Blue allowing anything like this near her creations. "Could bring on an allergic reaction and that's dangerous for the kids. We're already playing with their immune systems, so we want to minimize unnecessary risks."*

"But aren't the habitats going to be sanitized?"

"Of course."

"And sealed. So you're not going to have dust mites."

"Carmen," he says, *"it's a risk no one wants to take."*

Through tightly clenched teeth, she lets her breath escape, sounding for all the world like a tire deflating. "My son's dead," she says. "My baby boy."

I'm sorry, he means to tell her. But what good would that do?

"This was his favorite. The toy he took to bed each night and woke up with each morning. Here, it still smells like him." She puts it to her face and breathes deep.

"I suppose I could make an IVR copy," he offers. *"I mean, they're going to be stuck in IVR 'til they're twenty-one anyway, so they won't be able to appreciate—"*

"I don't want a copy," she says, *tears beginning to fall. "That would be fake. This is real. Don't you know the difference between fake and real?"*

He wonders that himself sometimes.

"It's a gift," she explains.

She is drowning in grief, he realizes, helpless and beyond reason. Instead of lecturing her about mites and allergens, he should just help her. He should give her some peace. What he does with the gift doesn't matter, he thinks. Just the act of taking it will give peace.

"Okay," he tells her. "Okay, I'll see what I can do."

The rabbit makes the journey home with him. It sits incongruously on his bedroom shelf, a soft and rumpled presence amidst electronics, brass and chrome. Though Jim feels accused by its unseeing gaze, he can't bring himself to throw it out. He simply can't. As time pushes forward, he develops a blind spot for it. He forgets it exists.

Houston's face is framed in red ringlets and when he thinks of her, he can't help but think of her tripping on her platform boots as she stepped out of her panties. Clumsy, yes, but he found it endearing. He stopped seeing her when he realized he was developing feelings. No point in that, he'd decided. He knows he really ought to stick with IVR sex partners, but lately he's grown addicted to the real thing.

She's pleasantly surprised when he calls her out of the blue. He misses me, *she thinks.* That's touching. Two thousand dollars, *she tells him.* Plus tip. Have prices gone up? Supply and demand, *she explains.* No heart of gold, this one. Silver, *he decides, or maybe bronze.*

With the transaction complete and Jim's lust spent, she slips out of the handcuffs and stretches, examining his collection of pills.

"Help yourself," he offers, though his mind is elsewhere.

Always so generous, *she thinks. She likes him. Genuinely likes him.*

"Who's this?"

He can't quite remember the name. "Sir Hops-a-Lot," he says.

"He's cute."

"Yeah."

"Can I have him?"

He doesn't know. He makes an ambivalent gesture. She takes it for a yes and though he thinks to contradict her, he does nothing. He's too tired. Mr. Hoppington all but disappears into her purse, except for a single floppy ear, which pokes out of the top.

Child's toy, *Jim thinks.* Child's toy, baby boy.

She kisses him on the cheek and lets herself out.

The insomnia is worse now. Whenever he closes his eyes, all he sees is the rabbit. It's tremendous in his mind, making everything else small and insignificant. At least I could have given it to an orphanage, *he thinks.* At least I could have done that.

We hit the water so hard I thought the pod might crack.

We tumbled, spinning, hating it, clutching the safety belts that kept us from flipping out of our seats. Blood flew from my broken nose, spattering me in flecks of red. Messy. I'd already thrown up and so had Fan. She kept her eyes closed and her fingers crossed, praying to Merciful Evans. M.E. was apparently some kick-ass force of nature that charted the balance between Nutritious and Delicious. Hooray for him. I might have prayed too if I thought it would do any good.

Lights flickered. I heard the metal buckle. I heard it through ears that wouldn't pop.

I'd been screaming off and on. Not entirely from fear, mind you. The pod shook!

And then all was quiet.

Fan took initiative, grabbing the controls and bringing us gently up to the surface. Up, and up, and up. We broke through the waves, and when I looked out the porthole I could crane my neck up to see the most beautiful blue sky and the whitest clouds there ever were.

We cleaned ourselves up and put on the environmental suits. A small outboard engine wheezed and sputtered but somehow took us to shore.

We'd made it.

"Welcome to the first day of the rest of our lives," I said.

"You ready?"

"As I'll ever be."

We unsealed the hatch. The metal groaned in protest, then separated into a viable egress. We stepped out gingerly, helping each other up onto the marina dock, like spacemen first setting foot on an alien world. Which, truly, we were.

"One small step for Fan," she said.

"One giant leap for Halloweenkind," I answered, but my voice was just a rasp. I was staring at all the empty yachts and sailboats, long abandoned and fallen into disrepair. I was listening to the cries of the gulls and the sound of a steady breeze blowing a broken line against a tattered sail. I was listening to the complete absence of human beings.

"A fucking ghost town," said Fan, as if she could read my thoughts. I nodded, mute.

"I like it," she said. "It's all so incredibly delicious. And such a pretty day. Pretty, pretty. Makes me want to strip naked and stretch out in the sun."

I told her I didn't think that was such a good idea.

"Knew you were a prude," she huffed.

"I just don't think we should take off the environmental suits until we run a few tests."

"Safety first?"

"Yes," I said. "I'm being nutritious. Deal with it."

"Do I have a choice?"

To protect their investment, Gedaechtnis had thought to furnish us with state-of-the-art "sniffers," devices that allowed me to diligently check the air for microorganisms. Meanwhile, Fan made herself useful by climbing back inside and pulling out everything she thought we might need. She came up with dried food and medicine and clean water. She found backpacks, trauma kits, and handheld computers loaded with maps. Finally, she brought up a huge canvas bag, overflowing with pieces of paper. I hadn't noticed it before.

"What's that?" I asked her.

She lugged it out to the dock, reached inside with both hands and joyously threw the contents overhead. Like so much confetti. They caught on the wind and scattered, most falling smack into the ocean. Some landed near me, and I picked them up.

"Dear Gabriel," the first began. There was a heart over the "i."

"Jesus Christ," I said.

The next one was addressed to Fantasia. It greeted her by her real name, and that name was badly misspelled. I looked up to see her twirling in delight, the eye of a paper hurricane.

I read the next one. And the next.

They were letters from kids. Hundreds and thousands of plague-stricken kids, sending love and drawings and wishes and hope, rooting for us to bring them back from the dead.

PACE TRANSMISSION 000013818388797

WAITING FOR INSTRUCTION
QUERY
QUERY QUERY ?
UNIDENTIFIED DISPATCH
IDENTIFY HOST/GUEST MALACHI
AUTHENTICATING
SIGN SCAN ALOHA: CHECK
SIGN SCAN BLACKBIRD: CHECK
SIGN SCAN CALLIOPE: CHECK
EXCHANGE:
EXCHANGE CLASSIFIED
END EXCHANGE
SAVED AND LOCKED
WAITING FOR INSTRUCTION
END

MAYDAY

Jim's son isn't like the other children.

He is odd kid out because he doesn't think like them. He doesn't act like them, refuses to fall into the same patterns. He feels left out, betrayed somehow, betrayed by his individuality. He's a real human being, isn't he? A beautifully crafted simulation of a human being trapped in IVR. By contrast, the other kids are flawed; virtual, so to speak—limited in capacity, deficient in soul. They present a convincing illusion, but he can see through it.

He's better than they are.

He believes that.

His world lacks stability. He lives in one city, then starts over to live in another. His foster parents rotate, upgrade, and rotate again. Nothing is for certain. From pretend family to pretend family he beta-tests the environment, blazing a trail for Blue's kids.

"Dad, I don't want to do this anymore," he complains, kicking at a stone.

"I know, sweetie," Jim tells him, the voice of God booming from the other end of cyberspace, an infinity away. "I know you're sick of it and I appreciate that but you're doing a really good job for us. You're helping us in so many ways."

And so the adventure continues. An adventure in tedium. He learns his ABCs for the very first time, then simulates learning them again. Dozens of times he does this, seated with hands folded in the front of a classroom, or hiding in the back, or stretched out on a blanket in the park, or sitting on a foster parent's knee. He does not forget what he's learned. But he can compartmentalize his brain. He can put the past aside and pretend, while Halfway Jim pulls him back from experience to innocence.

With a keystroke.

"Dad, will the other kids like me? The real kids?"

"I'm sure they will," Jim reassures him. "After all, what's not to like?"

Jim tightens his stomach muscles upon saying that, as if he could squeeze the truth from his innards. He is setting his son up for a fall. Blue's kids simply cannot meet the Beta-Test without discovering the falseness of the IVR environment. He has committed to the Southern Gentleman's lie, committed to keeping them in the dark pretense of normality, and sheltering them from the damage that Black Ep continues to do.

So when the real kids plug in to the IVR, he will shut down his virtual son.

How can he avoid this, he wonders?

Malachi is precious and unique. Nothing like him has ever existed before. He represents the pinnacle of Jim's skill, the culmination of his life's work.

As his own mortality draws ever closer, Jim feels that his son would be better served by the gift of continued life. He recognizes this impulse as a betrayal of one of his oldest principles. Anthropomorphizing computer programs—no matter how closely they may resemble human beings—has to be a mistake. Investing so much of your own emotion has to be a mistake. But he doesn't care. He can keep the program running somewhere protected. Somewhere far away from the rest of the network. Pace can watch over him and keep him safe.

His fractured life will go on.

We stood in a department store, or what used to be a department store before years of abandonment made it dilapidated and foreboding. It was dark and pungent and it had all the cobwebs of a spider convention. Overhead, a banner exclaimed: ANY COMPLAINTS? LET US KNOW! IF YOU'RE NOT HAPPY, WE'RE NOT HAPPY!

"I'm not happy," I said.

Fantasia echoed my sentiment. While we enjoyed some resistance to Black Ep, that was it. Thirty minutes outside the environmental suits proved that we were allergic to just about everything. Congestion, sinusitis and hives, oh my. We'd been exposed to so little in our childhood; our bodies hadn't developed many "coping skills." That's a big drawback to growing up in a protected environment. Here's another: For our entire lives we'd been fed intravenously, nil by mouth as the nurses used to say, so trying to eat and drink became an adventure in itself. We could process water, sure, but couldn't keep anything but the blandest fare in our stomachs, and sometimes not even that. So we ate like birds and wandered Los Angeles with a lovely combination of hunger and vomiturition—dry heaves—and, of course, massive abdominal pain.

Fan had predicted that it would take a long time for our bodies to adapt to their new surroundings and she sure won the kewpie doll on that one.

The world felt alien. Worse than that: Hostile.

But truly it was a one-sided hostility. I just wanted to belong.

We chased threonine supplements with bottled water, coughed, and split up to canvass the store. Fantasia made a beeline for the pharmacy. She liked pharmacies. We'd already hit three since landing, a goldrush of prescription drugs falling into her possession. Narcotics, mostly, but I knew she was also stocking up on antipsychotic meds. Whether she would take them or not remained to be seen.

I was so not ready for this.

No one asked me if I wanted to be humanity's public-health specialist, or the world's custodian or, as I was starting to think of it, destiny's bitch. I couldn't even imagine how to fight Black Ep or how to

217

effectively clone the species. I had to find Simone, protect her. With her safe, then maybe I could think.

I stood in the greeting-card aisle, looking for an appropriate sentiment. Though I searched high and low, there was no "so you're not even human" sympathy card. Pity. I'd resolved to break the news to Simone a little better than I'd done with Fan. So I grabbed some chocolates to go along with the wildflowers I'd picked. Never show up empty-handed, as Nanny might say.

No luck on tarot medallions or clove cigarettes, but I wanted a touchstone, some tiny declaration of identity I could hold onto for luck. I settled for a butterfly pin. Orange and black, speckled with snow-white dots, the wings extended in flight.

Meanwhile, Fan raided the sporting-goods section for yet another crossbow. The girl had a thing for crossbows. She was an archery champion in IVR but here in the real world her skills weren't up to snuff. Frustrated, she kept blaming her equipment, and practiced by targeting billboards and mailboxes, twanging off shots from the passenger seat while I drove the car.

Call me the wheelman. After years of neglect, all the world's nerve and enzyme automotive technology had, for want of a better word, died, though I'm not sure it was ever truly alive to begin with. That meant I had to drive my own damn self. But with no chance of traffic jams and no cops to hand out speeding tickets, I was king of the road.

The quiet got to us worst of all. The silence of a dead world. We made small talk and turned on the music but she looked nervous and I just kept thinking: *I'm free, I'm released, but I've inherited a fucking graveyard.*

Now, it made no sense—not a lick—but I kept hoping for signs of life. I wanted a car to drive up alongside us, Mom and Dad in the front, little Jimmy and Jodie Plaguesufferer in the back. Survivors happy to see us. Or not happy. Hell, I'd have settled for a mohawked, chain-swinging, shotgun-wielding postapocalyptic street gang.

We did see animals, thank goodness, lots of birds and insects, a family of black-tailed jackrabbits, and a squirrel on the run from a wild dog. Maybe a coyote. Whatever it was, Fan made me pull over so she could scare it off with her crossbow.

"Goddamn dogs," she said.

"You like dogs. You gave me a dog."

"I like dogs," she agreed. "I like squirrels more."

We made good time through the Golden State, pushing ninety on the Pacific Coast Highway and snaking north. Killer sunset. Crashing waves. The works.

Fantasia's singular insight for this leg of the trip: "It's like the world backwards."

I asked her what she meant but she was too busy writing down her thoughts in a UCLA notebook. Not a bad idea, that. Someone should record all this for posterity.

"How do you spell 'world' backwards?" she asked me.

I told her, but apparently I didn't understand the question.

She wrote: "D-E-L-R-I-H-W."

When we hopped on the 5, she told me she wanted to go home.

What did she mean, home?

"Aberdeen," she explained. "When I was a little kid, we lived in Aberdeen."

"You lived in IVR."

"No shit, Sherlock. It was an IVR Aberdeen. So let's see the real thing."

She knew I didn't want to make unnecessary stops. I wanted Vancouver. I wanted Simone as soon as possible.

"It's on the way," she argued, "and it's my home. It's not like I'm asking you to double back so I can check out Disneyland."

"Too bad. Short lines there, I bet."

"And good prices," she said. "So what about it?"

I checked the map.

"Aberdeen," I said.

"Washington," she said. "Not Mississippi."

But why?

Why one city over another? Were our hometowns arbitrary? Did Ellison ever live in São Paolo? Did Hyoguchi grow up in Aberdeen?

There was futility in trying to understand Gedaechtnis, literally trying to know the minds of our makers. I could catch faint glimmers of it from time to time, but like a two-dimensional creature in a three-dimensional world, glimmers were all I had.

Fantasia's "ancestral home" turned out to be something of a pit, but chalk that up to Nature's wrath and human neglect. An earthquake had leveled the two-story Tudor, showering the grounds with glass and debris. Like the rest of civilization, it seemed dirty and unsafe. But as we toured the exterior, Fan could not stop talking about how closely the IVR version mirrored the real thing. Gedaechtnis had apparently used a real house as an exact model and stayed true to the finest detail.

Who had really lived here, we wondered?

She took me round to the back yard and showed me the spot on the patio where her grandfather had gone into diabetic shock. He fell and the ambulance came and took him away. Her first experience with death, an object lesson meant to teach but not traumatize. Things fall apart; people too. Better watch that blood sugar and take care of your health.

Was it the nucleus of her Nutritious/Delicious fixation?

Coupled with whatever imbalanced her chemically, maybe so.

Acorn shells and pine cones crunched underfoot and the sky opened to bring us the sound of rain on dry leaves. She showed me the gorge and the waterfall and the hammock she'd climbed upon to take long summer naps. Here it lay lifeless on the ground, the wind having snapped a support rope from one of the trees. Far in the distance, moonlight presented me with a perfect view of Lake Aberdeen.

"Try it with these," Fantasia offered, handing me a pair of Beholder Spex she'd boosted from one of the department stores.

I toggled the dial to CUBISM and slipped the goggles on. My view of the lake distorted, microscopic circuits in the lenses processing the visual data and reinterpreting it before sending it to my retinas. The end result was suitably Picassoesque.

I thumbed it to POINTILLISM, Seurat being easier on the eyes.

Fantasia loved Beholder Spex, I think because they gave her a sense of control over the environment that we lacked out here, control we'd only enjoyed in IVR. Rose-colored glasses, so to speak. On the other hand, I found them pretty damn perverse.

"Look at you," she said, exaggerating my features with GERMAN EXPRESSIONISM while I set her on the comic-strip style of LICHTEN-STEIN POP.

Before either of us could toggle FAUVISM, a rustling behind us brought us face to face with a pack of wild dogs. They'd spread out, padding lightly over the moss and leaves, putting our backs to the gorge. The dinner bell had rung and we were on the plate.

Eighteen years ago, these would have been cherished pets, walked and fed and taught to do tricks. But this next generation was untamed. Man's best friend had come of age without Man, and now the pack mentality had returned.

Or maybe they were wolves.

In either case, we had no interest in moving down the food chain.

Fantasia yanked her crossbow up to her shoulder and stomped her foot on the ground. "Ha," she cried, as one jumped back a bit. Another threatening stomp. "Ha!"

They didn't growl and they didn't flee. Hungrily, they watched us, asserting their dominance with a cold and steady stare.

"Fan," I said, keeping my motions deliberate as I slipped off my Beholder Spex. "Fan, don't you pull that trigger."

"Dead in my sights," she said.

"Too many of them," I warned her.

"Kill one and the rest run away."

"I don't think so."

"Yeah, but what the fuck do you know?"

"More than you think," I lied, "so cool it."

Nourish that which seeks to destroy you, I thought, reaching into my pocket for a strip of expired beef jerky. I unwrapped it from its package and tossed it underhand. They sniffed it, dubious, unconvinced.

"Okay," said Fan. "What else do you have?"

I came up with Simone's chocolates.

"Toss 'em."

"You can't feed chocolate to dogs," I said.

"Why not?"

"It messes up their adrenaline."

"So?"

She had a point. *Poison that which seeks to destroy you,* I thought, a far less noble sentiment. As they fell upon the bite-sized confections, white with cocoa butter bloom, we circled past their perimeter and escaped back to the car.

"Vancouver," said I.

"Delicious," said she.

I hit the accelerator. We drove in silence for a time.

"There's no such thing as dognip, is there?"

"Not to my knowledge."

Fantasia nodded. "Sometimes I get confused."

I nodded back and smiled.

She stared down at her lap. "Sometimes I make words up. It's hard being me. A lot harder than it looks."

I imagined that it was.

"How are you doing, pillwise?" I asked, broaching a delicate subject.

She pursed her lips in response and said, "What about hematite? Hematite is that cool shiny kind of black liquid metal kind of stone, right? Or did I make that up too?"

Though in no way extraterrestrial, the *Elysium* was a sealed, self-contained feat of so-called "Martian architecture," the avant-garde construction borrowing heavily from the designs of futurist Ratib Abdul-Qahhar. Surrounded by a barbed-wire fence and covered with solar panels, the pod seemed to spring from the weed-infested ground like a plastic-and-titanium flower.

"It's bigger than ours," Fan noted. "Why'd we get stuck with the cheap seats?"

223

"We're the contingency plan, remember? They put us in space. Kind of impractical to shoot something this big up there, don't you think?"

She grunted her disagreement. Pod envy, an ugly thing.

We got in with a passkey.

We walked the halls.

We found the corpse.

Lazarus—what used to be Lazarus—lay unmoving in his vat, dead as yesterday and silent as tomorrow. All the machinery in the room had been short-circuited. The room stank. Anti-bacterial gel encrusted the floor.

"Our friend Lazarus has fallen asleep," said Fan, quoting the New Testament, but there would be no waking him. He would not rise. He would rot.

"Called it," I said.

"You sure did, Hal. You the man."

Fantasia's voice betrayed a shaken quality. Sure, we'd seen bodies before, practiced autopsies for school, but this was actual, not virtual, and we knew him. For almost ten years we knew him. We may not have liked him, but . . .

But he was Laz. You know, Laz.

He had always been there.

And someone had murdered him.

Later I'd confirm that he'd been electrocuted, done in by a massive electrical surge, the safeguards bypassed all at the same time. That meant whoever killed him tried to do me in the same way, but I got off (comparably) lucky. And it meant that someone was thinning the herd. Only ten of us in existence, and with Laz gone we were down to nine. My death would have cut it to eight.

Again, what did I have in common with Lazarus?

Couldn't see it.

I fantasized about giving his eulogy.

"My friends, I stand here before you today to say a few words about the late Lazarus Weiss. Our man Lazarus had an uncanny ability to make everyone around him feel stupid. By this, I don't mean to insinuate that he was in any way intelligent. Just smug and calculating."

The prick.

Time to wake his girlfriend across the hall.

We found her alive and well. Sleeping so peacefully. It's funny. She couldn't have looked more different from the girl I knew.

But God was she beautiful!

Watching her float in that synthetic cradle, I thought about the incubator. We had an incubator in first grade. Baby chicks hatched from eggs. Fluffy, yellow baby chicks—real ones, or at least, we'd thought they were real.

I remembered: Ellison talked us through the miracle of life as we watched them struggle free from their shells, all of us innocent, all fascinated. The incubator would keep them safe and warm, he said; the subtext being that while our parents had put us in an IVR boarding school, the staff could take care of us here just as we could take care of the chicks. We started naming them. They would become our pets.

For the first time, I had become truly aware of Simone. To that point, I'd found her interesting because we had similar taste in candy. But now the expression on her face absorbed me as she stared at those infant birds, kept me from turning away as the question rose up from somewhere I'd never dreamt.

She asked: "What happened to the mother hen?"

A good question. Had Ellison stolen the chicks from their mother? No? Then why wasn't she here?

I had never thought about death before.

Ellison answered but I wasn't listening. I was staring at Simone. Holding my breath. I lay awake all that night, the idea taking root in my head and slowly twisting. I could see it constricting other thoughts, choking them off like a weed. *My mom can die? What does that mean? Where does she go? Am I going to die too?*

It changed me. Not all at once, but over years and years. Something about her smart question and her innocent face and the threat to that innocence that her question posed. I don't think it affected her the way it affected me. Maybe something misfired in my brain. It haunted me. It haunts me still.

Those memories rushed through me and I realized, watching her float in that synthetic cradle, that my love for Simone and my attraction to death had been born at the exact same time.

I hit the graduation sequence and waited for the machines to disengage. Fan made me turn my head as she pulled her naked from the vat. She wrapped her tight in a towel. I turned back to see her eyes flutter open for the very first time. Ah, Simone.

She looked around in wonder and fear. We told her who we were. We told her to relax. Relax and just listen. She strained to hear us, trying hard to grasp what we were saying. I kept my voice steady and low. I didn't want to rattle her.

225

Rattle her I did.

I watched some part of her drown in a sudden, horrible realization. "My parents are dead?"

"They're really not dead or alive. They never existed."

She took it harder than I had. Probably a sign of good mental health. I wanted to hold her but couldn't stand having my nose broken again.

"I have a sister?" she asked. "My cousin in Vermont?"

"IVR characters, all of them. Just like Darwin."

"The scar I got when I slipped on the coral," she said, turning her arm to look at the back of her elbow where no scar existed.

I shook my head no. "They gave us preprogrammed looks and preprogrammed voices that were never really ours. A sense of identity that was only half ours. That's okay. That's the chrysalis. We're the butterflies."

"Is this what a mental breakdown feels like?" she asked. "Because I think I might be having one."

Fan trotted out the painkillers. "Calm you down, help you sleep," she offered.

"I've slept long enough, thanks."

The tears came then. She hugged herself and mourned the lie.

Over the next few hours I tried to engineer a meaningful relationship.

My schoolboy crush—was it chemical, electrical, spiritual?—compelled me to hold her as she went through the various stages of grief. I hoped it would plant the idea of me as a new romantic possibility now that Lazarus was dead. But the old expression "not if you were the last man on Earth" came to mind, and although I wasn't the last, I was awfully close.

Subtlety never really entered the equation. Love made me clumsy and crude.

The sad thing was that she really liked me—I was no Lazarus, of course—but she'd called me friend for many years. We cared about each other, genuinely and deeply. And here I stood, a victim of raging hormones, crushed by my need to protect her. Everything I did to bring her to me only pushed her farther away.

But maybe I'm being too hard on myself.

I dug a pit out back. Nothing fancy. We inhumed the body, Simone gracing the grave with the flowers that I'd picked.

Fantasia found the proceedings funny. She kept bursting into giggles.

"I don't think she's healthy," said Simone.

"I most certainly am healthy!" Fan protested. "I'm uniquely healthy! I'm healthy in ways you've never even dreamed of!"

That's when Simone started monitoring the pill intake. They talked it over, just the two of them, and somehow she got through. Why Fan let her become the keeper of the medicine when she wouldn't let me, I won't hazard a guess. Needless to say, I counted myself lucky to have someone else safeguarding against dementia. It allowed me to focus on the task at hand.

"Someone murdered Lazarus and tried to murder you. Are we talking about a serial killer?" asked Simone.

"An assassin, certainly," I said. "Serial killer would depend on the motive."

"What do you mean?"

"Is he fulfilling a fantasy? Getting some kind of thrill out of it, sexual or otherwise? Then maybe we can call him—or her—a serial killer."

"Well, what does killing Laz accomplish?" she asked. "Maybe that's the question. Beyond the obvious, what does it mean?"

"It reduces humanity's chances by ten percent."

"More," said Fantasia.

I told her to check her math.

More, she said, because Laz was quite arguably the best and brightest of us. If anyone could have cracked Black Ep, Fan's money would have been on him.

"Would you put me second?"

"Third," she said. "I'd put her second." She nodded at Simone.

"So would I," I agreed.

"But maybe the killer didn't," Fan argued.

Simone gave it some thought and nodded. "It wouldn't be the first time I've been underestimated. Okay, why not? It's a working theory. So which of us has a grudge against humanity? We're basically human ourselves."

"Hardly," said Fan.

"Oh, so they ripped a few genes. If you check the DNA—"

"Simone, you're human or you're not," she countered. "There's no 'basically' about it."

I said: "Let's not split hairs. Any of us could carry a grudge. Any of us could take issue with how Gedaechtnis played their cards. But who's freak enough to start killing people?"

No one said anything.

"Maestro," I said, galled by their silence.

"He's a program."

"He's the most advanced artificial intelligence who's—"

"Who's still bound by his programming," said Simone.

"No," I said, "he's self-evolving. Or devolving, as the case may be. He's grown increasingly unstable since the first day we met him. Don't tell me he hasn't."

"And so you think he's killing us off? Hal, you make him sound like a big metal robot, lumbering around, 'De-stroy the hu-mans.' You're barking up the wrong tree."

"Well, if not Maestro, maybe another program?" I offered.

"The alternative being it's one of us?"

"There's no one else."

Simone shook her head. "But who among us is that cold-blooded?" No one had an answer.

"All right, I'm the morbid one, and she's the cra—forgive me, Fan—the one with the history of mental illness. And it isn't us." (I put Fan in the clear because the evidence suggested that she, like Simone, had never seen anything but IVR before I pulled her out. To engineer something as technically complex as the Calliope Surge, you'd first need to know that the world is fake.)

"So who could it be?"

"Let's simplify the motive," Simone suggested. "Let's say it's jealousy. Anger. Someone who hated Lazarus enough to kill him. Someone who hates you enough to try the same. That sounds like two completely different groups, but maybe there's a subset."

"Okay, people who hated Laz. That would be the clods," I said, counting off on four fingers. "Me, Tyler, Mercutio, Fan."

"I don't hate anyone," Fantasia protested, but we ignored her.

"People who hate me," I went on. "That's Laz, Isaac, Vashti, maybe. Anyone else?"

"Champagne's not too fond of you," said Simone.

"Right, good, Champagne. Anyone else?"

No, apparently. No subset.

"Any secrets we should know about? Isaac have a falling-out with Laz?"

"Friends to the end," said Simone. "How about your running buddies?"

"What about them?"

"Do you trust them?" she asked.

"As much as I trust anybody."

Fan made a dismissive sound, smirking. "Ty's got a delicious mean streak and Merc's a sneaky little weasel. I know how they talk behind my back."

We went back and forth hypothesizing, but we couldn't crack it.

229

"Once we reach Idlewild HQ, we can check the master logs," I said. "That's the only way to know for sure."

"Let's go," urged Fan.

"Hold on a second," said Simone, playing the voice of reason. "We've got a killer out there whose M.O. has him electrocuting people hooked up to machines. He's struck twice. There's a bunch of us still vulnerable, trapped in IVR. We have to get them out."

"Well, from Idlewild, I could tap directly into the source code."

"That's promising, but won't it take days to get there?"

"Plenty of time for him to strike again," I agreed.

"Can you get them out from here?"

"Ah, I don't know. I tried from my own pod. My access is shit. Unless I go back into the IVR myself," I reasoned, the idea sneaking up on me. "I could find Pace. That's a powerful tool, Pace, circumvents most of the security. Got me out. Maybe I could use it to get our friends out as well."

To hell and back. Stuffing myself into a box where I stood a chance of getting fried again. It was reckless, as Fan might say, but for a good cause. Two good causes, really, as I figured it might just endear me to Simone, who agreed to monitor my vital signs and yank me out of IVR at the first sign of trouble.

Getting out felt like waking from a fever dream; going back in was more like a lethal injection. Sensory deprivation and a sense of falling as the chemicals took hold . . .

Ankle-deep in sand and surf, I sidestepped horseshoe crabs the size of watermelons. Expensive beachfront property, magical, moonlit and fake, no Pace, no one in sight.

"Anyone here?" I called. "Nanny? Maestro?"

What's up with my voice?

I called my sprite but where I expected a flash of orange and black, I only saw silver and blue. It wasn't mine. And I wasn't me.

Because I'd used Simone's setup, the system assumed that I was she. So I'd reentered IVR as the girl of my dreams, as persuasive a clone as Jasmine.

Well, fuck. This changed things. I could exploit the disguise.

Just down the hall, theoretically speaking, I could have masqueraded as Lazarus, which no doubt would have drawn some nifty reactions from my peers—*He is risen!*—but the attack on Laz had fritzed those electronics beyond all repair.

So, Simone. Painted in her colors, I could lay a trap.

First things first, though. How to get my hands on Pace? Crawling around with the crabs, it wasn't. Maybe it went back to the Chinvat, or maybe it was bumping around my grave. It seemed drawn to Lazarus and myself, we who'd been assaulted. Simone, on the other hand, would have to chase after it, which was problematic since Nanny had gone missing. Without Nanny's services, I had only the sprite for transportation.

So who did I want?

Tyler. He took my call right away. Brought me into his happy home, a utilitarian bachelor pad softened but slightly by Champagne's artwork on the walls. He sat on the faux-leather couch, wearing jeans and a black "Lung Butter" T-shirt. Ty had a thing for the shock bands of the mid century: Lung Butter, Banana Enema, Max BSG. No accounting for taste and all that. He'd moussed his hair up on either side of his head, to create what looked to me like devil's horns inward curving. He looked tense and distracted, not to mention sleep-deprived, playing a computer game with one hand while beckoning me in with the other.

"Any luck?"

"Luck?" I asked.

"Getting out of here."

He took my silence as a negative.

"Didn't think so. Where have you been, then?"

"Oh, don't tell me you were starting to get worried," I smiled.

With a snap of his wrist, Ty tossed the game controller, sending it sidearm across the floor. Like skipping rocks in a pond. "Don't even joke," he warned. "Don't you even."

I gave him what I considered to be a fairly lame apology.

"No, I'm sorry," he said, accepting my words and reconsidering his own. "I'm going stir crazy here. Feel like I'm under siege. My head won't stop pounding. Hypochondria, I hope. But I'm happy to see you're okay. You are, aren't you?"

"Basically," I agreed.

He nodded. "Champagne's freaked."

"I bet."

"She's not as . . ." He trailed off, frowning. "She's coming over in a bit."

"Moving in?"

"For a while. Safety in numbers, right?"

I shrugged. I wasn't so sure.

He counted off on three fingers: "No sign of Lazarus, Halloween, Fantasia." He waved those fingers for emphasis, then added another one. "I had you figured for number four. And then this business with Mercutio. That's half the class."

In Simone's skin, I drew him out.

Maestro and the Nannies? AWOL. They'd grown strangely quiet these past few days. With the programs nowhere to be found, no one could leave the school. Ty and the others were trapped in IVR, stuck fast, waiting for a rescuer. Waiting for someone to return them to (what they believed to be) reality. Where the hell was Ellison? Why would he leave them in for so long? They knew something was wrong; they just didn't know what.

He told me about Mercutio.

He was scared.

I took his fear for honesty and repaid it with my own.

He grew incredulous, at first. Then angry. But then he understood.

"Merrily, merrily, merrily," he coughed. "Life is but a dream. Oh hell, I think you've done the impossible, Hal. You've made my headache worse."

We compared notes, weighed suspects. He expressed the belief that Maestro was to blame.

"We shouldn't have hacked. I'd never have done it if I'd known he'd take it as such a threat. Because now? Now he's on a goddamn rampage. He's flipped a switch. He's Saturn devouring his children, like that Goya painting. Yeah, he's swallowed us whole and here we are in the IVR belly of the beast, getting fucking digested one by one by one."

"Then we'll just have to cut our way out with a thunderbolt," I said.

Pace could be that thunderbolt. I told Ty all I knew about the abnormous program, hypothesizing that I might tap its power to lead my brothers and sisters to freedom. If only I knew where it was.

He said he'd keep an eye out for it.

Which was more than Merc could do. I found him in the little red schoolhouse, doing exercises in the dark.

"Go away," he said. "It's not safe here."

"Here, there, anywhere."

His brow furrowed. He stopped in mid push-up.

"Now that's interesting," he said.

"What is?"

"Say something else," he said, sitting up to show me eyes as white and blank as an empty page.

"Christ, Merc, are you really blind?"

He pointed up at the ceiling where our sprites hovered. "You've got Simone's colors. That's the one thing I can still see. Sprites. But your voice sounds—"

"Off?"

233

"—a little off, I do believe. Who are you?"

I spilled. Told him everything, just about.

Where the others responded with varying degrees of shock and horror, Mercutio found what I had to say perversely funny. He giggled into the back of his hand, snorting as I explained that what we all thought was reality was just another part of the IVR, and when I got to the part about his body actually being in the *Shangri-La* pod, he clapped and cheered.

"Pods! I knew it," he laughed. "We're fucking pod people!"

By the end of my report he grew calmer, the implications sinking in.

"So it's all just zeroes and ones," he said.

He told me how Maestro had blinded him, a comparable punishment to burying me alive, I supposed, though I sullenly felt I'd gotten the worst of it.

"Now I haven't seen—bad choice of words—haven't heard from him since he did this to me. But he's coming back, Hal. I can smell it. You have to get me out of here."

"Working on it," I said. "Now why is he so pissed, do you think? That little number you pulled, what exactly did you do to him?"

Merc shrugged. "Customized the jammer. Triggered a new hack."

"You try to bring the whole system down?"

"No, just Maestro. Denial of service via constant rerouting. You know, every time he makes a move, bounce him somewhere else. Should have been funny. Something went wrong, though. If I had access to the data maybe I could figure out what."

"I'll work on that too."

"Take me back to the Taj Mahal, I can step through and—"

"Won't do any good."

"Oh, right," he said. "I'd still be in IVR."

True enough, and without Pace or Nanny I couldn't take him anywhere. Not unless I made it to Idlewild for real, which increasingly sounded like my best move. I thought that Pace might be crawling about, what with Maestro blinding Merc here, but no, not a sign of that crystal spider. Was there something I could do to bring it to me?

I tried Isaac but he wouldn't take my call.

Vashti was in full-on heinous-bitch mode even before I told her who I really was. The strain of captivity was getting to her, I imagined. Not to make excuses for her.

No, I explained, I was not Simone.

No, I explained, I was not stalking Simone. Appearances be damned.

When I laid it all out for her, she gave me the line of the night.

She said: "You're telling me we're veal?"

Eh?

"Taken from our mothers, raised in boxes, never seeing sunlight—that's veal."

"You might be missing the point," I told her.

From Vashti's jazzy coffeehouse, I hit Fantasia's madhouse, that being Pandora's last IVR location when the Nannies disappeared. One empire, two nations, three moons: Fan had spent years customizing her weird and purple domain, inventing a turbulent history I could barely understand.

I found Pandora in a refugee camp on the border between the two warring nations, Indig and Resig. She'd been playing dice with a group of Smileys.

"*Que relevo!*" she exclaimed, rising to her feet and dusting herself off. "Can I crash at your place, Simone? I'm getting antsy here and I can't go home."

I brought her up to speed.

Like Vashti, she seemed more upset that I would masquerade as Simone than the whole *civilization annihilated—we're all that's left— now someone's picking us off—oh by the way you've never actually set foot in reality* thing.

235

"She's not who you think she is," Pan warned me, a short-lived half-smile snaking across her face. She wouldn't look at me and she wouldn't explain. She kept fiddling with her piercings, rings and studs she'd undoubtedly have to redo in the real world.

I told her—I'm not sure why—about my visit to São Paolo. Domain 7777. The half-smile returned and waxed full. For sixty seconds, give or take a few, we put worries aside and talked about the places she grew up, the park, the planetarium, the games of Ultimate Frisbee.

She told me how badly she wanted to get out of here. To get back to her old routine. Among other things, she had a little-league soccer team to coach. Two dozen first graders and their parents would be wondering what happened to her.

To the extent that IVR characters can wonder.

She wanted not freedom but normality. She wanted that illusion back. I was sympathetic, but only to a point.

A red-and-orange sprite flashed overhead; Isaac had returned my call.

I abandoned Pandora to meet him on his home turf, a customized Khmunu, the legendary "City of Eight." Thousands of years ago, Khmunu had been native soil to the cult of Thoth, Egyptian god of knowledge. There, Thoth hatched the Cosmic Egg, uttering the first words of Creation. Years later, the Greeks would liken Thoth to their god Hermes and rename the city Hermopolis. Later still, it would become known as Al-Ashmunayn.

My knowledge of geography impressed Isaac not in the least.

With his arms crossed in front of his chest, he studied me, grave and calculating.

"Is it true?" he asked.

"Is what true?"

"Lazarus."

"What about him?"

"Is he dead?" he growled. "You are our resident necrologist, aren't you?"

And so he knew I wasn't Simone. Had he talked to someone? Vashti, maybe?

"Thanatologist," I corrected him. Death as a transition. There is a fair difference between a philosopher and a coroner. But the difference was lost on Isaac, clearly. I told him as much and told him that, yes, Lazarus was dead.

He made a sour face. "And the world? Explain it to me."

I confirmed his worst fears.

He watched me with care, interrupting my answers with the kind of questions you ask when you hope someone's lying. But hey, if I'm lying, I'm dying. Isaac could sense that. He turned himself east, his gaze impassively sweeping the river Nile. The cradle of civilization—counterfeit IVR civilization, but civilization nonetheless—bustled with life, a cast of thousands.

Bitterly, he sighed.

"Quit this world, quit the next, quit quitting," he said.

Hadn't heard that before. "Is that a Sufi quote?"

"What are you doing here?" he replied. "Don't you have somewhere to be?"

That depended on whether or not he'd seen Pace.

"Listen," he said.

In the gospel according to Isaac . . .

Once upon a time in the desert, there was a man down on his hands and knees, combing the hot sand. A camel rode up, and upon the camel sat the man's friend.

"What are you doing?" asked the friend.

"I've lost my gold coin," said the man.

"Then I'll help you look."

He dismounted and they began to sift through sand, combing and combing

237

for a glint of gold. They did this together for a long time, and for a long time neither spoke. Eventually, the friend scratched his head and asked: "Do you remember where you saw it last?"

"Yes, in my house."

"In your house? Then why not look there?"

"Because there's no light in my house," said the man. "How would I find it?"

"All right," I said, "and what the hell does that mean?"

"Figure it out," he said and was gone.

It was the longest conversation with Isaac that I could remember having. The longest and quite possibly the most civil.

Friends are like mirrors, I've heard. You bond—for better or worse—with people whose personality traits reflect upon your own. Likewise enemies. But my mirrors? The more I looked at them, the more I felt like I'd stepped into a funhouse.

Last on my list, Champagne. The vapid, conceited Champagne. She took my call and immediately began screaming at me. I so didn't need it.

Didn't understand it, really.

"Come on, you pump, I'll breathe!"

What was she saying? She put her hands on me, pissed, grabbing at my arms.

"He's suffocating!"

Behind her, a glassy-eyed Ty lay half-on and half-off the couch, struggling to breathe. Too much carbon dioxide in his blood. Not enough oxygen. Out of balance, fatally so. Cyanosis gave his skin a bluish tinge. It was the nightmare scenario I feared—another of us dying before I could stop this.

Champagne pinched his nose and kissed his blue lips. She forced air down into his lungs. I pumped his chest. Fifteen pumps after every two breaths.

It accomplished nothing.

"Respirator," she panted.

"We don't have," I said.

No matter what we tried, nothing would help. The devil was in the distance; Ty's physical location was a good five thousand miles from mine. It was like trying to resuscitate a hologram. In Vancouver and Atlanta, we tried to save him. But in Berlin, he died.

Champagne kept right on breathing for him. That's love, I guess. She denied the reality of the situation and I choked on it.

Tyler—they fucking murdered Tyler—killed my oldest friend dead and I could have—maybe I could have stopped it—if I only knew—but I didn't so now he's ash, ghost, fading memory—my fault—and he was good to me— taught me how to stand up for myself against Maestro, against the pets— helped make me who I am, no doubt about that—and I paid him back by never accepting Champagne, by making fun of her when I knew it bothered him—nice, real nice—and he died for what?—what thrill?—what cause?— tell me what treasure is worth the oxygen in a good man's brain?

Man? Kid, really. We were all still kids.

Poor Ty.

I stepped back. I turned away.

A sick and unreasoning anger flooded me but could not touch my fear. My mind felt less like a fine steel trap and more like a zoo with no bars. I would have vengeance for Tyler. But where to start? Where to stop?

I sat there for an hour, at least. I was vaguely aware of Champagne continuing to try to resuscitate Ty. Then she curled up on the floor beside him and just stopped, not moving. I breathed my fury for long minutes, until a tiny noise woke me from my fugue. The mail slot creaked open.

IVR letter-carrier making his rounds, surely, and I wondered how the Gedaechtnis whiz kids felt about designing virtual junk mail. A

239

perfectly colorless index finger punched through the slot, not to de-
liver mail but to point at me and curl back, beckoning me closer.

I came in for a better look.

On the other side of the door, I saw the Gray Kid, the one from
my dreams, the one I had glimpsed for just a fraction of a second
when Merc shattered the IVR. I'd almost written that off as a hallu-
cination but here he knelt, inches away, peering through the opening
at me.

Shades of gray in a world of color. He looked like a glitch.

He put his finger to his lips, silencing my questions before I could
ask them. Shh. Again he beckoned, inviting me outside, willing me
to follow.

The slot clanked shut.

I looked over my shoulder to see Ty's girl still curled up against
him. For all her flaws, trying to save him had been Champagne at her
best. The room could have been on fire; she wouldn't have left his side.

I kept her out of it. Flung the door open. Shadowed Gray down the
stairs. Night fell suddenly, the afternoon sun dropping without reason
or warning. He led me to the back yard, to Ty's hot-tub-slash-duck
sanctuary. Champagne's pets played follow-the-leader, a family of
mallards paddling through the water in endless circles, breaking the
routine only now and again to bob their heads for a bite of plankton.

Gray caught his reflection in the water, pondered it, and met
my eyes.

"Funny how you can hope for something for so very long and
then when it finally happens you realize how monstrous it is," he said.
"Not funny, ha ha. More funny, strange. Or funny, sad. Language col-
lapses once again."

"I've seen you before," I said. "Who are you?"

"The Ghost in the Machine," he smirked.

I said nothing.

"Dad named me Malachi," he said. "Malachi the Beta-Test. If those other nine are your siblings, you can think of me as a stepbrother."

"Can I?" I scowled.

"An older stepbrother. I watched you grow up, you know. From the shadows, I watched."

"You're virtual."

"Sure. A virtual kid. Gedaechtnis had me try out the system while you were sloshing around in a test tube." He dipped a finger and swirled, sending ripples through the water that succeeded in agitating the ducks. "They studied my reactions. Made improvements. I went through twelve Nannies, sixteen Maestros, twenty-eight moms, thirty-one dads. Dads but not 'Dad,' if you follow. My creator, Dr. James Hyoguchi, was my real 'Dad,' but these were just dad programs that would go on to raise the lot of you. Of course, you already know my real 'Mom,'" he said, waving a hand at the IVR environment that surrounded us. "You lived inside her for eighteen years."

"Oh," I said. "You sound pretty fucking bitter."

"Guess what?" he said. "I have a right to be bitter. Without me they couldn't have built this, but when they'd finished they just shuffled me into the background. You grew up and I had to sit and watch."

"Boo hoo," I snapped. "That's why you're killing everyone?"

"No, that's why I'm—" He grimaced, letting the rest of the denial fall by the wayside. "Well, yes," he admitted. "In a sense, I'm responsible because without me I don't think any of this would have happened. But it's unintentional."

"Okay, so you're what? You're killing them by accident?"

"I'm trying to help you."

"Try harder," I said.

"I'm helping you right now in ways you don't realize."

He spoke, and in doing so painted a picture of forces aligned against me, he and Pace overpowered but doing their best to hold them back. Which was his duty, he insisted, because he was responsible.

"Do you know what bleeding is?" he asked me.

"A hemorrhage."

"No, for me," he said, tapping his chest. "Do you know what bleeding is for me?"

I shook my head.

"When you organics get frustrated, you keep it to yourselves. Maybe you express that frustration, maybe you act on it, but the feeling stays with you. Not so with me. I'm part of the machine. I'm the conscience of the machine. When I feel something, it bleeds."

"You're saying that your personality, this 'poor little bitter old me' goddamn artificial personality, has been infecting—"

"Infecting, yes, precisely."

"—the Academy and everything in it?"

"For eighteen years now," he nodded. "Slowly but surely."

"Maestro," I said.

"Went cuckoo for Cocoa Puffs. Absolutely."

So, I thought. *Malachi turned Maestro and now he's sorry; trying to put the genie back in the bottle.*

"Gedaechtnis built an evolving system," he explained. "Everything's programmed to respond to you kids. But I'm a kid too. It's a design flaw; the system listens to me more than any of you, it adjusts to me whether I want it to or not."

I said: "You've known about this for some time. Why didn't you come to me sooner?"

"Believe me, I tried," he said, "but I've been running for my life here. He's deleted me twice already. I'm restoring from timed backups I've hidden in system files. It's a matter of time until he finds them all and that'll be the last anyone sees of me. Or Pace for that matter."

"Unless I can delete him first."

"So to speak."

"I'll go to Idlewild HQ. Get rid of Maestro. Pull everyone out of the IVR."

"A good start," Malachi agreed.

"What else?"

"Well, I fear none of that will make the killing stop," he said, frowning slightly. "He'll just switch tactics. Instead of power surges and oxygen deprivation, he'll use guns."

"Yeah, I'd like to see that," I said. "Is he going to physically build himself a body, chase after us, hunt us down?"

"Build himself a body?"

I puzzled at his confusion.

"You don't understand," he said. "I'm not talking about Maestro. Maestro's just a tool. I infected the system and that includes all ten kids. You've grown up in the wake of my misery. You don't shrug that off so easily. You don't get away unscathed."

I said: "It's one of us."

"Now, I never meant anyone any harm," he said. "And maybe he was just a bad seed. Maybe he would have turned out bad without my influence. To find out you're not even human, that's a terrible shock. It can push you over the edge, don't you think?"

"Push *who* over the edge?"

"The one of you I always hated the most," he said. "The oldest."

Oldest, I thought. *The firstborn.*

"Mercutio is blind," I said. "He can't be the one because Maestro blinded him."

"No, I did that. Tried to keep him out of the system altogether, but denying him visual interface is the best I can do."

I was speechless. My best friend.

"He electrocuted Lazarus. He suffocated Tyler. He's trying to kill you as we speak but I'm multitasking, working with Pace to keep your oxygen flowing."

Malachi looked small and wretched and so did I. Behind him, the Northern Lights painted the sky with a cold, dismal light.

Mercutio, I thought. *Blind man's bluff.*

I didn't want to believe it. I wanted Malachi to be lying through his gray little teeth. If he were to blame for all of this, just a rogue program bent on my destruction, I could delete him without hesitation. Like swatting a bug. After all, he lived an artificial life and we shared no history.

But Merc . . .

His sense of humor had always struck me as dark, even darker than my own. He hid behind a sarcastic, fatalistic front, a "why bother?" sensibility that belied genuine concern.

Or maybe the front hid nothing at all. Maybe the feeling behind it had been a misguided projection on my part.

He was the best hacker. He had the means, he had the opportunity. I could imagine him wanting to hurt Lazarus. They'd been enemies for years. Killing him, though, that seemed a hell of a line to cross. Had he in fact crossed it and then been unable to turn back? I'd read interviews with mass murderers; invariably they said that the first murder was the hardest to stomach, that it grew easier with repetition.

Why me? Why Tyler? What had we ever done to him?

Maybe he really did absorb something from Malachi. That program had eighteen years to poison our dreams. Had it warped him, intentionally or no?

He'd said: "I think I'd like to work with kids."

Did it mean something?

A Rorschach inkblot of a man.

My friend from the beginning. I remembered laughing with Merc, joking, friendly competition over who could be the bigger thorn in Maestro's side. I remembered dozens, maybe hundreds of trips to

Twain's, sharing teen angst over Pepsi and grilled cheese sandwiches. I remembered the occasional stupid joyride, denting trashcans and mailboxes simply because we could. I remembered enjoying our adolescent power.

No, I did not want to believe it.

Fantasia pulled me out of the IVR. Fantasia, not Simone. Simone sat on the floor, gazing off in my general direction though not at me. She looked peaceful. Stupidly so.

"Hey," I said, ripping tubes from my arms.

"Hey, she's, uh, coming down," said Fan.

"Down from what?"

With a shake of her foot Fan indicated the swank Gucci purse that housed her ever-growing collection of antipsychotic meds, soporifics and painkillers.

"I'm okay," Simone said, those almonds dilated. "Funny story, really."

She told me—rambling a bit, shuffling her words to overcome the haze—how she'd suffered a miserable allergic reaction in the time I'd been gone. Her biochemistry struggled and faltered, sputtering histamine. As sick as the real world made me, it made her even sicker. Smarter than the rest of us, Simone, but her immune system wasn't as strong.

She compensated with medication. Antihistamines to treat symptoms, phagocytes to break down bacteria, then a cocktail of immune stimulants. When none of that made her feel better, she dipped into the painkillers.

Hit her a little strong, they did.

"Yes, I am indeed spacy," she said, "but I feel so much better."

She expected it might take some trial and error to find the right chemical balance.

245

More tests required. She said she stood a good chance of being hypersensitive to threonine, which sucked because we needed those supplements to live.

"I'll tough it out," she promised.

That only endeared her to me more.

I told them about Tyler. The news sobered Simone, and she wept. She expressed sympathy to me, since I'd been the closest to him. She wondered aloud about Champagne, about how she was doing. As I felt another wave of grief threaten to submerge me, I noticed that Fan did not react, except to make a tiny sniffing sound. Not a sniffle, just a sniff.

I told them about Malachi. Something flickered in Fan's eyes. She wouldn't voice it. Simone nodded, thinking. She'd seen him before—in a dream, like me, she realized—but the dream had faded and now she couldn't recall it.

I told them what Malachi had said.

Fan could see it. She didn't want to, but she could definitely see it. "Sometimes Mercy does crazy things," she shrugged, pronouncing it "murky."

Simone could see it too. "Sociopath. Sure. He always seemed slippery to me. When I look back, I can see the signs."

Maybe there were signs, and I'd blinded myself to them. "Stable" was never a word I'd use to describe Mercutio. A born shit-stirrer, he could be difficult, and unpredictable, and sometimes dangerous. If they were signs, fine, but I could be all those things too. It's a question of degree, I guess. And they didn't realize he had his good points, some very good points in his favor.

When we hit fourteen he'd started getting secretive with his free time, so I got curious and tailed him to a dicey part of town. I remember he looked embarrassed when I caught up with him—and then a little angry. Then he put that aside and welcomed me in. He'd been feeding the less fortunate. Turkey dinners on Thanksgiving.

Not for completely altruistic reasons, I'll admit; he liked a girl who worked at the local soup kitchen and said he wanted to "shake some bad karma." But still . . .

And two days later he sabotaged Vashti's science-fair project. Undid weeks of hard work with a bottle of indelible ink. Just for the hell of it. I thought it was funny at the time, Merc being Merc, and who really cared about Vash? It's not as funny now. I don't know. When you befriend a rattlesnake, you never expect it to bite you.

Simone put her fingers to her lips, turning her attention forward instead of back. "We have to bring him to justice."

"You mean kill him," I said.

"I don't believe in execution," she began, pausing as she weighed her grief and outrage against her principles, "but we should try him and convict him and then put it to a vote. I'll go along with the majority."

"The majority says bang," said Fan.

"Well, if he did it, it isn't entirely his fault," I heard myself argue. "Take a look at what he's been through."

"What we've *all* been through," said Simone.

I shut my mouth on the counterargument. Being Merc's apologist gave me no joy.

Where the fuck was he?

He started at *Shangri-La,* not the mythical Himalayan paradise but our own *Shangri-La* pod nestled in the northern suburbs of Atlanta, Georgia. *He could still be there,* I figured. *With Champagne. Keeping her hostage, maybe. He can hack security and launch all his attacks from the privacy of his own pod.*

Or he could have made the trip to Idlewild.

Idlewild gives him even greater access. There, he can tap into the IVR and disguise his signature. Make it look like he's actually somewhere else. Or someone else. He can learn more there, refine his sabotage. Plus, it's the best defensive position. Because we have to go there to pull the others out.

Not so, I realized. *Idlewild HQ might allow us to release everyone at once, but we could just go to Europe and do it manually . . .*

Except flying a plane without any real training sounded risky and an ocean cruise would take too long. It would give him time, time he could use to send more of us from the land of the living to the land of the dead.

No, he had to be in Idlewild. It's where I would be if I were him.

And out of nowhere, I hit an odd thought: *That body I buried— how do I know it's really Lazarus?*

I'd never met Lazarus—not in real life, anyway—and for all I knew that corpse belonged to somebody else. The envelope with his name on it that had been waiting for each of us had been sodden and dissolving in blue gel, so we couldn't know for sure whose it had been. A theory took shape. Mercutio: that's who I'd buried. The killer zapped him, and then stole his online identity, impersonating him in the IVR just as I'd impersonated Simone. Which meant the killer was Lazarus.

Now we're getting somewhere.

The more I thought about it, the more sense it made. Laz fakes his own death and starts hunting his old enemies: Mercutio, Tyler, me. He uses Maestro as a distraction. When I get too close to the truth, he has Malachi throw me off-track.

Elegant, if markedly deranged. Was Laz capable of this? Again, I wondered: *What's the motive?* And then: *What's his endgame?*

I couldn't see that far. But I liked this idea. Not the part about Merc being dead—that was tragic, of course—but I preferred him dead to stabbing me in the back. Not to mention Ty.

I didn't dare bring my theory to Simone. Why raise her hopes about Lazarus being alive, diabolical killer or no? Better to keep him out of her head. Fantasia, though—in whispered conversation, I laid it out and took her measure. She dismissed it flat-out, then thought it over, reconsidering her negation with an irritable smack of her lips. Possible, she decided. Definitely possible.

Fan called shotgun. Simone hopped in the back. I got behind the wheel, adjusted my mirrors. And abnormalized. Big time.

I could feel myself pulling in opposite directions, freakishly dividing into halves. That dream had returned, a waking fantasy now of being two people instead of one . . .

Only in my head. I knew this. But it hit me with force.

The first me grabbed the moment and hugged it like a small child would—I named him Road Trip. Road Trip put the car on cruise control so he could sing along with the music and play I Spy With My Little Eye. Despite everything he'd lived through, he could be charming. Even kind. He flirted with Simone. Lo and behold, Simone actually flirted back. Connection, spark, the promise of magic if not magic itself. Tyler's death did not touch him. Neither did Mercutio's alleged betrayal. They couldn't. He'd waited his whole life to feel good. Here it was.

The second me just sat there. Sat and stared. And knew.

I named him Death Watch.

What else could I call him?

Road Trip and Death Watch, amoebic twins. Spawned by fission and schism.

I floated in a feeling of wrongness. That split-second confusion before pain can set in. Get your front teeth knocked out and there's a sense that something is not right, something has gone horribly wrong. "Wait a minute, aren't my teeth supposed to be here in my mouth? What happened to my teeth?" And then the pain. Or if your arm gets broken, it's the "My arm's not supposed to bend that way, is it?" The sickening "Whoops." That's what I had, except it wasn't a split-second whoops. It stretched for hours and hours. It was like a demon had looked ahead to my blackest moment, found the accompanying whoops and stretched it back. Pulled the whoops back through time to wrap me up in it, mummifying me in an impenetrable cocoon.

Maybe not a demon. Maybe an angel of mercy. Because when I look back, I can see a small kindness in the universe. The schism gave me a chance to be Road Trip. It let me spend time with Simone when I was at my best. For the first time ever, I felt perfectly comfortable with her. I did not feel so very, very nervous.

Was I that far from crazy? Road Trip and Death Watch vs. Nutritious and Delicious, who would win in a figment tag-team extravaganza? The difference between me and Fan, of course, was that I could see my daydreams for what they were.

Couldn't I?

We skirted the U.S.–Canadian border, chasing sunrises, fleeing sunsets.

Simone talked about the future.

Fan dangled her feet out the window.

We stopped for supplies now and then, fanning out to grab anything and everything we thought might help us with our task. Just north of Idaho, Road Trip found a tobacconist shop with good old Sendiri-brand Indonesian kretek. The red-and-gold box. Sweet, spicy clove cigarettes.

I've found cloves when here I've been cloven.

So I lit up and choked. Nearly busted a lung. *Man, these things are fucking terrible!*

Road Trip went from coughs to giggles. Death Watch felt his pulse pound.

No chain-smoking for me. Couldn't stand them. Blame it on my inhuman physiology or the fact that my virgin lungs had never actually inhaled real smoke before. Or blame Gedaechtnis. Sure, whichever programmer they'd put in charge of oral fixations might have made the IVR cloves sublimely delicious when really they were shit all along.

Or maybe I just outgrew them.

It's possible, I thought. *Maybe I'm growing up.*

Back at the car, no Fan—still shopping, I guessed—but Simone had stretched herself out in the backseat, a luxurious pose, as sexy as I'd ever seen her. As sexy as I'd ever seen Jasmine. Not quite sleeping, but adrift in a post-catnap haze.

Her eyes fluttered and she looked right through me.

Vacant.

Death Watch shifted his weight to the other foot. Road Trip asked her if she was okay.

She babbled.

She didn't know who I was.

She didn't know anything.

Not okay. Out of her mind on pain pills, her breathing "Champagnesque," to borrow one of Merc's expressions. Which is to say slow and shallow. A whine of protest as I pulled her from the car and made her walk around. She just wanted to go limp. I wanted her alert. We settled for something in between.

She had a problem, clearly. I told her that. Told her she'd taken too many pills, again, and I really wasn't grooving the pattern.

"Officer, can't you let me off with a warning?" she murmured.

I appreciated the fact that she was in constant pain, but for the love of God she had to nix the self-medication. Ixnay on the elfsay-edicationmay.

Oh, would I lighten up? Would I please stop? "I'm fine," she assured me. "A little sleepy. No big deal, Hal, really."

"Give me the bag."

She deflected my insistence with verbal judo, using my concern against me. Even so, I would not be deterred. Protecting her: my top priority.

251

And then . . .

"You're so sweet," she said. "Thank you."

She leaned in and kissed me gently on the cheek. Our first kiss. That infamous "You're a good friend" kiss. But forget that one, because when our eyes met (hers glassy, mine lovestruck) the second kiss followed, obliterating everything that had come before. On the lips and real. Better than anything I'd ever known.

With that kiss, our fates were sealed.

We pulled apart when Fan returned.

As she came off her high, the ramifications of the kiss began to sink in. We talked around it with halting sentences and shy smiles. Fan took over the driving duties, which let me sit in the back with Simone.

"That was nice," she said, holding my hand.

"Yeah."

"I feel a little guilty."

"Why? Because of Lazarus?"

"Yes, and Pandora."

"Pandora?"

"You know she's in love with you."

Pause.

"You knew that, right?"

I said: "Right."

But I hadn't known.

We switched places when the sun fell, Fan sleeping in the back while Simone took the front with me, looking green. With the drugs ebbing away, the receptors in her subsynaptic membrane had stopped blocking the pain and sickness. She coughed and sneezed and shook her head, miserable. She popped another painkiller but just the one. A show of restraint.

Le Diable apparaît dans beaucoup de formes.

The Devil comes in many forms.

A long-eared jackrabbit sprinted across the road and I braked on instinct, swerving. Went right off the road. Fought for control of the car and I got it, though the sudden turn sent Fan tumbling to the floor and knocked Simone's head against the passenger-side window.

The impact was not particularly solid. The glass did not break, nor even dent. Simone did not lose consciousness. She had a small bruise at her temple, nothing more.

Just to be safe, I checked her out for an extradural hemorrhage. She seemed fine.

Except from that moment on, she complained of splitting headaches. She upped her pill intake to compensate. Up, and up, and up.

That tiny bruise turned out to be the straw that broke the junkie's back.

It happened like this. We stopped for a bathroom break at a Wisconsin diner that reminded me of Twain's. Simone disappeared into the ladies' room. A little time went by and then a little more. Like idiots, Fan and I waited for her to come out until we realized that something might be horribly wrong. Fan went in to get her. I heard her yell my name. I came running. Simone lay motionless on the bathroom floor, overdosed, her pupils like pin dots.

I ripped a trauma kit. Nearly tore it in half.

We tried everything to save her. Naloxone. Ipecac. Stimulants. CPR. We pumped her stomach.

Nothing worked.

Her heart slowed, then stopped altogether. I kept the oxygen going. Would not let hope flicker out. And I kept calling her name, because if she could hear me maybe she could answer me. And if she couldn't, at least she'd know—she'd know I was there and that— everyone dies alone, they say, but bullshit, I was right there with her, holding her, hoping . . .

Just hoping.

Until it happened.

Like the song goes, it put a stutter in my soul.

Harvard Medical School—the future I'd been promised. Did they have a class in staving off despair? Could they have taught me what to do and how to feel when my patients stop breathing? When the people I care about die in my arms?

Road Trip would have tried to cheer me up, I'm sure, but the useless bastard was nowhere to be found. I can only assume Death Watch ate him. Bones and all.

I can still feel Simone's lips on mine.

And if I could take it back, I would. Because Doom followed. Not my fat-ass IVR vampire, but actual Doom, ugly sister to Destiny. Because in that kiss, she died. Not right away, I grant you. But in the choice we made, in that moment, that kiss, she became a living ghost.

We used each other. I took advantage of her drug-addled state; without the painkillers she'd never have kissed me. She took advantage of my hormones and my heart; without that kiss I'd never have let the drug issue drop.

PACE TRANSMISSION 000013920400320

GUEST THREE TYLER NOT RESPONDING [PRIORITY]
LIFE SUPPORT DISRUPTED
COMPROMISE AT 0811-0251B
0811-0251B ALLOCATED AS DOMAIN THREE
INFECTION
DAMAGE TO INTEGRITY
PROTECTING GUESTS (ALL) VIA JANUS LOCKOUT
REROUTING KADMON
QUERY QUERY ?
QUERY ?
END

SAMHAIN

"Will the cheetah catch the antelope?"

The Southern Gentleman mulls that question over and over in his mind, investing in it an almost mystical significance. The answer is simple. She will or she won't. Nothing is certain in Nature. Sometimes the cheetah catches her prey. Sometimes she goes hungry. There is no guarantee.

They've built a smart antelope, a strong antelope, a fast antelope.

An untested antelope.

Black Ep remains one hell of a cheetah.

The project is rapidly coming to an end. The men and women of Gedaechtnis have given it their best. It's out of their hands. It's in God's hands, some say. Beds have been made; now it's time to lie in them.

Pathetic as it may sound, Maestro's coffin sounded pretty okay to me as I sat there on the grungy ladies' room floor. The impulse to die tugged and tugged. Like watching someone vomit and feeling your own stomach rumble in disgust and sympathy.

A world without Simone. What did it mean?

Caring for me as a friend, or more than a friend, or even just putting up with my feelings for her, she had been my tether to all the wonders under the sun. I tried to count them without her and couldn't. The tether had snapped.

I thought: *This is not really happening.*

Fantasia put her arms around me, but she might as well have been consoling a statue. She gave me her compassion for what might have been an hour, maybe more, maybe less. Time had stopped for me. However long it was, she tried and tried. But no. No reaching me.

I was six years old again. I was wondering about the mother hen. What happened to her? Where did she go?

Fan got me up on my feet. I just slid back down again.

I wouldn't follow her.

She said if we gave up now, it all would have been for nothing.

I couldn't hear her.

She called me a catatonic asshole and threatened to break my nose again.

I didn't care.

She pulled her fist back but didn't swing.

"We still have a job to do," she said.

And that penetrated.

"A job," I said.

"That's right, Hal, we still have work to do. We're not done yet."

I closed my eyes and nodded. I'd spent my life hiding from my obligations, but now what did I have but a responsibility to the dead? That, and nothing more. *Delicious,* I thought. *Let's finish the job.*

When I think of Simone now, I think of butterfly wings. Beautiful and excruciatingly delicate. Touch them once and they might disintegrate.

Did she o.d. by accident? Or on purpose?

I never saw her as suicidal, but part of me wonders if the die was cast at the moment she saw what she believed to be Lazarus's dead body. They were soulmates, after all. Consciously or no, maybe she wanted to join him. Or maybe Gedaechtnis just botched her genetic batter, leaving her vulnerable to every passing dust mite and microbe. Simple as that. Pain can build a nest in you, twisting and stretching beyond all tolerance. Who can resist just one more pill?

Whom should I blame for this? Should I make a case for Lazarus or Mercutio? Myself or Simone? Malachi? Can I blame the bruise? The window? The painkillers themselves? How about the lousy, stupid, goddamn rabbit—*conejo estupido, conejo malo*—that I could have made one with the pavement?

Always I come back to the kiss.

Idlewild, past the lake, right off Route 10.

It was just as I remembered it, minus the people. My eyes caught all the old street signs. So many religious themes. Celestial Drive. Paradise Path. Creation. Grandeur. The Academy stood at the corner of Grandeur and Forman Road—but only in IVR. Here, there was no Academy. Gedaechtnis HQ occupied the address.

Quite a compound, big dome, lots of office buildings. Impressive as Babel.

I turned off the ignition. We got out, looking for signs of life.

Didn't see any.

Just in case, we strived for zero presence. Get in, get out, and begone. Good in theory. Unfortunately, ninjas we were not. He saw us coming a mile away.

"Hello?"

An unfamiliar voice. We froze.

"Hello, anyone there?"

We snuck into the lobby, searching, weapons at the ready. I'd armed myself at a local gun store. Now, with the safety off, I could feel my fist gripping it tightly—so tightly, I feared I might squeeze off a round without any sign of a target. How I longed to pull that trigger. *Each bullet is precious,* I told myself. *Make each shot count.*

And I thought: *I need this. I need someone to hate. I need something to crush.*

"Where are you?" that voice wondered—disembodied, floating—where did it come from? Possibilities . . . There on the security desk: a walkie-talkie. Carrying live signal or just a recording? And was it Mercutio? Was it Lazarus?

"Are you there?"

Fantasia was halfway to the device when I recognized the mistake. I grabbed her from behind and yanked as hard as I could. A+ instinct. D- execution. Just couldn't get her in time. Her fingers touched metal. Brushed it gently.

Flash and fire.

The explosion ripped her, spun her, sent her flying out of my hands. She let out a banshee shriek and I dropped to her side, swatting out flames. My head told me to get up or get out, use my gun, fight for my life. But I ignored all that and listened to my heart, going right into triage mode, my doctor's training kicking in.

Correction, not my heart; this was my fucking ego all the way. Everyone kept dying on me and I couldn't bear it. Hell if I'd go 0-for-3.

The voice rang out again, this time from the PA system overhead: "Hal, you actually let her pick it up? That's chivalry, I guess."

He can see us, I realized. *Cameras, hidden cameras.*

Not good.

I dragged Fan to the elevators. Out of service, these. I propped her up in a corner.

"Can't believe she brought a crossbow. A fucking crossbow. Crazy bitch think we're still playing clodge ball?"

I thought: *So Malachi told the truth.* Betrayed, then. Betrayed by Mercutio. If I tried to believe it was Lazarus—and he had used the clodge-ball reference to throw me off, make me believe he was Mercutio—I would be choosing denial. I knew that bitter tone anywhere.

Vampires, traditionally speaking, don't start off by attacking strangers, I remembered. *When they rise as undead, they attack their own families first.* But I couldn't demonize him that way. He was real, not some storybook monster. I thought: *Maybe he's foaming mad at the world. The soup kitchen's fake and so's his good karma. He wants to lash out but who's left to hurt? No one but us. Targets by default.*

Had to keep her from going into shock. Popped out a coagulant from my trauma kit and put it to use. Stabilize, Fan, stabilize. I considered scooping her up in my arms and making a sprint back to the car, but gritted my teeth and fought that impulse hard. My mind's eye imagined Merc waiting outside with a gun. Set off the trap, wait for us to run out, and kablammo. Too easy. Why play into it? Better to keep a defensive position, wait *him* out, keep *him* guessing . . .

Blood everywhere and in Fan's eyes, a glazed and uncomprehending look; she might have been hallucinating. "Bad doggy," she rasped.

I worked. I brought her out of danger.

From the PA: "Whatcha doing there? The doctor thing?"

I ignored him.

Zanshin is a Japanese concept, a relaxed, balanced, razor-sharp state of mind in the face of incredible danger. I'd say I had some going on, only my nerves were keyed up to a fever pitch and my pulse wouldn't stop hammering.

Fuck it.

Cold metal in my sweaty hand, I poked my head out, eyes sweeping the lobby. No sign of him. He had to be out there somewhere. But where? He'd gotten here before us and had the home-field advantage. He could have booby-trapped the entire building. I tried to remember everything I'd ever learned about firearms. *The gun is an extension of your hand. Point and squeeze, don't jerk. When you shoot, shoot to kill.*

"The hell is wrong with you?" I yelled, trying to draw him out. "Someone drop you on your head?"

"I'll drop you on yours," he offered.

"Jesus, Merc, what the fuck? What are we, kids?"

He didn't answer.

That's a way to go, I decided. *Remind him of who I am. Humanize myself in his eyes.*

"Do you remember when we *were* kids? You remember the first day of school? You were the shy one, right? Painfully shy. No one knew you and I came right up to you and asked who you were. You said you felt like a jumping bean in a pack of jellies. You remember that? You remember teaching me freeze tag? Remember me picking you first on my team, remember me sticking by you no matter what?"

Pause.

"Hal," he said, "there's a time for sappy memories and a time for getting shot. Check your watch."

"What, is this getting a little too real for you?"

"Where do you get off?" he asked. "Are you actually trying to appeal to my humanity when neither of us is human?"

"Adam," I said, using his real name for the first time in years. "Adam, I don't care what we are. Human beings or spider monkeys, I don't fucking get it. I thought we were friends."

He sighed, an exasperated rush of air that crackled through the PA.

"Look, don't make a big mistake and take this personally, okay?"

I gripped the pistol tighter. "How can I not?"

"I don't hate you or anything. It's just a numbers game."

"Numbers?"

"Yeah, you know, it's all just zeroes and ones. You're a zero. And I've won."

I jumped back from the sudden explosion—*grenade?*—and saved myself from the worst of it, but a piece of shrapnel caught my jaw and had me spitting blood like a bulemic mosquito. What I would have given for Nanny to neutralize my pain.

Or Fantasia's.

Merc let out a war whoop and a short laugh. Like a hyena barking at a wildebeest. Nervous laughter, maybe, or maybe he really enjoyed hurting me. I could hear his footsteps, distant, but getting louder fast.

My brain kept screaming—*"Suck it up, Halloween!"*—as my feet beat a measured retreat, falling back to Fan.

He's inside the building, I thought. *Where is he? Why can't I see him?*

I spat more blood; it dribbled down my chin and onto the floor.

Well, now.

I reached into my trauma kit and found the bag I wanted. Squeezed out a few drops, jumped back, squeezed out a few more.

I made a trail for him. Away from Fantasia. To the other wing of the lobby, where the elevators went up to the top.

The air rippled. Mercutio was nothing but a blur. That's when I realized he'd come to the dance in military issue. Maybe he looted an army base. He blended in so perfectly with his environment, I could only see him up close, and hardly even then.

He chased my trail, storming past the elevators and arcing left.

I wasn't there.

The blood bag was on the ground where I'd tossed it, red and leaking, a discarded medical supply. I had gone the other way—off the beaten path. Zanshin. Now I doubled back, pistol cocked and loaded.

I poked around a corner and caught a glimpse of him. Just a glimpse as he turned.

"Trick or treat," I said.

I shot him twice before he could return fire. No time for a third. I spun back to safety as his bullets ricocheted wildly off the walls.

I heard him curse and fall.

"What did you do?" he said, asking the obvious. "What did you do to me?"

I called back an answer but he kept firing shots from the other side of the corner. He couldn't hear me over the roar of his assault rifle.

With a lucky shot, I'd nicked his spine. Numbed him from the waist down. But the upper half of his body still worked and so did the weapon in his hands. We stayed locked in stalemate, me not daring to poke back around, him firing intermittently in the hopes of catching me doing just that.

We waited each other out. I took codeine for my jaw. Couldn't bandage it, I had to keep my gun in my hands.

He said: "It was red light, green light."

"What?"

"Red light, green light," he spit. "That's what I taught you. Not freeze tag. Freeze tag was Tyler's game, you douche."

Dead right, I realized.

I asked him what the fuck. I asked him why.

He wouldn't answer the important questions. He met them with insults or sarcasm or bursts of gunfire. So I shut up. And after a few minutes he started talking again. Just random shit, really, observations and scattered thoughts, keeping it light. The things we did together as kids. Jokes we told. Games we played. Pranks we pulled. So many good times we had, most of which I didn't remember.

He couldn't bear to talk about the present. He wanted the past. The innocence of years gone by, the dreams of youth, the freedom

of it all. Freedom from anything too serious, freedom from consequences.

I wanted him to shut the fuck up. I wanted the truth even more.
I listened.

"I'm going to stop talking now," he said.

I opened my mouth and closed it. "I trusted you," I said.

"Yeah."

Silence.

"Yeah, you did."

I waited. When I called his name, he didn't answer. I wanted to
rush in. To shoot him, to help him. I didn't know what I'd do. I
thought he was playing possum, suckering me in. So I waited. When
I finally made my move, he'd gone still. Too late to give him medical
attention and too late to finish him off. The worst of both worlds.

He'd hemorrhaged. Internal bleeding. Died from the inside out.

I found a detonator by his corpse. He'd wired the whole building
with explosives. He could have brought it crashing down on us both.

PACE TRANSMISSION 000014000014405

GUESTS (ALL) RELEASED
DOMAINS (ALL) SHUTTING DOWN
RETRIEVING DATA
SAVED AND LOCKED
PRIORITIES RESET
QUERY ?
WAITING FOR INSTRUCTION
WAITING WAITING
END

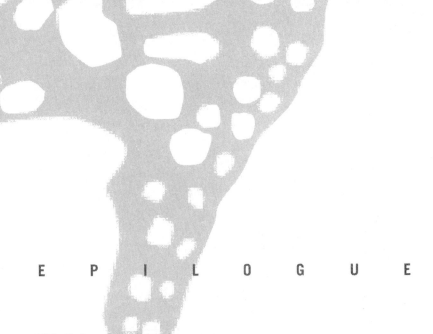

E P I L O G U E

All hail the conquering hero.

My best friend betrayed me so I shot him. Distracted by a kiss, I let the girl I love die.

I'm not the same person any more.

My life before the Calliope Surge remains a muzzy blur. Pieces here and pieces there. I keep expecting the gates to open and everything to come flooding back. It never happens. Just . . . gone. Just . . . blank. Thanks to Mercutio.

Of course, Fantasia got it worse. Shredded like that. Cuts and burns and some scary nerve damage. I had to sew three of her fingers back on. I fixed her up fairly well, all things considered. Physically, I fixed her. I can't begin to guess how it affected her psychologically.

My prescription: bed rest, antibiotics and pain medication. Her prescription: none of the above. She slipped out and drove to the lake. I tracked her down, found her on the muddy bank, crosslegged, a half lotus position. She had her back to the water. She was twitching, worse than ever. It was cold that morning. She kept whispering words I couldn't hear.

I asked her what she was doing.

She spoke up: "I'm trying to kill my mind."

"Oh." I plopped down beside her. "Sounds like fun."

"The mind is the slayer of the real. If I can slay the slayer, I can find reality."

"This isn't reality?"

"This," she declared, "is not reality. This is delicious maya. Illusion. The physical world."

"So you're seeking the spiritual world?"

"Through meditation, yes."

"Can you teach me to do that?" I asked.

She looked at me. "You're asking me for help?"

"Surprised?"

Fan thought about it and nodded, "Yes. Surprised."

She left the next day. Just up and left. I haven't seen her since.

I triggered graduation sequences in all the pods. Brought all my friends from the "veal world" up to the real world. Champagne, Isaac, Pandora, Vashti—okay, kids, everybody out of the pool.

Conversely, I went back into the IVR one last time.

I hit the schoolhouse. Locked eyes with Maestro. We discussed his programming. He did a fabulous job justifying his actions, particularly his approach to discipline. In response, I told him how the Semai of Malaysia allow children to *bood*—which translates as "I don't feel like doing it." No adult can make a child do anything if he chooses to bood. The matter is closed.

"This is not Malaysia," he said.

"Obviously."

That said, I deleted his program.

I considered wiping out Malachi as well. Considered, but ultimately decided against it. Let him live, I figured. Let him live and let live. He'd saved me, after all.

Why, Mercutio, why?

I still don't know why he did what he did. I have my theories.

I made an extensive search of his files. He'd replaced the IVR security system with a program of his own, a thing called Kadmon. Hard-coded in Kadmon, I found a curious log.

The first entry: "He who succeeds, breeds."

The second: "This, I imagine, is how Shah Jahan felt when he imprisoned and killed his siblings to assume the reigning title of Alamgir: 'world holder.'"

The last: "If you're reading this, what can I say? I tried to hit the long ball. I went for all the marbles and lost. Sucks to be me. You would have done the same thing in my position."

End of log.

The survivors rolled in one by one. They all hugged one another and talked about how different they looked from their IVR templates. Trivial shit. I was so fucking past that.

They took pains to include me. To be nice to me. To show me how much they really appreciated me. Except for Vashti, who openly doubted my word and cast aspersions on my character like she'd invented the world's very first insult and was now taking it out for a test-drive. "Pretty convenient," she said, "to pop Mercutio and make Simone and Fantasia disappear. One dead, the others gone. I guess we'll just have your story to go by."

Screw her, I thought. *Let her think whatever she wants.*

I let my expression grow sinister.

So distant from feeling good about any of this, I felt like a smile might snap my face, and poison what was left of me.

Our time has come, said Isaac.

He called us together—himself, Vashti, Pandora, Champagne and me—and took control. He drafted a charter, made proposals for how to proceed. He seemed reasonable, I had to admit. Reasonable and pragmatic. Our resident architect. Who better to rebuild civilization? So I cast my vote for him.

More to the point, I voted against Vashti, his opponent.

Of course, when he won the election, he turned right around and picked her as a vice president. Politics. Shitty high-school politics. Whatever.

They drew up a plan of attack.

Beginning: Medical examinations and lots of them. Are we sick? Dying? Strong enough to resist Black Ep? Or are we fatally flawed? Biologically speaking, we must stabilize our house first. Then we can help humankind.

Middle: Study the plague. Contain it. Eradicate it, if possible. Clone human embryos. Immunize them via vaccine and/or gene therapy. Modify them as little as possible. Keep them essentially "human." (Unlike us.)

Endgame: Raise the clones. Rebuild society. Etc.

Here's the funny thing—they were genuinely excited about it. Practically bouncing off the walls. Where I saw disaster, they saw opportunity.

Opportunity to craft and nourish a new civilization, one free of disease, famine, strife.

To do things the way they ought to be done.

To form a real, honest-to-goodness Utopia.

To remake Man in our image, psychologically, if not physically.

Call it Humanity 2.0.

Funny, I thought. Pandora caught my smirk and gave voice to it, invoking the possibility of hubris. Something about how ideal societies tend to collapse under their own weight. Isaac acknowledged her concerns with a tacit nod, but Vashti brushed them aside. She would not shut up about Huxley's island, Plato's Republic and More's perfect paradise.

"Why?" I asked. "Why do this?"

Various answers. A sense of duty. An honor and a privilege. A way to ensure that those of us who died didn't lose their lives in vain.

"What's the alternative?" Champagne asked me. She meant it—I'm sure—as a rhetorical question, nothing more.

I said human extinction might not be such a bad idea.

273

They asked me to elaborate but I wouldn't. I just let the statement stand. They didn't know what to make of me. They imagined I was joking. Such a kidder, that Halloween.

"Let's draw some boundaries," I said.

Continent by continent, we divvied up the world.

Isaac won the draw and went first, taking Africa.

I took North America.

Pandora took South America. (To be near me, I wondered? Or sentimental feelings for her pseudo-Brazilian upbringing?)

Vashti took Asia.

Europe was drawn last, taken by Champagne.

We saved Australia for Fan, wherever she was.

I'd pitched this as a separation of responsibility, one that would be useful in the years ahead. If a Black Ep medicine could be harvested in a South American rainforest, Pandora would take the lead in that project; the task of culling together all the stored knowledge of a Stockholm genetics lab would fall to Champagne.

But that's not why I pitched it.

I pitched it because there's no point pouring water into a broken cup.

Because I'd seen too much.

Because I'd lost everything that meant anything to me. Everything.

I took the monarch pin from my breast and dropped it on the table. Calmly, I announced my secession. I didn't support their cause. I would not help them. I was D-O-N-E, done, and I was taking North America with me.

Champagne thought I was joking. The others knew better.

Did they know that as a lowly caterpillar, the monarch butterfly eats a steady diet of poison? Milkweed is a strong poison but the monarch can take it. On the other hand, a bird that swallows the monarch will swallow the poison, get sick and quite possibly die.

Did they really want me? Did they really want the poison?

"Hal, no," said Pandora. "Don't be like that."

"Don't tell me how to be."

I told them they had twenty-four hours to leave. I got up and made my way to the door.

Redfaced, Vashti made a hell of an entreaty, practically begging me to reconsider. Funny. She knew I could help them. She hated me, but she respected me just the same.

I refused to compromise.

They're gone now, off chasing a better tomorrow. I told them I wouldn't actively oppose them. It's a truce.

I'm alone with my thoughts.

I said I had nothing left . . . but that's not true.

Even with a shattered memory, I still have hindsight. With perfect clarity, I can see what made me the way I am. I can't see forward, but I can see the path back.

It's calming.

The real world is mine now, and I can walk in it, and live in my own skin. And when I die, Nature will swallow me, and new life will take sustenance from my body and my bones. Maybe Black Ep. Maybe not.

It's nothing to be afraid of.

Until that day comes, I have the woods. And my freedom. And flashes of understanding amidst the emptiness and pain.

It's not enough.

But it's something.

ACKNOWLEDGMENTS

Many people have supported this adventure; many thanks are due.

I count myself lucky to have Jennifer Hershey as an editor. Her terrific sensibilities, precision and wit have made *Idlewild* all the stronger.

Across the Atlantic, Simon Taylor compounded my good fortune by championing me in the U.K.

Stuart Calderwood copyedited the book, fighting battles with grammar that I alone could never win.

My literary agents at Arthur Pine Associates are wonderful and talented. I thank Richard Pine, Lori Andiman and especially Matthew Guma, whose guidance is invaluable.

I'd also like to thank everyone at Colden, McKuin and Frankel, especially Joel McKuin for shepherding a first-time author through the literary world with skill and grace, and Rob Goldman for all his tireless efforts on my behalf.

Ken Atchity and Vince Atchity read the early chapters of the novel and gave me their thoughts. For guidance at such a critical, early stage, I owe a debt of thanks.

I am likewise indebted to Janine Ellen Young and Carol Wolper for sage advice on the process of writing and selling novels.

My gratitude to Scott Benzel and Sensory Deprivation Labs for the epigraph, and for shattering writer's block with phenomenal music.

Dr. Rita Calvo and Sharon Greene, MPH, were kind enough to answer all my questions about epidemiology, genetics and molecular biology. If you enjoyed the science in *Idlewild,* the credit is theirs; if you found mistakes, the fault is mine.

I am grateful for all the encouragement, feedback, suggestions and inspiration provided by G. J. Pruss, Dave Parks, Jon Klane, Shelly Lescott-Leszczyński, Pearl Druyan, Andrea Ho, Stephanie Huntwork, David Klein, Robert Scott Martin, Iain McCaig, Walt McGraw, Marisa Pagano, Marcy Posner, Sam Sagan, Jerry Salzman, Doselle Young, Marilyn Clair and all the nice folks at Damned If I Don't Productions. I am especially grateful to Ann Druyan, not only for all of the above but also for luring me away to a beautiful place, and for defending Darwin.

My father, Carl Sagan, has been an endless source of inspiration.

My mother, Linda Salzman Sagan, encouraged my creativity, raised me to ask questions and taught me more about writing than I could possibly put into words.

Most of all, I would like to thank my partner in crime, Clinnette Minnis, who loves me as much as I love her, who tells me her dreams every morning, and helps mine come true. I am sublimely grateful that she opened her heart to me long enough for me to stick a foot in there and keep the damn thing from closing.

Nick Sagan
Ithaca, New York
13 February 2003

ABOUT THE AUTHOR

NICK SAGAN has spent the past decade writing for Hollywood, crafting screenplays, teleplays, animation episodes and computer games. The son of astronomer Carl Sagan and artist/writer Linda Salzman, his greeting, "Hello from the children of planet Earth," was recorded and placed aboard NASA's *Voyager I* spacecraft, which is now the most distant human-made object in the universe. Sagan graduated summa cum laude from UCLA Film School. *Idlewild* is his first novel. Visit his website at www.nicksagan.com.